Campus Confidential
An Academic Thriller
Sid Stark

Newsletter Signup

Want to find out how it all started? Want to stay in touch and get all the latest news, updates, and offers? Get your FREE copy of the prequel novella **Foreign Exchange** and sign up for my newsletter (but only if you want to) by scanning the QR code below.

1

They say knowledge is power. Those people must never have gotten a PhD.

Case in point: the way I sidled into the room my first day at my first job. If my power corresponded to my knowledge, I would have stridden in like a conquering hero. But my knowledge of the sigmatic aorist or the Onegin stanza only seemed to weigh me down as I slithered into the faculty meeting room, smiling like a meek little idiot and wishing everyone would stop staring at me.

"You must be our new Russianist. Rowena Halley, right?" The speaker was a big bear-like man, a rarity in a foreign language department, where the faculty tended to be mainly female and inclined to the childish or the wizened. His joviality, though, had the manic edge common in academics, honed through decades of politically correct bullying into a weapon capable of inducing suicidal depression in everyone who encountered it.

"Yep."

"They say you're from Georgia."

Now everyone was staring at me, like they'd never seen anyone from Georgia before. Which was all too possibly true.

"Originally," I said.

The all-white group did a collective grimace as they bit down on their reflexive desire to berate me about racism and segregation. No doubt it was coming.

"But I did my PhD in Indiana," I continued, triggering another collective grimace at the mere thought of the Midwest.

"Indiana..." said the bear-like man. "That must have been...different. Was it the first time you saw snow?"

"I lived for several years in Moscow. So no."

"Moscow! I bet you have lots of opinions about Putin!"

There was a chorus of titters.

"Is what they're saying about police harassment true?" continued the bear-like man, his eyes avid. "It must not be safe to be an American there these days, is it?"

"It's at least as safe as it is here in New Jersey," I said, and sat down on the one remaining empty chair, between a woman who was vaguely familiar to me from my Skype interview for the position, and the only other man in the room. The woman was wearing chunky gold earrings and a thick necklace that hinted enough at Central America to leave her open to accusations of cultural appropriation, so even though I couldn't remember her name, I was guessing she was from the Spanish program. The man was slender and had bristly dark-blond hair, dark-blond stubble covering his face, and looked like he hadn't yet turned thirty.

"Good to see you again, Rowena," whispered the woman, but didn't remind me of her name. The man gave me a sideways flicker from his eyes, and then went back to looking straight ahead, stony-faced. His left leg, though, was quivering slightly under the table, hidden from everyone except me, as if he could barely contain his pent-up energy and desire to be out of this room.

There was an awkward silence, and then printed agendas were handed around and the meeting broke out, starting with pointed introductions to the one newcomer—me.

The bear-like man was John Greene, Associate Professor of Spanish and chair of the Department of Modern Languages. Of the other fifteen faculty members there, eight also taught Spanish, and three taught French. The Spanish instructors kept inserting bits of Spanish into their speech, some with better accents than others—John Greene's was particularly shaky—causing the French instructors to laugh sycophantically and nod to show that they, too, spoke a Romance language.

Aside from the Romance contingent, there was one German instructor, one Chinese instructor, one Arabic instructor (the man sitting next to me), and me. We all sat in nervous silence as the Spanish contingent discussed business that had nothing to do with us and swapped in-jokes, with John Greene occasionally making little digs at Georgia until he got caught up in an argument over something that everyone kept referring to as "C. Diff."

"Why is everyone talking about c. diff?" I whispered to the woman sitting next to me. "Was there an outbreak of diarrhea here last semester?"

She gave me a weird look, but got distracted by the argument over whether or not the Department of Modern Languages was adequately supporting C. Diff's mission.

"It's the Committee for Diversity, Inclusiveness, and Fairness," the man to my right whispered, bending close enough that I could feel his stubble brush my ear. "C-D-I-F. It's a student-faculty collaborative, interdisciplinary initiative to increase the presence of under-represented minorities and engage in town-and-gown outreach in order to encourage local members of the community, especially potential first-generation college students, to apply to TLASC." He delivered the words in an inflectionless whisper, but when he broke away, his whole body was now quivering, I assumed with suppressed laughter.

Meanwhile, an argument had broken out between a Spanish and a French instructor over item three on the agenda, the cross-listing of survey literature courses with tempting titles such as "French

Neoclassicism: An Introduction" as comparative literature, or CLIT (pronounced See-Lit), classes.

I looked down at the agenda to confirm my suspicions of the spelling of the course identifier, and then sideways at the woman sitting to my left, but she sat there impassively. If she had ever found it amusing to teach classes labeled CLIT 101, those days had long since passed. The man to my right was running his hand over his face, maybe from tiredness, maybe because his stubble itched, or maybe from the desperate need to keep from exploding with mirth. I fought the urge to ask if Introduction to Differential Equations was labeled DICQ 101 on the course bulletin, and narrowly won.

The argument was settled in favor of foreign language instructors teaching courses cross-listed as CLIT 101 as they apparently always had in the past, but with a motion to request that the courses be listed as FORL first and CLIT second, instead of the other way around, as they currently were.

"After the latest curriculum survey they're obviously planning to reduce the foreign language courses as much as possible, maybe phase out the requirement altogether!" said the French instructor who had been arguing in favor of getting the courses listed as FORL first and CLIT second. "We need to remind them that we're still here!"

"Which is why we want to get in on the CLIT listings!" cried the Spanish instructor who had been arguing against her. "Raise our visibility!"

"I've heard they're thinking of cutting the CLIT program entirely," put in a third person, a bird-like woman whose tiny stature was balanced out by a large mane of wispy, hay-like hair that appeared to have last been brushed sometime back in the Bush administration. The first Bush administration. I couldn't remember her name or what she taught, but odds were it was Spanish.

There was a vociferous outcry against the perfidy of budget cuts aimed at foreign language programs, which united the room long enough for us to move on to the next item on the agenda: the promotion of our LCTL (pronounced "Lictle") program.

"Now, I know you haven't been here long, Rowena, if I may—you don't mind if I call you Rowena, do you? I know how touchy some new PhDs can be, especially young women, about being called by their first names—of *course* you have to stand up for yourselves, I understand that, and in the classroom you should, but here we're all not just colleagues, but friends—but you must have talked about growing our LCTL program during your interview? In fact, that's part of why we hired you, isn't it?—because you had some *really* good ideas for outreach and development for our LCTLs, which is something we *really* want to do; the Provost has named it a priority, and anything the Provost wants that might raise the profile of foreign languages on campus, well, we want to get behind that, and it's always *so* exciting to bring in promising young scholars, even from places like Indiana; I mean, maybe you have some great ideas you've gotten there that you can share with us"—there was a reflexive giggle from a number of my new colleagues at the thought of great ideas coming from Indiana—"and so, why don't you and I, Rowena, meet after this to talk about some of those ideas, just the two of us, to really hammer out some plans?"

John Greene fixed me with a bright stare at the end of his speech. I smiled weakly back. Before I could say anything, we had moved on to item five, the cut in the office supplies budget and how this would force us to act in a more environmentally responsible manner by not printing out so many handouts (the man to my right looked down at the printed-out meeting agenda, caught my eye, and then looked swiftly away, rubbing his hand over his face once again) and then briskly to item six, student mental health reporting.

"After what happened last semester"—there was a pregnant pause, during which everyone, even John Greene, appeared to shrink a little in their seats—"the Office of Student Wellness has instituted a new protocol for notifying them and the authorities of students who appear to be a danger to themselves or others. There was some question over whether the new mandatory reporting rules violated FERPA, but it was decided last week that they are in fact FERPA-compliant, so everyone will need to do the online training seminar prior to the start of classes, which I don't need to remind you is in two days' time. Rowena, you'll have to do your regular FERPA, Title IX, and Health and Safety training at the same time. It's all online; shouldn't take more than an hour or two, but it *has* to be done before classes start or we could be facing a potential lawsuit."

Now John Greene did wait for me to promise that yes, I would complete the FERPA, Title IX, Health and Safety, and Student Wellbeing training within the next 48 hours.

There was some grousing about more mandatory online training, and a little tiff between two Spanish instructors, but no further explanation of what had happened last semester, and with that, my first faculty meeting as a real professor was over.

2

"Rowena, this way please," said John Greene, bustling out of the room in an oddly feminine manner for such a burly man. "And Alex, Emma—you too, please. My office. And Kate, you come too. I know German isn't technically a Less Commonly Taught Language, but"—he uttered a nervous laugh—"here it might as well be. So why don't we all put our heads together. I'm sure with *so much* youth and brilliance we'll come up with some *marvelous* ideas for promoting the LCTL program. I hope you don't mind, Rowena, if I invite the others—I know I promised you a tete-a-tete, but this way you can benefit from hearing what some of your more experienced peers have tried, things that have worked—or failed. I'm afraid we haven't had much luck getting students to sign up for our more...exotic language offerings, but now with *you* here, I'm sure that will change."

He gave me a Hollywood-starlet-level bright smile while shepherding us through the department front office and into the chair's office. I hoped my face didn't betray how I felt when he shut the door behind us. After my dissertation defense, I had made a promise to myself that I wouldn't attend any more closed-door meetings with senior faculty, and here I was breaking it already.

"Pull up a chair—do we have enough—not quite—Alex, I see you're leaning against the bookcase anyway—pull up a chair. Now,

Rowena, what were some of those *brilliant* ideas I heard you had during your interview?"

"Well," I said, perching on a rolling chair with one broken armrest. "Of course, there's ROTC..."

But John Greene was already shaking his head regretfully. "The ROTC presence on our campus is *so* small, I'm afraid, that that's just not a pool worth pulling from, and Arabic already has that pretty much sewn up, don't you, Alex? Of course, with your Navy record—can I just say once again how *proud* TLASC is of your service—that's no surprise."

Alex, the man who had been sitting to my right earlier and was now leaning against an Ikea Billy bookcase that had, like the chair, seen better days, shrugged. His earlier amusement had gone, and now his attitude was saying that he might be here physically, but mentally he was somewhere else. "Arabic has something like 50% of the current ROTC cadets on campus," he said. He turned and focused on me, fully present for an instant. "But there's always the other 50%. I'd be happy to talk to you about recruitment strategies."

"That would be great," I started, but before I could say anything else, John Greene was talking about the Chinese film series that Emma had started last semester, that had been such a *brilliant* idea but had suffered from poor turnout.

"I'm afraid it's hard to get students to show up to anything these days," he was saying, shaking his head regretfully again. "So many of them commute in or are working, and the ones that live and work on campus are already so overcommitted with social events these days. Kate, you tried holding an Oktoberfest fair, but..."

"We couldn't get permission to hold it on the quad," Kate told me. "Only the basement of the Union. So no one showed up."

"Um, okay," I said. "Study abroad—"

"Yes, of course, of course...why don't you drop by the study abroad office this afternoon, Rowena, see if you can make some contacts there? Get a *full day* out of your first day on campus! Now I'm afraid I have to go. A chair's work is never done!" And we were ushered out of the office with as much bustle and nervous laughter as we had been shepherded in.

"Well, I've"—he looked at his phone—"gotta run, but I'll see you around," said Alex. "Let me know if you want me to hook you up with my contacts in the ROTC office, Rowena." He slung his bag over his shoulder and set off at a semi-jog. Unlike most academics, he appeared to be at least somewhat familiar with the act of running.

"Yeah, me too," said Emma. "Welcome to Lib State, Rowena." Her tone and the smile that followed it were not particularly welcoming, and she set off almost as fast as Alex, but less athletically.

"Do you know where your office is?" asked Kate. "Will you be with the rest of us in the adjunct office? Wait: you're not an adjunct, are you? You're a VAP, aren't you?"

"Sort of," I said.

"But only for one semester, to fill in for Professor Cahill, while he's...out."

"Yes," I said.

"So no possibility of renewal, then," she said, sounding unsure whether to gloat or sympathize.

"Not that I know of."

"Well, they put the Spanish adjuncts in Cahill's office while he's...out, so you won't be getting that. Probably you'll be with us. Mary Beth, do you know what office Professor Halley will have? Mary Beth's our current work-study," Kate explained to me, as the blonde girl sitting at the department front desk frowned at being asked this difficult and unexpected question. "So are you going to be with us again this semester?" Kate asked Mary Beth. "I thought you said you might be transferring to Math."

"They're keeping me here at least until the end of the week, I think," Mary Beth said. "Then I don't know. Linda's out to lunch; you'll have to ask her about Professor Halley's office."

"Linda's our admin," Kate told me. "But she must have emailed you already. She's the only one who knows how anything works. But I'll show you around, and then you should go to HR if you haven't done that yet. Here's the copier. Have you gotten your copy code? Ask Linda for it when she gets back. You have to have your copy code to make copies, not that it'll do you much good. As you just heard, they made it so we only get 100 copies a month, down from 200."

"I have thirty students," I said. "What do I do when I run out of copies?"

Kate shrugged. "Make your own copies? That's what I do. Or you can have them take quizzes online."

"For Russian 101? Asking them to type in Russian seems a little harsh for first semester."

"Well, most of us make multiple choice quizzes."

I bit my tongue on what I thought about multiple choice quizzes, and allowed Kate to lead me to what she, in the privacy of the corridor, called the "adjunct warehouse," the single office, labeled simply "Adjuncts," shared by Kate, Alex, Emma, and now, it seemed, me. There were two desks and two computers and three chairs and a futon mattress rolled up against one wall.

"That's for Alex," Kate told me. "Sometimes he spends the night here when he's teaching an early morning class or an evening class, or rests during the day before he goes off to teach at Tech, since he commutes in from Yardley, from his parents' place. If you need it he'll probably let you use it too, although you won't be working a second job, will you? Professor Cahill has the only other Russian position in the area, doesn't he? He used to do the same thing—spend the night in his office or rest there during the day so he wouldn't have to go home between jobs, although his second job was at Rutgers, not Tech. I think he's still teaching there this semester, even though he's been put on administrative leave here after...what happened last semester. Not that it's connected, not officially, but..."

"Uh...what happened?" I asked, dropping my voice to a whisper even though no one else was in the room with us.

"They didn't tell you?"

I shook my head.

"Oh! It was...really tragic, actually. I'm surprised they didn't tell you, although it's not something you'd bring up in an interview, I guess, but you'll want to know before walking into your 201 class, since everyone there knew him. And maybe they'll ask you about it in 101 too. Someone really should have told you. Anyway, there was this kid—Brandy—who was in Russian. Really good, according to Professor Cahill, who took him under his wing, helped him find scholarships for study abroad, that kind of thing, sponsored him for student government. Brandy was the president of the campus Lambda group and wanted to run for student body president. Only," Kate looked over her shoulder before continuing in a whisper so low I could barely make out, "at the end of last semester he killed himself."

3

Before Kate could tell me more, a short, heavy-set woman, whose bright-green cats-eye glasses contrasted intriguingly with her frumpy brown tunic and palazzo pants, looked in and introduced herself as the mysterious Linda, the person who had been sending me vaguely threatening emails for the past two weeks, and led me back to the department office to sign my contract.

"And here's your copy code," she said, pushing a slip of paper in my hand, "but I'm not sure it will work this week. Your contract doesn't officially take effect until September 1, so you may not be in the system until next week. You may have to wait until then to be able to use the copier and log into the computers." She frowned. "Were you planning to use any of the smart classroom tech this week?"

"Probably," I said.

"Well...maybe someone else can log you in."

"Or I can just not use it," I said. I looked at my contract again. "Um...it ends December 15?"

"Yes, that's so Payroll can process your final paycheck before winter break."

"But finals week runs until the nineteenth?"

Linda frowned some more. "If the system locks you out, let me know, and I'll enter your final grades for you."

"But..."

"Now you'll want to take this over to HR and make sure they start processing you right away," said Linda. "And you'll need to get keys for your classrooms."

"Keys?"

"Yes, of course. How else are you going to get into them?"

I started to say that I'd never taught at a place that kept its classroom doors locked during regular class hours, let alone with physical keys, but before I could get the words out, Linda had shoved several more slips of paper into my hands, and hustled me out the door and pointed me in the direction of HR.

I left the rather dingy stairwell of the incongruously named Dreme (pronounced Dream) Hall and stepped out onto the front quad of The Liberal Arts State College, officially known as TLASC (pronounced T-LASC) but more generally known as Lib State. With a name like that I would have expected a year-round picket by the College Republicans, but maybe they didn't even bother. Maybe they didn't need to. The college seemed pretty well imbued with a spirit of rugged individualism, AKA grasping greed by the rich for more riches, already.

The quad itself, in contrast to the stairwells and offices of Dreme Hall, looked like a movie set for an adorable East Coast American college campus. Brick neoclassical buildings stood around three sides of a lawn that would have done a golf course proud, and strategically placed oaks and maples no doubt turned blazing reds and oranges in the fall. Broad footpaths, fenced off with knee-high black chains and signs warning people not to walk on the grass, crisscrossed the quad and made elegant little curves into each building, curves that probably drove everyone crazy as they rushed to their 9:00am classes. I wondered what would happen if I were to hurdle the black chains and sprint across the grass and along the hypotenuse of the triangle I was being forced to traverse, directly to my destination, instead of following the path into the middle of the quad and then taking a 90-degree turn onto the next path. Could faculty be fined for something like that? Probably they would dock my pay for despoiling campus property.

Of course, in order to dock my pay, they'd have to pay me first, and technically what I was doing now was unpaid, since it was August 25 and my contract didn't start until September 1, even though classes began August 27, which meant for the first few days I would be teaching students without being an official employee of TLASC. Surely that was at least as big a legal breach as any sins I might inadvertently commit against FERPA (the Family Educational Rights and Privacy Act). TLASC had ample reason to believe I was too poor and desperate to sue them, but if I were to do something that instigated a suit by a student's family, well...I wasn't sure what the college's legal position would be, but I *was* sure it would end up with me getting kicked out on the street. But since that was going to happen in December anyway, what did any of us have to lose? Other than my self-respect, but that was being eroded ever more quickly.

I obediently kept between the chains until they dumped me out of the quad and into the backside of the campus, where elegant neoclassical brick gave way to prefab and trailers. I spent an hour in the HR building filling out forms that mostly had to do with how I would allocate the pension and life insurance that the state of New Jersey was going to withhold from my paycheck, despite the fact that I was a temporary employee who couldn't actually access said pension and life insurance. When I tried to object to that and to the start and end dates of my contract, the woman processing me stared at me with a look of flat disinterest, and then went back to contemplating her three-inch sunburst yellow nails, so I signed everything without further protest and made my escape as fast as possible.

Next stop was Campus Facilities, which turned out to be a trailer that was also out in the unattractive hinterlands, but on the far side of campus, requiring me to walk all the way around the football stadium.

A walk that turned out to be for nothing, since Campus Facilities had not yet received the official key requests to hand over my classroom keys, and the slips of paper I had been given by Linda in the department office, and the copy of my contract I was still clutching after my run-in with HR, were insufficient to convince them to hand over the precious keys to Dreme 301 and Angelo 027.

"Angelo—that's the new building," the man who had refused me the keys told me. He looked and sounded so much like an extra from something like *The Sopranos* I had to struggle not to laugh. "Brand new, from the Superstorm Sandy money."

"Was the campus much affected?"

"Power was out for a week!" said the man, whose nametag read—I struggled even harder not to laugh at how all my stereotypes were being fulfilled—*Tony*. "Here and Princeton! We had trees down all over the place. That's how they got the money for a new building. They'd just started on it when the storm hit, wiped out the building project, so they started all over again, decided to build something twice as big. Have you been in there?"

"Not yet."

"It's fancy," Tony told me proudly, as if its fanciness reflected on him personally. "And they have electronic locks on all the doors, but they haven't set up the campus-wide system yet, so we're still using regular keys this semester. They won't be able to set up the electronic locking system until they sync everything with your CubID—do you have your CubID?"

"Um..."

"Your TLASC ID," Tony explained. "The school mascot is a bear cub. We're the Bear Cubs." He grinned. "You think we're cuddly enough to be bear cubs?"

"I guess. They took the picture for the ID at HR. They said the ID itself would be coming this week."

"Yeah, it might. Or next week. They're not the fastest. One of the reasons we don't have the central system working yet. You got your Cubmail account up?"

"In theory. In practice I haven't been able to log into it."

"Probably you won't be able to till they get you in the system, and then you'll need to go to the IT department with your CubID so they can log you in. You're supposed to be able to do it from home, but no one ever can. When do classes start? Wednesday?"

"Wednesday," I confirmed.

Tony sucked on his teeth doubtfully. "You're not gonna have everything ready by then. Why'd you leave it so late?"

"This is when they told me to show up."

"Yeah, that sounds like 'em. Well, if your first class is after nine someone else will have probably already opened the door. Just wait outside until the 9:00am class lets out, and jump in before they can lock you out. Sorry you had to walk all the way out here in this heat."

"Oh, well...87 degrees isn't really hot where I come from."

"Where's that?"

"Atlanta."

"Atlanta!" Tony rocked back like I'd said I came from Mars. "That must be different."

"A bit."

"What do you teach?"

"Russian."

That also rocked Tony back. No one was ever expecting to meet a genuine, real-life Russian professor in the flesh.

"They musta brought you in to replace Professor Cahill while he's...out."

"Yep."

Tony shook his head. "It was terrible what happened. Hope nothing like that happens to you while you're here. Hey—you don't think it had anything to do with studying Russian, do you? What happened to that kid?"

"Um..."

"Probably not. We always lose a few every year—drugs, car crashes...you know how kids are. But he was the first suicide in a while. Surprising, really. You'd think we'da had more, the way college kids kill themselves these days."

"I guess..."

"I read an article 'bout it recently. But the Provost is really big on this new Student Mental Wellness program. They tell you 'bout that?"

"Uh-huh."

"He really took what happened to that kid to heart, had a big memorial service, paid for the kid's parents' hotel himself out of his own pocket, the whole thing. And now they're pushing mental health. Have you done the training yet?"

"Not yet."

"Don't see what all these kids have to be upset about," said Tony, and after a few stories about his early days as a pipefitter and how kids these days didn't know how good they had it, and more wishes that I not have anything bad happen to the Russian program like what had happened last semester, I was able to escape.

4

When I got out of Tony's office it was 1:00pm. Although the temperature had not even touched 90, the air had a breathless, polluted sizzle to it that made me glad, once I had skirted back around the football stadium and found my car, to get under cover.

I turned the key and mentally cheered when my car cranked over. A fifteen-year-old Honda Civic, it was the most reliable car I had ever had, which meant it started at least three days out of four. I got it into reverse on the second try and rolled slowly towards the parking lot exit, which was gated. At the moment the gates were open, but I wondered how I was going to get in when classes started and I still didn't have my CubID. TLASC seemed particularly inefficient even for a university, and I shared Tony's skepticism that everything would be set up for me by my first class, which was currently 45 hours away.

I pulled out of the parking lot and onto the main drive that circled central campus and offered a picturesque view of the front quad. I had only been there for three hours and I already wanted to escape. I engaged in a brief fantasy of galloping off like a wild Haflinger pony, snorting and shaking my silver mane as I raced away to freedom, my butterscotch hide glistening in the sun...

"Oh crap!"

My fantasies about being a wild Haflinger pony had distracted me from the crucial task of shifting into second gear, something my less-than-trusty steed could only manage two tries out of three at best. After a quick look around told me that no one was barreling down on me as I sat stalled out in the middle of the road, or had even noticed me at all, I restarted the car and, this time concentrating carefully, made it all the way into third gear and out the main campus exit.

My apartment was two exits down Route 1 from campus, but my experience of driving on it in the morning had been so shattering that I decided to try a back way home. I had thought Atlanta had prepared me for anything the traffic gods could throw at me, but Route 1's ancient entrance ramps and homicidal drivers demanded more from my car's transmission than it was willing or able to give, and so, still shaken from having stalled out on perfectly flat ground for no reason, I drove past the entrance to Route 1 and followed my GPS's instructions for the alternate way that was one minute longer than its preferred route back to the Pleasant Hill Apartment Complex.

I found myself dumped into a neighborhood full of old Victorian houses that had once been fancier than any other architecture I had ever seen in America. Now, though, they looked like they needed to be pulled down, or maybe set on fire. Some of them looked like they *had* been set on fire, but people appeared to still be living in them. There were no lawns or gardens, only waist-high weeds sprouting out of dirt and cracks in the pavement. Grown men were sitting on sagging porches at 1:15pm on a Monday, staring at the passing cars with blank eyes. Other than me, everyone I could see was black. It was good to see that racism and segregation had been overcome and drop-kicked into the dustbin of history here in the enlightened north. A corner café, although "café" was much too upscale a word for such a hole-in-the-wall establishment, advertised grits and greens, the comfortingly familiar words like a beacon of hope and home.

I made it past the grits-and-greens café with only a hint of a stall-out, and then past a building that at first I thought was a minimum security prison, especially since it was right next to a down-on-its-luck-looking police station, but turned out to be an elementary school. Then there was a weed-filled vacant lot, and then a series of pawn shops, dollar stores, cash-for-gold traders, and payday loan places, that gradually morphed into Dunkin' Donuts, Mexican restaurants, Italian restaurants, and the road to the Pleasant Hill Apartment Complex, which this morning had seemed like a pit to me, but now seemed welcomingly upscale. Bloomington, Indiana, where I had spent the majority of the past six years, had no shortage of panhandlers and street people, Atlanta had its share of poor neighborhoods, and Moscow was, well, Moscow, but never had I had such a visceral sense of being in a third-world country as I had driving from my ostensibly elite campus to my ostensibly safe apartment complex. For a moment the urge to keep driving, get on Route 1 and then I-95 and drive south, south, south, until I was back in safety and civilization, rose up in me so strongly that I could feel my hands turning the wheel of the car, steering it away from my new life.

Fevronia is waiting for you! I reminded myself. *And besides, it's not like you've got anything else on offer. It's this or nothing.* So, instead of fleeing, I pulled into my parking space.

The Pleasant Hill Apartment Complex had probably once been nice, or at least not as dismal as it was now. But as it currently stood, the parking lot was as full of cracks and divots as a newly cooled lava field, all the paint was peeling, and rust and mold stains decorated the walls at every corner.

I got my door, which was unlikely to keep out an intruder but more than capable of resisting me, open on the second try. "Fevronia!" I called. "I'm home."

No fluffy tan face appeared. Fevronia, the long-haired cat I had adopted this spring and who had helped me immensely in completing my dissertation and hindered me much more than I had expected in finding an apartment, had not handled the move well. I searched around through all the unpacked boxes until, as I was standing with my back to the bed, a soft paw reached out and gently patted my ankle, making me do a creditable standing leap as I bit back a shriek.

Feeling the need to cuddle something familiar, I got down on my hands and knees and tried to lure Fevronia out from her hiding place, but she only glared at me balefully and retreated to the far side of the bed, crouching up against the wall and hissing at me, so I left her and busied myself setting up my printer.

I had set up my modem and router and my wifi connection as my second order of business when I'd moved in that weekend, stopping only to let Fevronia out of her carrier before opening up my laptop and logging in. Or attempting to log in. Most of the day before had been spent calling the cable provider's call center in India and rebooting my modem, which they seemed to think would solve all my problems, even though it hadn't the previous four times I'd tried it.

But today the internet—fingers crossed!—seemed to be working. I even got my printer reconnected with my computer, and set to printing off my syllabi. I had planned to do so on campus this morning, but even if I had gotten all my IDs and codes set up, the 100-page limit meant I would be able to print off fewer than a third of the syllabi I needed before I was locked out for the rest of the month. I assumed we were supposed to upload the syllabi and other handouts onto The Den, TLASC's online system for course websites, but I didn't have access to that either yet, and in my experience, the best, or even only, way to guarantee that students had copies of the syllabus was to print them out and distribute them myself. So that's what I was going to do.

My plans hit a snag when I ran out of paper halfway through printing out the RUSS 101 syllabi, which were each a bloated 15 pages long. I had inherited them from Professor Cahill, via Linda, who had emailed them to me last week with the information that, as they had already been approved by CurCom (the Curriculum Committee), they mustn't be changed.

All TLASC syllabi are required to have appropriate language regarding learning outcomes, grading, the Honor Code, and access to essential student services such as the Learning Center, the Office of Disability Services, and the Student Wellness Center, she had written, in a statement obviously copied and pasted from somewhere else. *Remember that syllabi are a contract between the instructor and the student, and treat them accordingly. Failure to uphold the terms of the syllabus could leave the College open to legal proceedings.*

Unfortunately, the six pages of legalese that had been shoehorned into what should have been a simple document meant that the actually useful information, like assignments and when they were due, was hidden away starting on page 8, and also that after printing off ten of them, I had used up all my printer paper.

I searched around for another ream, but that must have been one of the things I had opted not to bring with me in order to save space and packing time. Well, I needed to go shopping anyway.

"Guard the house with extreme ferocity while I'm gone," I told Fevronia, and set off to have a new and exciting experience in my life: a visit to a Jersey mall.

5

With my head stuffed full of Jersey stereotypes from a lifetime of exposure to Springsteen, Bon Jovi, *Jersey Shore*, *The Sopranos*, and the Stephanie Plum novels, I had high hopes for the Franklin Mall, but in fact it was much like any other American mall I'd ever been to, although, like everything else I'd seen so far in Jersey, more worn down and depressing, and packed with rude customers on the inside and rude drivers on the outside. Lots of rude drivers.

After a couple of detours to get lost, get gas (an operation made unexpectedly complicated by the fact that there was no self-service option—turns out in Jersey you're not allowed to pump your own gas. I wondered what it would be like to work pumping gas, day in and day out, and if I could get a job like that if this professor thing didn't work out, like it was threatening to), get take-out Chinese, and get lost again, this time in another super-scary neighborhood that would have looked more at home in Haiti than in what was supposed to be one of the richer and more forward-thinking states in the US of A, I made it back to Pleasant Hill, clutching my ream of paper, my dinner, groceries for the next few days including the all-important cat food, and a burning awareness of how much money I had left.

$937 left on my credit card limit to be precise, with $429 in my checking account. Putting down first and last month's rent on the apartment, which cost an eye-watering $1,300/month for a one-bedroom, one-bathroom place with stains in the carpet and a kitchen faucet that threatened to rip out in my hand every time I turned on the hot water, plus a summer of COBRA insurance—my TA health plan had been cut the moment I had stepped off the stage at my hooding ceremony—followed by getting private health insurance for the fall, plus renting the moving pod and shipping all my stuff over here, had drained my already meager finances dry.

As a VAP—Visiting Assistant Professor—I was going to get a flat $15,000 for the semester, no benefits, to teach two classes. The actual adjuncts were probably getting $4,000-5,000 per course, also with no benefits. I was making less than what I had made per credit hour as a TA, and as a TA I had had health insurance.

My courses each met for four hours a week, not the more standard three, and I had agreed, since if I didn't do it, no one would, thus ruining some student's college experience and possibly scuttling their ability to graduate on time, to teach a 1.5-hour advanced independent study as well, so really I would be teaching 9.5 credit hours, while being compensated for teaching six credit hours. And I wouldn't get my first paycheck until September 30, and it would only be a half paycheck, for the period of September 1-15. And somehow I had to buy my plane ticket to San Antonio for the ASEEES (Association for Slavic, East European, and Eurasian Studies) convention in November.

"I hope you like cheap cat food," I said to Fevronia, who had come out from under the bed and was winding around my ankles hopefully, now that her internal clock was telling her it was the witching hour when cats were fed.

Fevronia fixed me with a stern yellow eye and waited for me to dish out her food, which she nibbled at for a moment before abandoning in disdain. I hoped it would grow on her with a little more hunger.

I opened the container of Kung Pow Tofu I had gotten in a fit of weakness and lack of enthusiasm for unpacking and washing all my kitchen utensils, and nibbled at it with an equal lack of enthusiasm. Maybe Fevronia had the right idea. It was certainly something that under other circumstances I would abandon with disdain myself. But since I was hungry and that $937 had to last 65 more days, since my September 30 paycheck would all go straight to making rent, I started forcing down forkfuls while going back online.

Out of habit I checked *Novaya Gazeta* and *Kommersantъ*, before opening up the site for *Nezavisimaya Pravda* (*Independent Truth*) and scanning it for a familiar byline...a text popped up on Skype.

John Halley: What the FUCK are the rooskies doing in Donetsk?

Rowena Halley: Um...what the Americans are doing in Syria? Or Afghanistan? Providing humanitarian aid and training? Isn't that what you're doing?

John Halley: Don't give me that shit. Don't make this about me. Plus, haven't you heard? We're going to be pulling out any day now.

Rowena Halley: Really?

John Halley: That's what they keep promising me. I'll believe it when I step back onto that sweet, sweet US soil.

Rowena Halley: I hope it happens soon. What time is it for you? Shouldn't you be—what do you call it—"getting some rack time"?

John Halley: Can't sleep. Thought I'd check on my little sister. How's the new job?

Rowena Halley: OK.

John Halley: Just OK?

Rowena Halley: Yep.

John Halley: It must really suck, then.

Rowena Halley: Yep. Pretty much.

John Halley: How poor are you?

Rowena Halley: It'll be OK.

John Halley: So pretty fucking poor.

Rowena Halley: Yep.

John Halley: Let me know if you need anything.

Rowena Halley: Sure.

John Halley: I'm fucking serious, Ro. Let me know if you need anything.

Rowena Halley: You're not exactly rich yourself.

John Halley: I can still bail you out if you need it.

Rowena Halley: Thank you. I appreciate it.

John Halley: Anyone try to mess with you at work?

Rowena Halley: Well, it's only been a few hours so far, so only a little.

John Halley: Just remember what I taught you about kicking people in the balls.

Rowena Halley: I don't think that will help in this situation.

John Halley: I find it helps in most situations.

Rowena Halley: Not if they don't have balls.

John Halley: ☺ ☺ ☺ *Well kick 'em wherever they're weak. But I'm serious, Ro: You're a professor. You're in charge now. You can't let people hassle you or give you shit.*

Rowena Halley: I know.

John Halley: I don't think you do, but maybe you'll figure it out. And I'm sorry the job sucks. At least it's only for a few months, right?

Rowena Halley: Right. It ends in December.

John Halley: Any prospects for January?

Rowena Halley: Not yet. There aren't a lot of jobs just for the spring semester.

John Halley: You'll find something. Or you can always move into my place if you have to.

Rowena Halley: You mean in Jackson-hell? Or is it Fayette-nam?

John Halley: No, Fayette-nam is where those Army mofos are. Jacksonville's nice. You'd like it.

Rowena Halley: I'm sure.

John Halley: At least you'd have a roof over your head. And I'd set you up with some of my buddies, but...nah. I can't be having them fucking my kid sister.

Rowena Halley: I appreciate the lovely, chivalrous sentiment.

John Halley: All the ladies do. So what are you going to do if you don't get a job?

Rowena Halley: Come begging for shelter in Jackson-hell, I guess.

John Halley: You know it's there for you. And there might be work. Uncle Sam's always looking for Russian speakers, especially now.

Rowena Halley: Yeah. Maybe we should have been looking for them a little earlier, and then we wouldn't be in this mess.

John Halley: Yeah...I can't even argue with you on that one. Too bad you didn't enlist like I told you to. Then you wouldn't be dealing with this bullshit. You would have gone to the DLI and have your pick of opportunities.

Rowena Halley: Yeah, my pick of interrogation booths at Abu Ghraib. And if I were a very, very good girl, maybe my very own black site. Maybe GITMO! I've always wanted to go to Cuba.

John Halley: God DAMN it, Ro! Idealism won't put food on the table.

Rowena Halley: Because it was hardheaded pragmatism that made you decide to become one of the Few, the Proud, and rake in the big bucks while sitting back in safety and comfort.

John Halley: Fuck you, Ro.

Rowena Halley: Face it: you'll always be Ivanhoe at heart.

John Halley: FUCK YOU, RO.

Rowena Halley: Mom and Dad still hope you'll go back to your real name—and one of these days you will.

John Halley: HELL NO.

Rowena Halley: What do your "buddies" think when they find out your real name?

John Halley: THEY DON'T. IT'S NOT MY FUCKING REAL NAME. MY NAME IS JOHN. WHY THE FUCK ARE YOU SUCH A FUCKING PAIN IN THE ASS?????

Rowena Halley: Because I'm your kid sister?

John Halley: Point taken. Okay, jobs. Do you have a plan?

Rowena Halley: Yes. My plan is to apply to all the jobs that come up.

John Halley: Even the shit ones?

Rowena Halley: I think the shit ones are the only ones I can get.

John Halley: Don't sell yourself short, Ro.

Rowena Halley: I'm not. I'm being a hardheaded pragmatist. I spent 11 months applying to 75 jobs, which were all the jobs in North America and most of Eurasia that I was remotely qualified for, and this is the one I got. Which is way better than what most of my peers ended up with. Maybe things will be better this cycle, but the job market sucks and it isn't going to get any better any time soon. So it's shit jobs or no jobs.

John Halley: Now is the time to put in that application with the CIA.

Rowena Halley: I'd never get a security clearance.

John Halley: You don't know that.

*Rowena Halley: Okay, I'd **probably** never get a security clearance. Besides, you know I can't work there.*

John Halley: For fuck's sake, Ro, they're not THAT evil.

Rowena Halley: It's not that. Well, it is, but it's not JUST that. It's that I'd probably have to cut off all contact with Russian nationals.

John Halley: I think in the case of the Russian nationals you tend to run with, they'd be more likely to want you to recruit them as assets.

Rowena Halley: Even worse! I don't want to do that. I CAN'T do that.

John Halley: Why the fuck not? What Russian is so important that you can't grab the one chance at the one job that might keep you from streetwalking?

Rowena Halley: Thanks, bro.

John Halley: Don't sass me, Ro. I heard you talking with your friend about becoming a stripper.

Rowena Halley: It was a joke. Sort of. It seemed less demeaning and more secure than academia.

John Halley: And maybe you're right. If you end up in Jackson-hell you can look into it. There's certainly plenty of opportunity there. But in the meantime, for Chrissake put in an app with the Agency. What Russians can't you give up? It's not still Dima, is it?

Rowena Halley: It's lots of people. Like three-quarters of my friends. Like my advisor.

John Halley: You hate that bitch!

Rowena Halley: Yeah, but you can't just break up with your advisor. It's like breaking up with your spouse. With whom you have a child. I still need her for recommendations, things like that. And it's ten years of college and most of my adult life.

John Halley: You'll make new friends, Ro. You'll find other people to write recommendations.

Rowena Halley: But not right away.

John Halley: Just promise me you'll put in an app ASAP. And look into jobs on—I can't fucking believe I'm saying this—Army bases (vomit vomit).

Rowena Halley: I applied. They didn't take me.

John Halley: Those motherfuckers! What do you expect from the Army, though. What about the Air Force?

Rowena Halley: There was a job at the Air Force Academy. I applied. Didn't even get a first-round interview.

John Halley: Bunch of fucking pussies. You're better off without them and their lacy panties.

Rowena Halley: Do I have to deconstruct the sexism behind that remark?

John Halley: Jesus Christ. Academia HAS fucked you up and good. Promise me you'll get out of there.

Rowena Halley: And do what?

John Halley: Just put in the app, okay? You don't need all those Russians you can't seem to give up. Especially not him.

Rowena Halley: Maybe.

John Halley: Do you know where he is now?

I looked at my laptop screen.

Rowena Halley: Apparently Donetsk. He has an article up about it.

John Halley: MOTHERFUCKER.

Rowena Halley: It's his job.

John Halley: Yeah, till he gets his super-brave, idealistic, I-hate-Putin ass blown to hell or tortured to death.

Rowena Halley: I know.

John Halley: And he kicked you to the curb anyway! He chose Putin over you!

Rowena Halley: Um...

John Halley: You know what I mean. He chose his obsession with Putin over you, after you went to grad school and everything for him, just to try and get a safe, secure job back in the States that would still let you travel to Russia while he screwed around deciding where he wanted to live ON YOUR MONEY. And how the fuck has that turned out? You're over in the States thinking about becoming a stripper in order to put food on the table, and he's yahooing around some fucking war zone, pretending it's because of his precious principles and not because he can't wait to get his next fix of fighting.

Rowena Halley: Because you would be any different.

John Halley: I know I wouldn't, which is why I fucking know how fucked up it is.

Rowena Halley: I know. I'm not hanging around waiting for him. But no three-letter agency is going to hire me now.

John Halley: They might be pretty fucking desperate right about now...shit, Ro, I have to go. Check in soon, okay? And let me know if you need to crash at my place.

Rowena Halley: Thanks, bro. I will.

6

After that bracing textual exchange with my brother, it was still only 7:00pm, which meant I had at least another hour, or better yet, two, of self-imposed work time. I put my newly acquired ream of paper to good use by printing off the rest of my syllabi and stapling them together and putting them in labeled file folders for each class.

7:30. I couldn't justify quitting now. Even though it was only August 25, I surfed through the AATSEEL (American Association of Teachers of Slavic and East European Languages) job listings, HERC (Higher Education Recruitment Consortium), and, even though it wasn't time yet for the fall listings to come out, the MLA JIL (Modern Language Association's Job Information List), before breaking down and going onto USAJOBS.gov just to tell John I'd done so. But the only job currently posted that required Russian expertise was as a park ranger in Sitka, Alaska. While I would have happily moved out to Sitka, Alaska, in exchange for work, it was a temporary position that asked for at least three years' prior experience as a park ranger in a northern environment. Preference given to those with extensive grizzly bear evasion training.

I wondered how difficult grizzly bear evasion training could be. I would totally do it, if I weren't sure that there were dozens of other, more qualified, candidates already lined up.

My evening ended like so many other evenings had for the past year, with me on The Wiki, as we called it, or the academic job search wiki for my field. The 2014-15 job search page for Russian/Slavic had just been put up this week, but so far there were no jobs except for a super-hurtful open rank chair search for a Modern Languages department that someone must have put up just to torment the rest of us.

Instead of actual job postings there were anxious anonymous messages about why there were no jobs except for that open rank chair search, even though we all knew that the tenure-track jobs wouldn't start being posted until next week, anyway, with the VAPs and better lecturer postings not coming until October at the earliest, and trickling in over the next two semesters, with the adjunct positions appearing in the late spring and summer, as the hundred-plus job seekers still remaining after all the tenure-track positions had been filled grew hungrier and hungrier, like snakes in a particularly overcrowded snake pit.

As I had told John, last year I had applied for all the jobs. All the jobs on the East Coast, the Midwest, the South, the West Coast, and most of Eurasia. At first it had been fun, imagining what it would be like to get that tenure-track position at Duke, that postdoc at Stanford, or that swish three-year visiting position with the possibility of renewal at Williams.

Then it had been less fun, but still interesting, to contemplate what it would be like to get that lectureship at St. Andrews in Scotland, or that fellowship in Hungary, or that instructorship in Israel, or that program development job in Kazakhstan. Then it had been even less fun, but still potentially an adventure, to imagine myself working as a Russian instructor at Fort Bragg or Andrews Air Force Base, clocking in at 8:00am and out at 4:30pm (at least according to the job description) like an hourly employee and riding herd over a bunch of over-confident recruits whose idea of a good time was to mouth off to their female instructors and then be smacked down in vaguely sexual terms. We got them in the Indiana summer program I taught at too, so I was wise to their ways and for enough money, or any money at all, I would have done it with a spring in my step and a smile on my lips.

But none of that had panned out. I had, as my advisor had told me, done exceptionally well, with not one but *two* first-round interviews for tenure-track jobs, although both at state schools in the Midwest, but there had been no invitations for that all-important second round, the campus interview, let alone an actual offer. As the spring semester had wound down and I still had no employment lined up for the fall, not even a visiting instructor position, my committee had started getting shorter and shorter with me, even as they became less and less patient with my requests for more letters of recommendation.

"We thought it would be *you*, Innochka," my advisor had confided in me, when I had confessed in April that the phone interview for the two-year VAP in an especially snowy part of Minnesota had come to nothing, and, according to The Wiki, the job had gone to the inside candidate, who had been there for five years but every two years was forced to reapply and complete the interview process all over again. "We thought that of all our grad students, *you* would get a job. Our hopes were on *you*. And now you've failed us!"

"Ummm...I tried?" My advisor was known far and wide for her blunt-speaking Russian ways, but that was harsh even for her, especially given the fragile state I was in, not only jobless but neck-deep in formatting the deposit copy of my dissertation.

"Isn't there something else you can try?" she'd said.

"Teaching English? That way I could go back to Moscow..."

"No! That's the kiss of death. Only undergrads and losers teach English. You will not teach English! You will teach Russian! Only

Russian! You're the only American here qualified to do so. You must teach Russian or you will be failing not only yourself, but our program!"

"Uh...thanks?"

"Although I noticed you used the accusative case after a negated verb when, although what you said *is* technically correct and some people might have spoken that way, in this particular case a native speaker would more likely have used the genitive..." And she'd gotten distracted from my failures as a job candidate by her dissection of my failures as a Russian speaker, but neither of us had forgotten that statement that I was a failure, not only of myself, but of the program. *I* was supposed to be the one that returned a little of the fading glory to our once-illustrious program by proving that PhDs from state schools could get jobs, *good* jobs, and not just go straight from grad school to SNAP benefits and part-time positions bagging groceries.

And then, in August, at the absolute, impossibly absolute, last-minute, I had gotten this crappy, crappy job, a one-semester fill-in position with no benefits and no possibility of renewal—but it was labeled a VAP, and it was in the Mid-Atlantic. My advisor had practically cried with joy when I had told her about it, and ordered me to take it, no matter what.

"No matter how bad it is, don't complain," she'd told me. "No matter what they ask you to do, always say 'Yes, I'd be happy to,' just like we told you—well, you know. Never say 'No' to them, no matter what, never let them know you don't know what to do. Tell them you do and you'll be happy to do it, whatever it is, and then figure it out afterwards. And be sure to let them know you're single and childless. They love single, childless women. We're the best workers. I'm so glad you didn't get knocked up like the other girls. I hope you're ready to work, Innochka, because it will be so much more work than you've ever done before, but it's in the Mid-Atlantic, Innochka! Only fifty kilometers from New York! This is *it*, Innochka, this is your big chance!"

I shut down The Wiki before I could get any more depressed, and, after contemplating my good fortune and my big chance as I tried to put away some of my dishes only to discover a dead cockroach in the cupboard, gave up for the night and went to bed.

7

The next morning I got up, and after as usual inviting Fevronia to join me, and as usual getting a refusal—Fevronia believed that cardio was best accomplished by periodically leaping out from behind the toilet at inopportune moments and scaring the bejeezus out of her humans—I set off for a dawn jog. A dawn jog that turned into a short but high-intensity dawn run when I stumbled into a neighborhood that appeared to be primarily inhabited by rotting sofas and used condoms.

Back from my exploration of the charms of Greater New Brunswick, I did a few hapkido forms as best I could on the sticky square of kitchen linoleum that had seen better days, followed by some asanas for flexibility and—ahahahaha—relaxation, followed by a shower in my apartment's icky cheap plastic shower, which I still hadn't gotten around to cleaning. I had lived in many sketchy, nasty places, but the thought of the $1,300/month I was paying for this one made the nastiness much less easy to bear.

It was now 8:00am on Tuesday, or 26 hours until my first class was set to start, and I still couldn't access my Cubmail or get into The Den, where fabulous prizes, such as my class rosters and the electronic grade books I was required to keep, were said to reside. I sent off an email to Linda asking her if I could get a print-out of my class rosters, and she sent back an almost immediate snippy response telling me she wasn't allowed to access that kind of information, but that I should go to the help desk at The Bear Cave and maybe they would be able to help me.

There was no point in going to The Bear Cave until at least 9, so I spent a few productive minutes unpacking my dishes and loading them into the doll-sized dishwasher, only snapping off two of the few remaining tines in the bottom rack in the process. I wondered if I should report that. Probably it would result in me losing my deposit and not getting a new dishwasher. I was wise to the ways of slum landlords, I just was having a hard time accepting that $1,300/month hadn't moved me out of slum landlord territory...I had to stop obsessing over this $1,300/month. After all, it could be worse. The other place I'd looked at had had a dead rat lying there in plain view of the front office, and had been $1,500/month. I should just accept the $1,300/month I was throwing into this pit and get on with my life.

Next week the monthly job list that came out of Ohio would be posted, and I could scan it for more jobs I wasn't qualified for, or would never get the requisite security clearance for. Maybe I really should have listened to John seventeen years ago and enlisted along with him...no! Black sites aside, I'd heard too many stories about what happened to girls in the Corps to think that a big brother would protect me, and I'd never felt like having to fit into the labels of bitch, dyke, or ho, anyway. And in a couple of years he was going to hit his twenty-year service mark, and then maybe he'd be chewed up and spit out of the institution he'd signed up for just like me.

I grinned at the thought of the outraged denials that comparison would garner, from academics and Marines alike, and, loading myself down with my laptop, my course files, and every form of ID I could think of, set off to beard the Bear in its Cave.

After only one mildly exciting stall-out, my trusty Honda was parked behind the football stadium, and I was hoofing it across campus to Parson Library, home of a small collection of books and a large collection of aging computers, along with the only Starbucks in a two-township area. I'd realized I was truly slumming it when I'd pulled into town and discovered the lack of Starbucks around me. And it wasn't because its place was being taken by little locally-owned coffee shops that sold fair-trade coffee and homemade scones, either. There was really no market for coffee shops with wifi here. There was Dunkin' Donuts, or nothing. Hopefully my apartment wifi wouldn't go out on me. Haha. How I was going to generate motivation to put in those extra-awful applications I didn't know. Drive into Pennsylvania and search for a Starbucks there, maybe.

But Parson Library had enough of a foot in the world of intellectual exploration to have an overpriced chain coffee shop, although with a limited selection and particularly sad-looking scones. This helped me keep my resolution not to buy any pastries as I sidled past them and across the lobby into The Bear Cave, where a pale skinny girl with lank dark hair sitting at the front desk gave me an unhelpful look and then pretended to ignore me until I was standing directly in front of her.

"I'm having trouble accessing my Cubmail," I said.

"What's your CubID?" she asked, still not looking at me.

"I don't have it yet."

"Students were supposed to get their CubID during orientation."

"I'm not a student. I'm faculty."

That rocked her back.

"Whaddya teach?" she asked, becoming marginally more animated.

"Russian."

"You're Professor Cahill's replacement!" she said, now sitting up straight. "I'm gonna be in your 201 class. I'm Madison."

"Nice to meet you, Madison. I'm..." Oh God, oh God, I was a professor now, and a fully-fledged PhD! I had to introduce myself properly. "Dr. Halley," I said, hoping I sounded confident but not too confident as I said it.

"Why don't you have your CubID yet, Dr. Halley?"

"They haven't given it to me yet. I was only hired a couple of weeks ago."

"But without your CubID you can't get into your Cubmail or get into The Den!"

"I know," I said. "That's what I'm here for. To see if I can at least access my course rosters."

Madison sniffed and wiped her nose on the sleeve of her ratty hoody, and then grinned. "Technically you're not supposed to be able to get into any of that stuff without your CubID, and technically I'm not supposed to give it to you. But since you're my new Russian prof, and you look cool, we'll see what we can do. How old are you, by the way? You don't look old enough to be a prof."

"Thirty-four."

"Whoa! You look way younger than thirty-four. I honestly really did think you were a student when you came in. Not a freshman, maybe, but one of those older students. Certainly not a prof. I guess you're like Professor Miller—you know Professor Miller? The Arabic professor? He's, like, ten years older than he looks too."

"A lifetime of virtue and clean living is its own reward sometimes."

"You gonna be like this all semester? Saying silly shit like that all the time?"

"Probably."

Madison sniffed and wiped her nose on her sleeve again. "Well, it'll be good for a laugh. Brandy..." Her face shut down.

"I heard about Brandy," I said. "That must have been very difficult. Did he have a lot of friends in the Russian program?"

"Yeah. He's the reason I got into it. I was gonna do Spanish like all the other dumbo losers, go for that easy A, since my GPA's not exactly something to write home about, not that I have to write home, since my dad...but Brandy—his name was really Brandon, FYI, but he went through this whole coming-out thing and started making everyone call him Brandy—anyway, Brandy talked me into trying Russian. It's super-hard, but the Cahill was fun, he was chill, you know? A real weirdo, but that's okay. Profs are supposed to be weirdos. Are you a weirdo?"

"Um...that would depend on your definition of weirdo, I guess."

Madison grinned. "Are you a strict grader?" she asked. "'Cause that's the important question, you know? You know Rate My Professor? You on it?"

"I haven't checked," I said. "And I think I'm reasonably strict but fair when it comes to grading."

"You should check out your Rate My Professor entry! I bet you got lots of peppers! You know? For hotness?"

"I know," I said. "I haven't checked. So do you think I could look at my course rosters? Maybe get a printout of them?"

"Just a sec. Jason! Jason!"

A twenty-something man came shambling up to the desk from the back office. He was plump and scruffy and vaguely bear-like. I wondered if they hired people based on their resemblance to the college mascot. I reminded myself that making jokes with Madison about the suitability of his appearance to his work location would be inappropriate, now that I was a professor.

"What is it, Maddie?" he asked, looking at a spot on the floor halfway between the two of us. I was willing to bet next month's $1,300 rent payment that he lived in a basement somewhere and spent all his free time playing *World of Warcraft*. I shouldn't be so judgmental about people and their peculiar obsessions, especially since his had led to employment that was more gainful than my own.

"This is Professor Halley," Madison said proudly, like she was responsible for me herself. "Our new Russian prof. Only she can't get into her Cubmail or The Den and see her course rosters."

"Do you have your CubID?" Jason asked, mumbling and still staring at the spot on the floor.

"Don't be silly, Jay-Jay, they haven't given it to her yet, that's why she's here! You know what asshole retards they are over in admin. Oops—I'm not supposed to say that, am I? The R word, that is. Or the A word. Sorry, Professor H. We had a whole training thing about insensitive speech."

"I've heard worse," I said. "But class starts in"—I checked my phone—"24 and a half hours, and I still don't have my course rosters, and I can't see if any students have emailed me."

"Jay-Jay'll check your course rosters, won't you, Jay-Jay? And I can check your email for you, if you don't mind me going in there. You don't have any porn in there, do you?"

"If I do, it didn't come from me," I said. "I've never been able to access it; that's why I'm here."

"Right. What's your first name?"

"Rowena."

"Whoa! Like in *Harry Potter*?"

"Yes, it's the same name, but I was born years and years before the first *Harry Potter* book came out—I know, crazy, right?—so it's like in *Ivanhoe*."

"What's that?"

"Um...a book by Sir Walter Scott?"

"Who's that?"

"A famous author," I said. "Like JK Rowling, but in the 19th century. *Ivanhoe* was made into a movie with Elizabeth Taylor."

"Did she play Rowena?"

"No, she played Rebecca."

"Huh. I think I saw a picture of Elizabeth Taylor once. You look kinda like her. And kinda like Rowena Ravenclaw, right? Do you look like the Rowena character in that movie as well? Did she look like us? Pale skin and dark hair? Only you've got sort of blue-ish eyes, don't you, and mine are brown, damn it."

"No," I said. "The Rowena in the *Ivanhoe* movie was blonde."

"Whoa, that's still cool, though. To be able to see a movie with someone with your name in it. Not a lot of Madisons in movies."

"Probably there will be in a few years," I said encouragingly.

"Yeah, maybe," said Madison, and, wiping her nose on her sleeve again, sat down at the elderly computer at the desk and clicked around for a bit until she declared, "Okay, I'm in. Here's your email. Wanna look?"

"Sure," I said. "Thanks. How'd you do that?"

"It was easy. For faculty and staff Cubmail is the first four letters of their last name plus the first two letters of their first name and then @tlasc.edu. So yours is hallro@tlasc.edu. And I got admin privileges in some of the systems, so I was able to look up your CubID. I'm writing it down right here. So I went in and changed your password for you—Jason showed me how to do that—and I was in. Your password's now Russian1, but you can change it if you want. Here's your BearCave employee page with all your info on it. It says you haven't done your F-E-R-P-A training yet. What's F-E-R-P-A?"

"FERPA," I said. "It's the law that says I can't show your grades to anyone without your permission."

"Really? There's a law about that?"

"Uh-huh."

"What, not even my dad?"

"Not even your dad. You're an adult now and those are your grades. You have control over who sees them."

"Uh-huh," said Madison, with well-deserved skepticism about her supposed empowerment. "My dad could see 'em if he wanted to."

"He can ask you about them, of course, but you're not obliged to show them to him if you don't want to, and *I* can't show them to him without your written consent."

"Haha! I can't wait to tell him that. Not that he'll give a shit. You wanna see your mail?"

"Is there anything interesting?" I asked, peering around the desk to read the screen.

"Doesn't look like it. Just a bunch of shit about faculty orientation—did you go to that?"

"No," I said. "It was only for incoming permanent faculty."

"Oh. And some stuff about convocation—you going to that?"

"Also only for permanent faculty."

"Oh. Whatevs. So what *do* you get to go to?"

"Class," I said. "Not that orientation and convocation are that exciting anyway, I'm sure."

"Right. *I* wouldn't go to them. Oh hey, Jay-Jay's here with your course rosters! I gave her her CubID," Madison told Jason.

"We're not supposed to give them out to faculty without a CubID card," said Jason, looking down at the floor as he handed me the printout of my course rosters.

"Don't be a re—don't be a dick—oh fuck—sorry, Professor H," said Madison. "Bet professors don't talk like this, do they?"

"They beat it out of us pretty hard in PhD school," I said.

"Yeah, that's what my dad says. He wants me to go to grad school, but I said fu—screw that. I hate this fu—sucking place, you know what I'm saying? 'Cept for Russian class, 'cause Cahill was such a spazz and Brandy was, well..."

"It must be hard to come back without him," I said.

"Yeah, well...your CubID number is there on your roster, so you should be able to access whatever you need now, set up whatever you need to. Just give us a holler if you need help, okay? I'll be here until noon."

"Thanks, Madison. You've been super-helpful."

"Anything for my favorite new prof," said Madison, with a sincerity that seemed only somewhat feigned.

8

Using my illicitly-gained access to The Den, I spent the next couple of hours setting up my course websites, with only occasional calls to Madison for help. Like most other university online systems I had encountered, The Den and Cubmail were clunky, opaque, and difficult to access for their legitimate users, but easy to hack, or so it seemed by the way Madison breezily got into the areas that were closed to me, even though I was faculty and she was a student. I resolved to keep all my grades on a spreadsheet on my password-protected personal laptop, and only post them occasionally in The Den, and double-check them before submitting. I also resolved to avoid online quizzes, saving paper be damned.

"Does everyone have this much trouble setting things up?" I asked Madison, after she had helped me upload my syllabi when the system locked me out for the third time.

"Yeah, most profs are totes clueless when it comes to doing any of this shit."

"*I'm* not clueless," I said. "I know my way around the web and a computer as well as most."

"Yeah, but our system requires a special touch, you know what I'm saying? You have to, like, wear your panties backwards and kiss the Blarney stone three times before you approach it. Most profs don't have the patience."

"Don't they have problems with people like you hacking in and changing grades?" I asked.

Madison grinned. "Of *course* not. Actually, that's harder to do than most other things. The actual, official grades are pretty secure. The registrar's office is behind a serious firewall, and they don't let work-studies have anything to do with that. But the course websites and Cubmail—anyone with admin privileges can get into that. And the algorithms for automatically calculating the grades can get fucked up all on their own—actually, that's where most of the problem come from. So I'd check the grades the site gives you before entering them into the registrar's site."

"Awesome," I said. "I'm so thrilled that using these systems is mandatory."

"Yeah, whatevs. If you post anything on Cubmail you don't want other people reading, you deserve to get caught, that's what I say."

"I have to agree." And I did. TLASC, like every other institution of higher education that I knew of, was freaking out about privacy, on the one hand, and inappropriate behavior and potential active shooters, on the other. All faculty-student communications were supposed to go through Cubmail, and all emails could be accessed by the administration in case of need. Or, apparently, by an enterprising work-study like Madison whenever she felt like it.

This led to some ugly complications with FERPA, since as I'd just told Madison, random strangers were not supposed to be able to see student grades, which could potentially happen if a student requested (in writing, of course) that their current grade be emailed to them, only to have that email read for whatever reason by someone in administration...not my problem, I decided. I would continue to provide students with their current grades upon request and generally act as I saw fit, and not worry too much over who was reading my emails and sneaking into my course websites. And I would keep my master gradebook and all sensitive or important materials on my own laptop, and only use Cubmail for TLASC-related communications. I wasn't going to be here long enough to bother switching over to TLASC-provided anything anyway.

Once the course websites were set up to my satisfaction, I briefly considered doing my FERPA, Title IX, Campus Health and Safety, and Student Wellbeing training modules, but those turned out to be video courses that would take ages, and I was starting to get antsy from sitting for so long in one place, so, thanking Madison for her help and getting a cheery wave, only slightly spoiled by her wiping her nose before and afterwards, in response, I packed up and headed home.

Once home I decompressed from computer work by unpacking a few more boxes, but that soon got boring, and I didn't want to unpack too much anyway, since it would all have to be packed back up in four months, so I shoved a bunch of still-unopened boxes in the bedroom closet, put the hanging rod back up after it fell down on my head as I was shoving in the boxes, checked on Fevronia—still in a snit—lurked for a few minutes on The Wiki in the hopes that some new, awesome, incredible, just-perfect job that the other 150 candidates currently on the active prowl wouldn't bother to apply for would have shown up since last night, and then, unable to put it off any more, did all the training modules.

When I was done it was mid-afternoon and I had gleaned many important pieces of wisdom, such as not using a rolling chair as a stepladder when trying to reach something on a high shelf, or not picking up broken glass with your bare hands, but instead sweeping it up with a broom and dustpan. I also correctly answered a number of questions about proper ergonomic posture, reducing eye fatigue, and maintaining proper mental health.

I also learned—for about the fifth time—that I could not release student grades to third parties without the student's written permission, and that I was required to report all suspected cases of sexual assault. No mention of what would happen once the case was reported, but if precedent was any guide, the assaulter would be given a slap on the wrist—probably while whining loudly about how Title IX was ruining his life and destroying his future and how hard it was to be a male in America these days—and the assaultee would be hounded out of the school and end up addicted and suicidal. And I learned how to report my concerns about student wellbeing, and what the college wanted me to do if I thought a student might be about to shoot themself and/or 27 of their peers.

The Office of the Provost has launched an innovative initiative to promote student wellbeing, I was informed. *Faculty and staff are a vital part of this important and timely initiative, and are essential to creating a safe campus atmosphere where students can flourish and unlock their full potential. TLASC is committed to creating an environment where students can not only develop intellectually, but where they feel truly cared for and part of a vibrant and diverse community, one that promotes the values of tolerance, civility, and mutual wellbeing. We all have a responsibility to care for each other and make our shared TLASC experience one we can all look back on with fondness!*

This was followed by instructions on how to have suspicious-looking students arrested, committed to a mental institution, or shot down by SWAT teams. I consoled myself with the thought that at least *I* was not required to come to class packing a gun—yet—and, correctly answering the necessary number of questions, passed my mandatory training with an A.

9

The next day was Wednesday. Class day. I started off with another dawn jog, this time ending up in a neighborhood that just had normal trash on the streets, not rotten sofas, used condoms, and discarded hypodermic needles, so I did my usual two miles and had a short but rewarding conversation with a couple of people stepping out of the grits-and-greens place I had driven by on Monday, which served as the boundary between the working-class neighborhood that was between it and my apartment complex, and the drug-dealing-class neighborhood that was between it and campus.

It turned out we—the two men stepping out of True Grit, as a faded, peeling sign proclaimed it to be, and me—all had family in Atlanta, which gave us something to bond over. The effect was only slightly spoiled by them remarking first on my bright blue running shoes and then on my legs and asking me if I had a boyfriend.

"Yes," I said.

"Back in Atlanta?" asked the more forward of the two men, who had introduced himself as Jimmy. Judging by the weathering on his face, he must have been approaching fifty, or maybe he was really my age but a lifetime of smoking and manual labor had worn him out before his time. He had the truly black skin you rarely saw on Americans except amongst immigrants and the very poor, and was missing half his teeth.

"He's deployed," I said.

This led to another brief round of bonding, as both the men had served and currently had nephews serving, and I was able to run off before they could demand to know more about my boyfriend and I would have had to decide how much to tell them of the truth and how much to pretend that John was my boyfriend. John wouldn't mind, and had in fact told me on multiple occasions to tell any men hassling me exactly that, but it always felt icky to me to pass my brother off as my boyfriend in order to escape unwanted sexual advances.

I fled fast enough to almost outpace the two men's comments about the pros and cons of my skinny white girl ass, but not fast enough to outpace the knowledge that if I were to complain about this to anyone, or even mention it, I would be treated to a double whammy of criticism, first for wandering into the wrong neighborhood and thus bringing about my own harassment, and second for being a white woman complaining about sexual harassment by black men, because it had recently been decided that complaining about or fighting back against street harassment of women was racist.

Which it was, in the sense that 98% of the street harassment I had ever received in America had been from working-class black and Latino men like that pair there. Lucky for me I had spent enough time being sexually harassed to have built up a high tolerance for it and a number of survival tactics, like being super-nice and then sprinting off down the sidewalk at a high turn of speed.

Once back at my apartment I fended off a sneak attack from Fevronia, did my forms and asanas, and then, wanting to make sure I got there in plenty of time to get someone else to let me into my classrooms, dressed in my teaching clothes and set off for campus.

The two exits I traveled on Route 1 were two exits too many, especially with the Honda's dicky transmission. I was just going to drive through the drug dealer neighborhood, I decided: my chances of dying were slimmer.

And once I got to campus, I almost had another wreck trying to get into the faculty parking lot behind the football stadium, which was now filling up rapidly with people who seemed even more stressed out than me. The delay caused by my exchange with the parking lot guard, who had to examine my TLASC parking hangtag, which HR had managed to get to me prior to the beginning of classes, unlike everything else, and interrogate me about why I didn't have a proper CubID to swipe myself in, led to a lot of honking in the line behind me, and then people trying to cut around me as I finally pulled through the gate and into the lot.

I found a spot in a far corner and, loading myself up with my laptop, my course files, my textbooks, my water bottle, and my purse, I joined the exodus of stressed-out, overladen people trying to run in badly-fitting suits without dropping piles of paperwork or very expensive laptops onto the pavement. Some had more success than others: the bag of the woman in front of me split open as she attempted to jog in a threadbare pencil skirt and last year's unflattering kitten heels.

"Here," I said, kneeling down to help her gather up what looked like dozens of handouts for an introductory German course. "Oh, hi, Kate."

"Thanks," said Kate, sounding too frazzled to be grateful. "Oh crap, is that the time. Gotta go!" She swept up the handouts in a crumpled armhold and dashed off in the run of someone who avoided exercise except under duress.

Feeling smug about my fitness and punctuality, I made my way at a more leisurely pace to Dreme Hall, where I dropped off my textbooks and files for my RUSS 201 class in the adjunct warehouse, spent a few minutes reviewing my roster and lesson plan for RUSS 101, got some rather vague directions from a harried-looking Linda on where to find Angelo Hall, and set off to teach my first class as a real, genuine professor. Well, sort of. A real, genuine, part-time VAP on a temporary contract with no benefits. But still, this was it! I was living the dream! Doing the job that I had spent so long and worked so hard to get! Granted, it was exactly the same job I had been doing for the past several years, except for less money, and it could be a little less humiliating and more glamorous, but it could be worse. I could be working in a chicken processing plant, for example.

Angelo Hall turned out to be a brand-new neocolonial brick building behind Parson Library. It was so new that they were still rolling out the sod on the landscaping around it as I walked up, staying carefully between the freshly painted black chains that lined all the walkways around the quad and the classroom buildings.

When I stepped in, the building still smelled like fresh construction, and the walls gleamed with new white paint, with hardly a scuffmark in sight. Big windows let in the morning light, and the whole thing looked like an advertisement for a modern liberal arts education, right down to the smart consoles at the head of every classroom, which looked like they could be used to guide a probe to Mars. I could just imagine myself setting up all sorts of fabulous learning experiences for the students...watching authentic news programs, getting Skype calls direct from Russia in order to chat with native speakers...these things never worked as well as I thought they should, but in *this* beautiful building, surely the tech and the timing would work, and the students would sit there with rapt attention, marveling at the opportunities their tuition dollars were buying them.

Angelo 027 was not, though, in one of the light and spacious classrooms near the entrance, but in a back corner in the basement with no windows and a distinctly chemically smell. I took shallow breaths as I waited out in the corridor, telling myself that there was plenty of oxygen down here, no problem, it would be no problem to keep my focus and keep everyone awake in this airless environment, and I wasn't claustrophobic at all, no way.

My lack of claustrophobia made itself ever more acutely felt as the corridor began filling up with students waiting to get into their 10:00am classes. The door to Angelo 027 opened at 9:53, and drowsy-eyed students began filing out. I slipped in past the last one, where I found Kate gathering up her things with shaking hands.

"Oh, hey again," I said. "This must be the department's go-to classroom in Angelo."

"Yeah, we're so lucky to get a room in the new building," she said, her voice trembling. "Only there are no dry-erase markers for the whiteboards, and I forgot to bring any for myself."

"What do you mean, there are no markers?"

"Didn't they tell you? They don't keep markers and chalk in the classrooms. You have to bring your own. Only I only brought chalk."

"They expect us to bring our own markers?"

"Well, the department will issue you with two a month. But you have to remember to get them from Linda, and she has to be in the right mood to give them to you. I always carry around a box of chalk with me, but I totally forgot my markers this morning. And there were too many students and not enough chairs, so some of them had to go out and steal chairs from one of the classrooms down the hall, and we got into trouble for that and someone from the history department came and complained and was *really rude* about it, and threatened to report the class to the fire department. It's not my fault they put me here and then overenrolled my class! And then I couldn't sign into the smart system, so I called IT, so that ate up, like, half my class time, and then they said the system was down on this floor anyway, so my whole lesson plan was pretty much down the toilet, and the students, well, they were sort of nice about it, I guess, but some were laughing at me, and some of them were pissed, I could tell, and to be fair, I'd be pissed too, if I were them. I mean, we wasted the entire class session, just wasted it, and you know how precious class time is, especially in 101!"

"That sucks. I hope your next class goes better."

"Yeah...it's 201, and I know those kids, so...maybe. Some of them are okay. And then this afternoon I have to drive over and teach a 101 class at Tech." Kate jammed the rest of her handouts into her bag, along with her laptop and her box of crumbling chalk, and made her sad way out of the classroom, stepping back and nervously letting in two big boys in leather jackets who had "immigrant from the former USSR" written all over them.

Warned by Kate's fiasco, I collared the bigger of the two boys, who introduced himself as Danila, from Odessa, and sent him off on a mission to steal any loose dry erase markers he could find. He and his new friend, Vitya from Minsk, brightened at the possibility of doing anything criminal, and ran off jauntily, speaking to each other in a mix of slightly accented English and broken Russian.

"I think they will be trouble," said a girl they had almost bowled over on their way out the classroom. She had big ash-blonde hair and a pouty mouth and an attitude I instantly recognized as Insecure Russian Girl Posturing.

"If they can get us some markers, they'll be doing a service to their Motherland," I said. "What's your name?"

"Ira," she said, sitting down and crossing her arms defensively over her ample breasts. "Are you Russian? I already speak Russian; I'm not sure I should be here."

"I'm not Russian but I've spent a lot of time there." Time on the ground counted for more amongst Russian speakers than formal education, which was both a blessing and a curse. "Can you read and write?"

"A little," she said, hugging herself more tightly in a way that said it was only a very, very little.

"Well, why don't you spend a couple of days in this class, see how it goes. You can always move up into 201 if that seems more appropriate."

"201 doesn't fit into my schedule."

"Well, in that case, this class might just be a very easy, relaxing experience for you."

She sniffed and hunched over her textbook.

Danila and Vitya returned bearing a faded blue marker that they claimed to have nabbed out from under the nose of an irate history instructor, and class began. Along with Danila, Vitya, and Ira, there was Riva, a short, dark-haired girl with a friendly smile and perfectly accented Russian, who was the only person who was actually able to read the phrase "What is your name?" when I wrote it on the board. We established that her grandmother had taught her to read and write, and that she should probably move up into 201.

Beyond the heritage speakers there were 14 non-heritage speakers, who sat there in a state of semi-stunned shock, mixed with a little delight over the incredibly badass, hardcore thing they were doing, especially when I wrote in Cyrillic cursive on the board, and promised them that by the end of the semester, they would be able to read what I had written.

Unlike my own undergraduate classes in Georgia, everyone was white, although with many more students of East European Jewish extraction than back home. They seemed to range from upper working class to upper middle class. None of them had blown me away with their brilliance yet. TLASC billed itself as an elite liberal arts college at in-state tuition prices, but thus far I had seen little sign of anything elite in either the students or the faculty. They all—we all—mainly seemed like Princeton's rejects, desperately clinging to any scrap of elitism by whatever fingerholds we could manage.

At exactly 10:50 all the students, who had been spending the last five minutes checking their phones as much as practicing the introductions I had taught them, rose as one and dashed out the door, with calls of "See you, Prof!" from Danila and Vitya, a snobbish toss of her head from Ira, a friendly smile from Riva, and dazed looks from the other kids. I congratulated myself on my completely tech-free lesson plan, which had allowed me to do everything I had meant to do without relying on the nonfunctioning smart classroom system, and on the completion of my first class as a "real professor," and, dodging what seemed to be imprecations from someone who thought we had stolen her marker, followed them out the door.

10

When I showed back up at the adjunct warehouse, I found a plump, pleasant-faced girl with glasses, messy brown hair that kept falling into her eyes, and an expression of terminal good nature waiting for me in the corridor.

"Professor Halley?" she asked as I approached.

"You must be Mackenzie," I said. "Hang on just a second." I juggled my books, bags, files, and keys as I tried to open the door, causing my textbook to leap like a salmon out of my arms and into Mackenzie's hands.

"Nice save," I told her appreciatively.

"Thanks. I played softball all throughout high school, almost got a scholarship for it, but then they gave me an academic scholarship at the last minute instead."

Mackenzie, my independent study, certainly didn't look like someone who would have ever been in the running for an athletic scholarship, which either went to show that you never knew, or that the bar for athletic scholarships to TLASC was extremely low.

"Wow, I remember this textbook," she said, following me into the adjunct warehouse. "Russian 101. Those were the days. Me and Brandy..."

"You were friends with Brandy too?" I asked, doing some more juggling as I attempted to create a place amongst all the Arabic, Chinese, and German textbooks and teaching materials to set my things down on and make some clear desk space for me and Mackenzie.

"Yeah. He was the best."

"I'm sure," I said, giving up on imposing any sort of order to the chaos on the desks, and setting my things on the floor and pulling two chairs away from the tables, into the tiny circle of clear floor in the middle of the room. "I'm sorry about what happened," I said. "That must have been very upsetting for everyone."

"Yeah. Me and Brandy, we were supposed to go to Russia this summer, but instead..." She made a small circling motion with her hand, and swallowed. "But it was great even so," she said, her naturally high-pitched voice even higher than it should have been. "Two months in St. Pete, right during the white nights! Have you ever been there?"

"I've visited it a few times," I said. "But I mainly lived in Moscow."

"Moscow's cool too, but so huge!"

"That it is," I agreed.

"Anyway, Brandy and I, we picked out the program together, we applied together, and then...I wasn't sure if I should go or not, you know, without him, but I didn't want to stay here either, so I decided to go ahead and go. You know, in his memory. Plus, it'd already been paid for. And it was great, but it would have been greater if Brandy'd been there. He wasn't sure at first, you know, with all the stories about what they do to gay kids there, but Professor Cahill, he said you didn't actually have to worry about it as long as you didn't do something stupid, and he should know...did you know that about Professor Cahill? I didn't just out him, did I? I mean, I don't think it was any kind of big secret...and professors are normally pretty cool about that sort of thing, aren't they?"

"We are," I said. "We may have our flaws, but most of us are indeed pretty cool about that sort of thing. We have to be, given how many gay professors there are."

Mackenzie giggled and then covered her mouth with her hand. "I mean, yeah," she said, once she'd recovered her composure. "Sometimes it seems like half my professors are gay. Not that there's anything wrong with that. It's kind of cool, you know what I mean? But I wonder why."

"Academia is a refuge for a certain kind of weirdo," I told her. "Or so they think. And Russian Studies particularly so."

She giggled again, this time not bothering to cover her mouth. "I didn't want to say anything, but...but it's okay to be straight, too, right? Because I'm thinking of going to grad school. Professor Cahill always encouraged me."

"It's okay to be straight as long as you don't think you're going to meet any straight men," I told her. "Or you're planning to have kids. If you're planning to go to grad school we should definitely talk. I know a lot of the programs and their pros and cons, so we can strategize. But in the meantime, let's talk about your independent study."

We spent the next half hour planning what Mackenzie would do over the course of the semester, which was basically to read up on current events in the Russian-language news and try to discuss them with me once a week in Russian.

"Of course, there's so much going on right now—but I suppose there's always so much going on with Russia, isn't there? But with what's going on in Ukraine right now—have you been following it?"

"Some," I said.

"Do you"—she suddenly looked shy—"do you know anyone over there? Where the fighting is? Brandy, he, well, he got really interested in the Maidan, he wanted to go down to Kiev and check it out while we were there, but, well...what do you think of the Euromaidan?"

"I think it's complicated," I said. "And I don't know a lot of people from there, but a...friend of mine is currently in the war zone."

Her mouth dropped open. "Doing what?"

"Reporting on it. It's what he does. He's a journalist."

"An American?"

"No, Russian."

Her mouth dropped open even more. "But...that's so dangerous...Russian journalists..."

"I know," I said.

"Have you ever heard of...Brandy kept going on about her...Anna something?"

"Anna Politkovskaya? Yes. Yes, I have."

"Have they ever found her killers?"

"They found some of them. They just convicted them in June after a retrial."

"But nothing like that is going to happen to *your* friend, will it?"

"I hope not. So what got you interested in Anna Politkovskaya?"

"It was mainly Brandy. He was always really into current events, political stuff, you know? Well, it made sense, since he was a big LGBTQ activist, but he was interested in all sorts of stuff, followed all sorts of stuff on the news. He wanted to be a politician, you know, the first openly gay mayor of New Brunswick, stuff like that." She smiled a sad smile. "I always used to tell him he'd have to shave off his mohawk, let the dye fade out, and then we'd all see he had mousy brown hair just like me. He was such a skinny little guy, really, no taller than me and much thinner, like you could just blow at him and he'd fall down, but he made up for it with his big mouth, you know what I mean? He never could shut up or back down. Until..."

"Sometimes bad things happen to good people," I said. "Really bad things."

"I don't know that you'd call Brandy a *good* person," said Mackenzie reflectively. "He was kind of a slut and he could be a real jerk sometimes. Everything that had anything to do with him, and a lot of stuff that didn't, was always all about him. But he was smart and he was fun and I wish he had been able to come to Russia with me this summer. Or maybe not. Probably he would have picked a fight with the OMON—you know what the OMON are?"

"Yes," I said.

"I saw some shut down some stuff that was happening after a soccer game this summer." She shuddered. "Glad we don't have people like that here. Anyway, I saw them and I just...ran away, but no doubt Brandy would've run straight at them and shouted at them that they were violating human rights, or something."

"Running away from the OMON is often the right thing to do," I said. "You can't do a lot about human rights when they're dragging you away by your ankles and throwing you into a holding tank. You're still alive and free, and that's more important that almost anything else, because that means you can still fight for what you believe in."

"Oh. Really? You, like, care about this kind of stuff a lot?"

"I do. Before I went into academia, I worked for several years for an NGO that investigates human rights abuses in developing democracies."

"Wow, really?! That must have been awesome!!"

"Mostly it was heartbreaking," I said. "But if you're interested in the NGO path after graduation, we should talk about that as well."

"Yeah, that would be...that would be awesome, actually. I'm really interested in working for an NGO when I finish school, maybe more than grad school, but my parents aren't so hot on it. They want me to get an MBA and then go to law school."

"You can still work for an NGO after you finish law school," I said.

"I don't think that's the kind of law they want me to practice," said Mackenzie. "I'm interested in human rights and immigration law, but they want me to become a corporate attorney."

"The important thing to remember is that only you can live your life, not your parents," I said before I could stop myself.

"Yeah, but they're the ones paying for it," said Mackenzie, and with that cynical thought, left for lunch.

11

Kate came into the adjunct warehouse while I was creating a gradebook for RUSS 101 on my laptop.

"You're supposed to do that in The Den," she said. "All grades are supposed to be kept in The Den."

"Yes, but I want to keep the master gradebook on my laptop, where it's safe. Safer," I said.

"Yeah, makes sense. Last semester something got off with my weighting in The Den's gradebook and all my grades were half a letter grade off and I had to go in and redo them all manually and then petition the dean's office to change every single one of them, and meanwhile I had students emailing me day and night, I had parents emailing me about it...a complete nightmare."

"Was your second class any better than your first?"

"It wasn't a complete disaster like the first, but...I'm just so tired!" she burst out. "I'm tired of sucking up to students who don't give a crap about German or anything else, and busting my ass to make great lesson plans that integrate technology with communicative methodology when the college can't even get the smart classrooms to work, not even in the new buildings, and I'm tired of schlepping all over Jersey and still not having enough money to pay rent! I'm thirty-five, I have a BA from Harvard and a PhD from Princeton, I work two jobs, and I still have to borrow money from my dad to make the rent every month!"

I was facing the open door and saw the hay-haired woman from the faculty meeting on Monday stop as she was passing by, stare into our office with a look of contempt, as if Kate's problems were the result of personal failure rather than systemic exploitation, and hurry off, probably to teach a class on queer theory and the systemic oppression of non-normative sexualities, or something like that.

"Yeah," I said. "The rent here is highway robbery."

"And my car needs new brakes—actually, my car needs to be a whole new car, but there's just no way I could afford to get a new car, not now, not any time soon. Are you going on the market this fall?"

"You bet."

"Yeah, me too. Any good jobs open up yet?"

"It's still August."

"Yeah, I know. How many tenure-track jobs were there in Russian last year?"

"Fourteen. But several of them weren't actually in Russian, and several were open-rank, so they weren't going to hire someone who didn't already have tenure. So really only about eight or nine."

"Jesus, that's even worse than German. How many people applying for them?"

"Probably about 100-150."

"Not as many as German but still way too many. Are there a lot of VAPs? Postdocs?"

"A dozen or so decent VAPs. A couple of postdocs."

"And then stuff like this."

"And then stuff like this," I agreed. "Are you going on the market too?"

"Yeah, of course, but I...I just don't know if I can do it. Not again. *And* I really need to submit this article I've been working on before I start sending out apps, but I just...it was rejected in the spring with some really hurtful comments, and I told myself I'd revise it over the summer, but I was teaching a summer course here, and you know how it is, you think you're going to get lots of writing done over the summer but when you're teaching it just sucks up every molecule of time and energy you have, and those comments...I just didn't. So now it's still sitting there staring at me, and the JIL will be coming out in a couple of weeks and I haven't done anything, and...I just hate it! I hate the way people treat me like a failure, like a baby, like I've brought this on myself! Everyone tells me they wish they had an easy job like mine, even though most of them barely scraped through undergrad, none of them have ever written so much as an article, let alone a dissertation, and ask them to get up and teach—*in a foreign language*—and they'd wet themselves, but *I'm* the one with the easy job! I can't...I just don't know if I can do it for another year. Oh crap! Is that the time? I have to get going if I'm going to make it to my two o'clock class at Tech."

Kate rushed out. As soon as she was gone, Alex came in, almost bouncing from restrained energy as he walked.

"Good first class?" he asked.

"Pretty good. And you?"

"Yeah. Are you going to be here all day?"

"No, I have class at one and then I'll probably go home."

"Oh, okay. Are you having lunch?"

"No," I said. "I don't normally eat lunch. I fast most days until midafternoon."

"Why?"

"I gained twenty pounds my first year of grad school, and then by the time I got that off, I started dissertating and gained thirty pounds. So I decided steps had to be taken. I started fasting, and got back into running."

Alex looked me over swiftly. "You look great to me," he said, and then looked away.

"Thanks."

"I used to run. When I was forced to during PT. My real thing is rock climbing, but these days I almost never have the time."

"Yeah, I know what you mean," I agreed.

"So'd you have a class in the new building today?"

"Yep. Me and Kate both."

"How was it? I'll be there this afternoon."

"They didn't have enough markers!" I said, my earlier outrage returning at the memory of this particular example of petty stinginess. Not being allowed to make copies was a given, but not being provided with chalk and markers was a new low for me.

"Yeah, we're not supposed to leave markers in the classrooms, in case they get stolen."

"Who would steal markers? Other than other desperate teachers."

"Students wanting to get high?" said Alex, one side of his mouth turning up in smile, probably at the thought of gangs of desperate teachers going on midnight marker raids.

"But the classrooms are kept locked anyway!"

"People still break into them all the time. I'll drop by and see if I can get a marker from Linda on my way out. Were the smart classrooms working?"

"Not this morning."

"Shit. I was going to show them a cartoon. Well, whatever. We'll figure something out. It'll be good to see inside the new building in any case, see how those illegal Superstorm Sandy dollars were spent."

"Illegal?" I said.

"Yeah, well...I mean, we got power knocked out, that's true, and a few trees blown down, and the building site was trashed a bit, but somehow the recovery dollars turned into a brand-new, state-of-the-art classroom building. Not that I'm complaining, but it's got a bit of an unkosher whiff."

"Yeah," I said. "Well, I'd better get to my second class."

"Have a good class," said Alex. "Well...if you're leaving...I guess I'd better get some rest between classes." He was already unrolling his mattress as I went out the door.

12

My 201 class was in Dreme 301, which I thought would be just down the hall from my office, which was Dreme 331, but turned out to be in an annex on the other end of a third-floor skywalk, and then around a corner and tucked away in the absolute back of the building. Discovering this delayed me enough that I arrived at the classroom at 12:54, as the instructor of the previous class was walking away down the hall, having already locked the door behind her. I shouted at her to wait, but she shrugged and mimed being in a hurry, and when I chased her down, she only shrugged again and told me she couldn't let strangers into the classrooms, even if she had the time, which she didn't.

I made it back to the classroom at 12:56, by which time what looked to be my entire 201 class had gathered and were milling about in the corridor, looking at me with wide-eyed curiosity tinged with a little youthful sadism.

"Professor H!" cried Madison, disengaging from a clique she had been huddled up with and jogging over to me with the jog of the non-athlete. Somehow today she looked even frailer and shabbier than she had the day before, with an even runnier nose and a manic look in her eyes.

"Hey everyone, it's Professor H!" she called out, making everyone stop their chit-chat and stare openly at me. "It's our new

Russian prof! Here to teach us some Russian, Prof?" She giggled at her pun.

"Maybe," I said. "Although we may have to hold class outside. I don't have a key to the classroom yet."

"That's okay, Prof! We all like it when class is outside, don't we, everyone! And this classroom sucks anyway."

That last statement was seconded by a fervent wave of nods by the rest of the students.

"Is this everyone?" I asked. "Is there anyone missing who you know should be here?"

"Only Brandy!" said Madison.

All the other students winced. After a short delay, Madison winced too. "I shouldn't have said that, huh?" she said. "Only...he *should* be here."

"Yes," I agreed, leaving it unclear what I was agreeing to, which was both statements. "Okay, what's a good place to hold an outdoor class? And does anyone have a piece of paper they can leave a note on telling any stragglers where to go?"

"The Caff is a good place, Professor H! They have outdoor tables we can sit on! At," she corrected herself. "Or on," she added. "They don't care."

"The Caff is the outdoor cafeteria seating, Professor," said an earnest-looking boy with very short hair, cheap glasses, and an Adam's apple that his throat hadn't quite grown into yet. "It's the only place on campus you're allowed to sit outside."

"Sounds like a winner. Quick head count." I counted off in Russian, eliciting impressed looks from the students. "Twelve of you—great. Let's go. Oh, *zdravstvujte*, Riva. Thanks for joining us. We can't get into the classroom, so we're going to The Caff to hold class outdoors."

"You're my second professor who couldn't get into her classroom today," said Riva, sounding out of breath but still game for whatever her first day as a college student would bring. "The first one just canceled class," she added, her voice betraying what she thought of that.

"The great thing about language is you can study it anywhere," I said. "Okay, who wants to lead the way to The Caff?"

"Me, Professor H, me!"

"Great. Madison, you lead the way. And we'll take the time on the way to practice our verbs of motion."

There was a collective groan, although not as loud as it would be by the end of the semester. 201 students still had no idea of the true horror that awaited them with Russian verbs of motion.

As we walked along I managed to squeeze out of a couple of students that the kind of motion we were doing was on foot and unidirectional, but no one could tell me what kind of verb you used for that kind of motion, although once I gave them the answer, Riva was able to say correctly both "I am walking along the corridor" and "We are walking along the corridor," and even "I am descending down the stairs," a sentence whose complexity was on the verge of triggering heart palpitations in the other students.

Riva then correctly described us exiting the building (on foot), walking across the quad, and even walking up to the cafeteria, with the correct use of case endings. By the time we made it to our destination, the other students were staring at her with the superstitious awe normally reserved for exceptionally powerful witches. And once we sat down, she was able to say, "Hello, my name is Riva Goldshteyn. What is your name?" which made her partner, the Adam's apple boy, so nervous he could only swallow convulsively. Or maybe it was the way she filled out her sundress.

I left Adam's apple, whose name, I eventually managed to squeeze out of him, was in fact Adam, to Riva's tender mercies, and moved on to the other students, who were either sitting in painful silence or horsing around like kindergarteners, with Madison the worst culprit. I spent the next several minutes getting them to focus on exchanging names, which some of them complained about because they all already knew each other, and then moved on to fielding complaints about how hot and thirsty they were. I tried to get them to say things like "I am hot" or "I am thirsty," but that was beyond them, so I set them to talking about how they spent their summer. That was also beyond them, but I told them to crack open the textbook and peruse the page on leisure activities and work through all the things they had and hadn't done.

"You mean...on our own?" one of the girls asked, her eyes big. "Not reading a dialogue, but making up our own sentences?"

"Yes," I said, less patiently than I would have managed two classes ago. "Go through the list and ask each other, 'Did you do X?' and then answer the question in a complete sentence."

This provoked complaints that it would be boringly easy, and then when they actually tried it, several of them found it impossibly difficult, as they had forgotten the past tense over the summer. Once they had reviewed the formation of the past tense sufficiently in order to be able to say, "I watched TV this summer," the fifty minutes were up, and I called a halt to the proceedings.

"For Friday do exercises 1.1 through 1.5 in the workbook," I shouted over the noise of students shoving textbooks into backpacks, as the tables filled up around us with laughing, chattering students from a neighboring engineering class that had just gotten out.

"Um...Professor?" It was Riva, hovering uncertainly at my elbow. "What should I do? About my enrollment? The Den won't let me sign up for 201 because you have to take 101-102 first."

"I'll find out," I told her. "I probably have to give you a Permission of Instructor code. In the meantime just keep coming to 201 as if you're going to be taking it. Unless you think it will be too easy for you."

"Is there a more advanced class?"

"Unfortunately not. Just independent studies."

"I think I'll try to keep taking 201. I need the hours, and I haven't worked on my reading and writing in a long time. My grandmother is so excited! Wait until I tell her I've moved up into second year." Riva smiled sweetly at me and, shouldering her backpack, incongruously large and sturdy against her small body and delicate sundress, headed off.

"Prof? Professor H?"

"Yes, Madison?"

"You need help with anything?"

"Not unless you can register Riva in 201 for me. I don't really know how the system here works yet."

"I probably could. If you needed me to."

"Are you authorized to do something like that?" I gathered up my materials, freeing my table just in time to avoid being pushed away by another wave of incoming engineering students, certain that this was their territory and that pathetic language students should get out of the way, and started walking back towards Dreme.

"Well...sort of." Madison skipped along behind me.

"I should probably ask our department admin about it. Probably that's something that should go through her."

"Yeah, but she won't help you," said Madison confidently. "She never does stuff like that if she can help it. So when she tells you no, you can come to me!"

"Is every work-study able to do this kind of stuff?" I asked. "Or are you special?"

She giggled, her laugh taking on a manic edge and threatening to get out of control. "I'm special!" she said. "Just like everyone else! That's what my dad likes to say. Right along with 'Actions have consequences.'"

"Dads like to say stuff like that."

"Does yours?"

"He used to sometimes. Once you're an adult they're supposed to lay off it some."

"I'm an adult! Technically. But I suppose you're more of an adult than me."

"Probably," I agreed. "I must be, what, 75% older than you?"

"Whoa, Professor H! You just did that math in your head like it was nothing! *And* it was right. Most profs who aren't math profs, and even some of the ones who are math profs, can't do mental arithmetic. Anyway, not all the work-studies have admin privileges, or if they do they don't know how to use them, but I do. I love computers! Do you like computer games? Jason and I play *World of Warcraft* all the time."

"I *knew* it!"

"You did?"

"Well, I knew Jason played either *World of Warcraft* or something like that."

"Do you?"

"No. Not a lot of time to play computer games with all the other stuff I have to do. And anyway, I'm not really into games."

"Like any kind of games?"

"I like sports. Not so much computer games. But that's just me. So do you think you'll do something with IT after graduation?"

"Not if my dad has anything to do with it! I've told him over and over again that I want to get into game development, that if I'm going to go to grad school, that's what I want to do—don't you think that would be cool? To get an MFA in game design? I could design a Russian game, wouldn't that be awesome? But my dad wants me to go to law school, or education. Although he says there's no future in being a lawyer these days. He wants me to go into education admin, like him. He also says there's no future in teaching—sorry, Professor H! Is that true? That there's no future in being a professor?"

"I wouldn't recommend going into it for the money. Or the job security. Or many other reasons."

"So why'd you do it, Professor H? Did you just really want to be a professor?"

"I wanted a job that would be safe, and that had flexible hours. And I got a fellowship."

"So you *didn't* want to be a professor?"

"No, I like some things about being a professor."

"Like what?"

"Like learning things. You get to spend years and years learning difficult, complicated things. And I like reading and thinking about literature. It's uplifting to read difficult things, like going for a hard run or maybe like playing a really complex game. And I like helping people, and you spend a lot of time helping students."

"Oh. So...you *like* working with students?"

"Yes."

"Really? Lots of professors I know just complain about them all the time. Us. Students."

"I know. That part of the job is a major shock to many people. But like I said, I like helping people. I like feeling like I've made a difference in other people's lives. And teaching is a way to do that in a very hands-on fashion. It's like being a nurse or a doctor, but with less blood and more tears."

"Oh." Madison considered that novel thought as we crisscrossed the quad between the black chains. "So, you're like an idealist, or something?"

"Pretty much."

"And your parents are okay with that?"

"First of all, I'm thirty-four. I call the shots about my career path and I have for a long time. Second of all, my parents are idealists too. They met when they were both in the Peace Corps. If anything, they consider being a humanities professor dangerously close to selling out."

"So were they mad when you decided to go to grad school?"

"No. They thought it would be a fun adventure. And they've always been very supportive of everything we've done, even when they didn't agree with it."

"Oh. Like...what didn't they agree with?"

"They were a little worried about all the time I spent in Russia. But mainly it was my brother. He rebelled big-time when he was a teenager and went to The Citadel."

"What's The Citadel?"

"A military college in Charleston."

"Where's Charleston?"

"South Carolina."

"Whoa, really! I've never met anyone from South Carolina before. Wait: is that where you're from?"

"No, I'm from Georgia."

"No way! I've never met anyone from Georgia before either! But...you don't have an accent. I mean, you don't talk like you're from Jersey, but you don't talk like the people in *True Blood* either."

"*True Blood* isn't set in Georgia, and the actors in it don't have real accents anyway. Besides, it's not an advantage to have a Southern accent, so I lost mine. It only comes back when I'm at home."

"Wow, really? But isn't that, like, discrimination, or something? To be forced to lose your accent?"

"No one 'forced' me to, I just realized I needed to. But yes. Technically it is discrimination to look down on someone because of their accent. But it's still not a good idea to have a Southern accent. Sometimes there are things you have to put up with to get ahead."

"Yeah, no kidding. So what'd your parents do when your brother decided to go to this Citadel place?"

"They said it wasn't what they would have chosen but it was his life to live and he would always be their son, no matter what."

"Whoa, really!" Madison stopped and stared at me, her pupils so dilated her hazel eyes looked almost black. It was astonishing she could see anything at all in that state. "That's like in a movie or something! A Lifetime movie! I can't imagine my parents ever saying that! I mean, if you, like, asked them if that's what they'd do, they'd say yes, but they wouldn't actually do it. Maybe *I* should have gone to this Citadel place too."

"I sincerely doubt you would have enjoyed it. Even my brother didn't enjoy it very much, although he enjoys telling people he went there now. It's the Lords of Discipline place."

"What?"

"You know Pat Conroy?"

"Who's he?"

"A writer from South Carolina."

"Oh." Madison spent the rest of our walk up to the front of Dreme Hall digesting the fact that there were writers from South Carolina.

"So what would you do, Professor H?" she asked as we approached the door. "If you were me?"

"If I were you? I'd graduate from here, get a job, and put myself through that MFA program myself, instead of letting my parents tell me what I could or couldn't study." My voice was more confident than maybe it should it have been, considering how very tenuous my own grasp on financial independence was.

"That is hard core, Professor H! I don't think my dad would be very happy about it if I did that, though. And I don't know that I could get in anywhere without him. I only got into *here* because of him."

"Oh. Well, that may be so, but the rest of your life is up to you."

"You should be like a guru or something, Professor H! Oh shit! That's my dad. Gotta go. Let me know if you need help getting Riva into the class." And she spun around and ran off before I could say anything else.

13

I briefly considered following Madison's example when I saw John Greene standing at the entrance to Dreme, talking to a man with a $100 haircut, a $1000 suit, and the kind of tan you get not from manual labor but from diligent self-care and vacations to the Bahamas.

"Ah, Rowena," said John Greene, catching sight of me before I could make a strategic withdrawal.

He's not actually dangerous, I reminded myself. *Neither of them is actually dangerous.* But that wasn't true. While they were unlikely to attack me physically, they could and very likely would leave me hopelessly mired in poverty, while their verbal jabs made me hate myself almost as much as an assault by a real rapist. And they'd probably congratulate themselves about "maintaining rigorous standards" and "upholding the integrity of the process" as they did so.

"This is our new Russianist," John Greene told the other man proudly, as if he were personally responsible for me, instead of just the person who had rubber-stamped the approval for my hire. "Fresh out of—was it Indiana?" He smirked a little.

"I didn't know Indiana had a big Russian program," said the other man. His expression on his expensive face was so smooth it was impossible to tell whether he was expressing an interest or being an arrogant jerk.

"One of the biggest," I said.

There was an awkward pause.

"So this must be your first real day teaching, Rowena," said John Greene. His voice took on a sugary tone more appropriate for someone at a daycare, not a self-proclaimed elite institution of higher education. "How did it go?"

"I've been sole instructor on a lot of courses before, so it wasn't anything I hadn't seen before," I said.

"Of course, of course, you have *so much* experience for such a recent graduate. And you had a class in Angelo Hall, didn't you? How was that? Isn't it *lovely* to be in a brand-new, state-of-the-art building?"

"Yes." I said nothing about the markers. No point.

"We're so lucky that the administration has granted the Department of Modern Languages permission to use two whole rooms in Angelo, just for us," John Greene was saying, half to me, half to the other man. "Of course, you were instrumental in that, weren't you, Provost? Rowena, this is Provost Johnson."

"Nice to meet you." I shifted my bags from my right side to my left in order to shake his hand. He gave me another super-expensive, super-smooth smile, and squeezed my hand a little too hard. I resisted the urge to squeeze back harder.

"Anyway," said John Greene, wriggling slightly with anxiety, "Provost Johnson and I were *just talking* about the possibility of expanding our offerings for the Department of Modern Languages. Language and cross-cultural competence *have* been declared key areas to target for improvement and expansion, and who better to lead the way than us, wouldn't you say, Rowena?"

"I would," I said.

"And while of course Spanish will *always* remain the backbone of our—or any—foreign language program, the LCTLs *do* hold a special place in our hearts, don't they, Provost Johnson? I hope you've been getting good reports about our advanced pedagogical techniques and our general focus on student wellbeing."

"Yes," said the Provost, flashing both of us another super-expensive smile.

"And if you want to hear more about our LCTL program, get *in person* reports from the ground, so to speak, I'm sure Rowena would be glad to talk to you about it in more depth, wouldn't you, Rowena? Because you had *such good* ideas for generating interest and drawing in students."

"I'm sure you did," said the Provost. "Well, John, it's been a pleasure. And...Rowena, was it? Is that an *Ivanhoe* reference?"

"Yes."

"Well spotted!" said John Greene, wriggling slightly again, this time with apparent pleasure. "You know, I didn't even think...but of course, you are an English scholar...Provost Johnson is our biggest champion in the college, I mean, the biggest supporter of the humanities in general, being a humanist himself, so no one recognizes the value of the so-called 'soft skills' more than he does..."

"Yes," said the Provost, cutting John Greene off with, I thought, the faintest hint of impatience that even his expensive suit and expensive tan and expensive corporate-academic veneer couldn't quite quell. "And I hope that we can all continue to get the good word out there, convince people of the importance of the 'soft skills.' And Rowena? I'm sure the college really would be interested in hearing some of your good ideas. Now is the time to push the study of Russian. We've been supporting Arabic for the past decade, and rightly so, but we can't neglect the development of area knowledge in Eurasia. I'd like to call a meeting with you and the other LCTL instructors to discuss practical opportunities to promote our critical need language offerings and how we might expand them, especially, as John mentioned, now that we have this new teaching space and have room to think about expanding our offerings, maybe create some permanent positions if the right circumstances and the right people should come together. John, is that meeting something you think you could set up?"

"Of course, of course, if you recall, I suggested something similar last semester..."

"Yes," said the Provost, cutting him off again. "Have your department admin get in touch with my office then, and set up a time. Nice to meet you, Rowena." He nodded to me but not to John Greene, and strode off with the air of a man on his way to a million-dollar budget meeting.

"Well, that went well," said John Greene. "I think you made a very good impression on Provost Johnson, Rowena, which is a *great* start to your time with us at TLASC. Provost Johnson is a person with ideas, a vision for the college, and he really is a friend of the humanities. He got his degree in English, like I said, British literature, I think, which is no doubt why he recognized your name right off the bat—are your parents academics? I don't think you ever mentioned anything about it."

"No," I said. "My mother is a doctor, and my father is a social worker."

"A doctor!" said John Greene, grasping at that happy word and skipping neatly over the much less happy sound of "social worker." "What kind of medicine does she practice?"

"Lots of things, but right now they both work at a non-profit addiction counseling service in Atlanta."

"Oh! Really? That must be...that's very worthy of them."

"Yes," I said. "It is. Although she's considering doing a stint with Doctors Without Borders."

"Really! You have...you must have quite the family history, Rowena! But didn't you do a period of non-profit work yourself? That's a wonderful experience to be able to draw upon for your teaching, don't you find that to be the case? Although these days

I'm afraid most parents are steering their children away from the non-profit sector into the, well, the for-profit sector. But it's still possible to make a profitable career, haha, in the non-profit sector, wouldn't you say?"

"More or less," I said. "I supported myself for years in one of the most expensive cities in the world doing it."

"One of the most expensive cities in the world?" said John Greene, looking lost.

"Moscow," I explained.

"Oh! Somehow you just don't think of Moscow as being, well, in the same class as London or Paris or Tokyo or New York, but I suppose it is, at least by some measures. Well, I really must go, Rowena. Linda will be in touch with you regarding the meeting with Provost Johnson. She knows your course schedule, so she'll be able to set up a time that works for you." He gave me a bright smile that was warmed largely by anxiety, and rushed off.

I stopped in the department office on my way back to the adjunct office, to see if I could get a marker and give Linda a heads-up about the possible meeting with the Provost and, if the moment seemed propitious, to ask her how likely she thought it was to actually happen. But the only person who was there when I stuck my head in was an unfamiliar work-study on her first day, who didn't know where the markers were and wasn't authorized to disburse them in any case. So I decided to leave things up to fate, and, after discovering that now Emma was taking a nap in the adjunct office, packed up my things and went home.

14

The next morning I jogged out to True Grit again, where I ran into Jimmy and his friend, who introduced himself this time as Mike. They were both garbage men, they told me, and laughed when I told them that I thought the politically correct term was "sanitation worker."

"You can call it whatever you want," Jimmy said, grinning and showing off his bad teeth. "It still stinks just the same."

I agreed to that, and then listened politely to the many complimentary things they had to say about my figure. It was technically offensive, but at least Mike and Jimmy were being open and upfront about their objectification instead of cloaking it in a veil of faux feminism. I smiled and told them I was glad to see them and agreed that yes, Atlanta was nicer than New Brunswick and its environs, and yes, I'd also been to Savannah, Charleston, and Charlotte, all of which were also very nice, and no, unfortunately I didn't have time to join them for a cup of coffee this morning, but maybe some other time, because yes, I sure did miss grits, and then I ran back home, passing the elementary school that looked like a minimum security prison and the shabby police station and all the cash-for-gold and payday loan places on my way.

I had to admit that, after seeing the neighborhood, the Pleasant Hill Apartment Complex was, just as it advertised itself to be, one of the nicest places in the area, difficult as that was for me to grasp. It wasn't that Atlanta didn't have bad neighborhoods, but even the bad neighborhoods in most Southern cities were newer and cleaner and more hopeful than even the good neighborhoods I'd seen so far in New Jersey.

Thursday was a non-teaching day for me, so I stayed at home, doing odds and ends to avoid taking care of the things I really needed to take care of, like finishing my unpacking and facing up to those article revisions that I, like Kate, had promised myself I would finish before going back on the market this year.

After a couple of hours of organizing my work email inbox and setting up folders for different topics, which took longer than it should have due to Cubmail's extreme clunkiness, and arranging for a roommate and booking a room for the ASEEES conference in November, something I could do because I didn't actually have to put money down for it, just give them my credit card number, and doing everything I could think of to do to prepare for Friday's classes, and spending more time than I should have surfing The Wiki and the job sites in case something really great had popped up since the last time I had checked twelve hours earlier, I forced myself to open up the emails with the comments from Reviewer A and Reviewer B, and actually sit down and start on the revisions for my article.

The good news was that Reviewer A's comments were more or less positive and even in some cases slightly helpful, with only a little bit of arrogant condescension bleeding through. But Reviewer B (Reviewer B was the title given to the more negative reviewer in the peer review process) was, in true Reviewer B fashion, in a snit that suggested they had read the article in a huge hurry, been mortally offended by something, possibly that I hadn't cited them, or possibly because just looking at someone else's work on a topic in which they were supposed to be an expert sent them into a tizzy of fear and inadequacy, and wanted me to make significant changes to the thesis of the article, changes that would go in the opposite direction of what Reviewer A wanted and would also make the article some other, completely different, article. The editor had made a feeble attempt to provide some guidance that only muddied the waters further.

I spent a while contemplating the myriad flaws of peer review and its basis on some kind of philosophical system that in no way resembled real life and actual human behavior, and some more time contemplating the nature of freedom and consent and how I couldn't stand up for the cause of advancing the sum of human knowledge because I needed to get Reviewer B to give me the go-ahead in order to get the article published, and I needed to get the article published in order to have any chance of getting a job next year and feeding myself. Then I thought about the parallels between this situation and cases in which people "voluntarily" provide sexual favors in order to keep their jobs, and whether a job that was supposed to provide me with physical safety was worth this kind of aggravation and degradation, and whether this kind of aggravation and degradation might have some kind of serious long-term consequences to my health and safety, and the impossibility of pleasing either bullies or random strangers, especially when it came to subjective matters of taste, and then I decided screw it, I'd been sitting around making myself unhappy for half the day over an article about a set of poems written in 1923 by someone who'd hanged herself in 1941, and thus was entirely beyond my help in any concrete way.

When I had written the article I had been fired with idealistic zeal to spread the word about "my" poet and get people to understand her poetry, and therefore, themselves, in a new and more enlightened light, or at least to sit back and go, "Wow, what great poems," thus bringing a little joy into their lives, but the reality was that no one other than the reviewers was ever going to read the article anyway. So I should treat it as a means to an end, just a tool to help me achieve my real aims, which were...what? Oh, that's right, a job with flexible hours and decent benefits, where the chances of being kidnapped or shot were low, so that Dima and I could get married and provide a safe and stable environment for his mother in her declining years. The flexible hours I had, sort of, but the rest was proving elusive. I did a "save as" of the article document, named it "draft 2," and started implementing the vague, contradictory, and mean-spirited changes the reviewers wanted to the best of my ability.

After a couple of hours of that fun and good times, my eyes were starting to water, and not just from frustration and rage, so I called it a day and went for a second run, this time, in a fit of self-destructive defiance against people who weren't there and wouldn't know about it, past True Grit and into the neighborhood where the streets were more holes than pavement, and grown men sat around on sagging porches in the middle of the workday.

No one bothered me other than a few remarks on the bright blueness of my shoes and the fitness of my legs, though, so after running three miles and briefly considering and then rejecting the notion of running all the way to campus and back, mainly because I didn't want to spend any more time than I could help on campus, I turned around and ran home and told myself I had made many important and meaningful accomplishments today, and made the world a better place for all concerned. When I said so to Fevronia, she hissed and took a swipe at me.

15

Friday dawned bright and clear and with a hint of pleasant coolness, and I set off for my classes with a certain cautious optimism that today would be less of a fiasco than Wednesday had been.

My optimism took a blow when I showed up for my first class and discovered that the door was locked, but then Kate came racing back from, she told me, a desperate bathroom break, to let me in.

"Everything's working today!" she said, smiling like the despair of Wednesday had been banished completely. "I was able to put up a PowerPoint no problem!"

"That's great."

"Yeah, they take *so long* to make, it makes it twice as bad when they don't work, doesn't it?"

"Yeah," I agreed.

"But once you make them once, you don't have to make them again, so that's good. If you're teaching the same thing, that is. I guess you're having to make all new lesson plans and materials, aren't you?"

"I've used this textbook before," I told her. "So I have some stuff prepared. I don't use a lot of PowerPoint, though."

Kate gave me a look as if I had unsettled her world view, and dashed off. I spent the next 50 minutes riding herd over Danila and Vitya, who went on another marker-stealing mission and then couldn't recover from the high, dealing with Ira's arrogant insecurity—she went into a big pout when she found out that Riva had moved up to 201, but that I didn't recommend it for her—and convincing the others to say anything at all. So a pretty typical 101 class.

When I showed up at the adjunct office, Kate, Emma, and Alex were already all there and had taken up all the chairs and desk space. Alex stood up and offered me his chair, and Emma and Kate said with a minimum of enthusiasm that they could clear a place for me on the desk, but I said no, I was fine, I would go sit—I scrambled to come up with a good place to sit, since the quad outside Dreme was a no-sitting zone—in The Caff and do my prep and grading there.

This was a good plan, or as good a plan as I could come up with on short notice, but The Caff was, it turned out, suffering from one of its periodic bee invasions, which apparently was a thing, so there was no bee-free place to sit outside, and all the inside tables were filled.

I carried on to the library, where I discovered that the Starbucks was full, as was The Bear Cave. I finally found a free desk in the basement, only to find out that I couldn't log onto the faculty and staff wifi. This necessitated another trip to The Bear Cave, where, after a half-hour wait for my number to be called, the tongue-tied Jason told me, still unable to look me in the face, that they had been having intermittent wifi outages all day and that was probably what the problem was, unless maybe it was because I wouldn't be officially in the system until September 1 and that had overridden the illegal override he and Madison had given me, but the problem would probably resolve itself in a few days, and if I still couldn't log in next week to come back and see them.

By then it was time to go teach 201, so I lugged my currently useless laptop and all my other stuff off to the annex of Dreme.

This time I got there before the previous instructor had left, and she, after my students had vouched for me as a TLASC faculty member and not a random stranger who had wandered in off the street and was teaching Intermediate Russian just for fun, let me in, so I counted that as a win.

The rest was not so victorious, as the room was barely big enough for the fourteen of us. In fact, a more accurate description would be "too small." Although it was technically designed for fourteen, as the occupancy notice at the door stated, in fact there were only twelve chairs. Which for the first few minutes of class was okay, since Madison wasn't there, but she showed up at the 1:10 mark.

"Oh," she said, looking around and seeing the chair shortage. "BYOC again, I see. Last semester this room was always Bring Your Own Chair too. Maybe I'll just sit on the floor."

"You'll have a hard time taking notes on the floor," I said. "And there's no room anyway." That was true: even with just twelve chairs the room was so jammed full with a giant table I couldn't walk around it, but was hemmed into one small corner by the chalkboard, which only had a tiny nub of squeaky green chalk that made marks almost too faint to read on the green board.

"I'll go get a chair," offered Adam Adam's Apple gallantly. "I think I saw some down the hall." He set off with a wistful look at Riva, who looked wistfully back before giving the most vicious side-eye a nice girl like her could give to Madison, who had flopped down on Adam's vacated chair and, complaining loudly about how tired she was, laid her head down on the table.

"If you're not feeling well, Madison, you should go home," I said loudly, to make up for the fact that I was trapped on the far side of the room and would only be able to make it over to her by sliding across the top of the too-big table, exotic dancer style.

"I'm fine, Professor H," she mumbled into her folded arms.

"If you're fine enough to be here, you're fine enough to sit up," I said, even more loudly. "If you're not fine enough to sit up, you're not fine enough to be here."

She sat up slowly. The circles around her eyes were so dark that at first I thought she had been punched in the face. She yawned and sniffled, wiping her nose on her sleeve. "Sorry I'm late, Professor H," she said.

"How do you say that in Russian?"

She shrugged and mumbled something.

"I'm sorry?" I said.

"I said," she said, with another jaw-cracking yawn, "Brandy would know. He was always late, and Professor C was always making him apologize for it."

I swallowed down my first retort, which was that it didn't seem to have done any of them any good. Brandy was dead and deserved better than that from me, the person who'd never met him, even if he couldn't get it from Madison, who supposedly had been his close friend.

"Let's review," I said instead.

By the time Adam had returned, lugging a chair with the expression of a conquering hero, everyone except Madison, whose eyes kept closing, had learned how to say, "I'm sorry for being late" and we were able to return to my planned activities, which I only had to modify slightly to accommodate the fact that we were all pinned in place and couldn't move around the classroom for group work.

I meant to grab Madison after class, but I was still trapped back in my corner when she eeled out of the room with an alertness that would have been much appreciated earlier, and before I could hurdle a few of the chairs and go after her, Riva snagged me and started talking to me earnestly about how she was really enjoying the class and her family was so excited she was taking Russian and she really thought 201 was the right level for her, but she still couldn't register, and could I help her?

This resulted in the two of us going to the department office together and sweet-talking Linda, who was not thrilled at having to do something for a temporary hire and a first-year student on a Friday afternoon, into doing her job and transferring Riva from 101 to 201.

Riva's good nature and effusive thanks won her over enough, though, that after Riva left, Linda asked me how things were going with something almost resembling interest.

"Fine," I said. "Although I've been meaning to ask for a marker. And has John Greene talked to you about the meeting with the Provost?"

"Oh! Yes! Here." She went over to a locked filing cabinet, unlocked it, and brought back a whole six-pack of dry erase markers, which she gave me with a conspiratorial look and the injunction not to tell anyone else, but this way I wouldn't have to bother her for a new one every time one ran dry.

"Janey over at the Provost's office and I have been trying to find a time," she told me. "You don't teach on Thursdays, correct? Do you teach somewhere else on Thursdays?"

"Nope. Just here."

"Lucky you. A lot of the other adjuncts hold two or sometimes three positions. But you're not really an adjunct, are you? Technically you're a VAP? This is your first position, isn't it? You *are* lucky. Anyway, how's November looking for you?"

"Um," I said. For some silly reason I had thought that the meeting, if it would be held at all, would be reasonably soon, like next week. Holding it in November, when my contract ended in the middle of December, seemed pretty pointless. "Fine, I guess. Except for the conference I'm going to, the week before Thanksgiving. I'll probably be leaving Wednesday, since I have a Thursday panel."

"Oh! Have you arranged for someone to fill in for you yet? Well, who would?" Linda frowned.

"I'll set something up," I said, not saying that what I would set up would be to not hold class.

"Well, let's see—I think Janey said the Provost's schedule was already filling up pretty fast—I'm not sure if we'll be able to fit in anything the first half of November, and then you'll be gone, and then there's Thanksgiving...we may be looking at December, then."

"Um," I said. "That's fine. Whenever works."

"Provost Johnson is *so* busy," Linda told me. "He's just full of good ideas. He really has a vision for the college. We were lucky to get him, although from what Janey says, part of the deal was his daughter."

"His daughter?"

"Don't you know? She's one of your students. What's her name? Margaret? Madeleine? Something like that."

"Mackenzie?" I suggested.

"No, that's not it."

"Not Madison?" I said.

"Yes! Madison. Part of the deal"—Linda looked around and lowered her voice—"according to Janey, part of the deal was that the school admit Madison. No one else would take her, you know."

"Gosh," I said. "I wonder why."

Linda smiled a not-very-nice smile. "If you don't know why yet, Rowena, trust me, you will."

16

I spent Saturday finishing up the revisions on the article and resubmitting it, which left me feeling dirty but enabled me to put it as "under review" on my CV with good conscience.

I was congratulating myself on my responsibility and hard-headed pragmatism until, on my regular roundup of the Russian news, I saw another report from Donetsk with the too-familiar byline. Unable to stop myself, I read through the entire article, which was filled with blistering condemnations of all sides, and then spent the entire evening hating myself for caving in to peer pressure—hahahaha, but not even that feeble pun could make me smile—and not standing up for what I believed in the way *some* people would have.

Instead, simply for the sake, not even of job security, but of the tiny possibility of some future insecure job, I had stripped my article of 90% of its new ideas and especially its feminist slant—funnily enough, all the claims that feminism was taking over academia notwithstanding, getting anything actually feminist published was turning out to be an insurmountable challenge—thus changing it from something that actually had meaning to just another piece of tedious scholarship that not only would not set the world on fire, but was actually making the world a more boring place. Good thing I had already submitted the revised version and couldn't take it back. Besides, in its original form no one was ever going to read it, because it couldn't be published, while in its revised form it had a slight chance of getting published, thereby doing *me* some good even if it would benefit no one else. Or so I told myself.

Sunday morning was by my Georgia standards almost freakishly cool for late August, so I went for a long run, exploring the rotting-sofa-and-used-condom neighborhood and confirming that indeed, it was not a place I should actually be running through, before doubling back the other way and stopping in at True Grit to buy a cup of coffee.

I could tell by the reactions I got that I was not only the only white customer currently there, but probably the only white customer who had come in all week, but Mike and Jimmy were there and called me over to sit down with them and eat grits and talk about Atlanta, which I did. My ability to tuck into a plate of grits elicited a number of appreciative remarks, almost as many as my running clothes, so I judged the four dollars and twenty minutes of my time to have been well spent, maybe the best spent twenty minutes of my week, and left with invitations to come back, or maybe drop by a church service, to which, judging by the hats, many of the other customers were heading.

Church would have been more fun, even for a mainly atheist sinner like me, than how I spent the rest of the day, which was starting my spreadsheet for this year's job search and entering in all the postdocs I wasn't going to get but that would make me feel like a failure if I didn't at least apply for.

This meant hitting up my recommenders for a fresh round of recommendations, which involved 1) actually speaking with them, despite my disinclination to ever have anything to do with them again after the way they had behaved over my dissertation, 2) giving them a much more glowing report of my current job than it deserved, and 3) providing them with enthusiastic plans for this year's search.

That was so disheartening that I spent Sunday evening turning my 8-page CV into a 2-page resume and submitting an application for a 1-year position as a resident study-abroad program director in Kazan. Babysitting college students and trying to keep them from ending up in jail or worse, as long as I could do it somewhere friendly and civilized, like the medieval seat of the descendants of Genghis Khan, was sounding a lot better than it ever had before, so I threw together a cover letter and fired off the application—non-academic applications were so ridiculously short it was laughable—before I could think better of it. What I would do if I actually got the job, I didn't know, since I'd sort of promised A Certain Person not to return to Russia without a specific request, but...whatever. Whatever. I went to bed with hopeful visions of me spending next year bribing petty officials and watching out for signs of alcohol poisoning in my charges, which sounded like a clean and honest way to make a living to me.

17

The next week, my first full week at TLASC, started off on a high note, in that my keys were, against all probability, waiting for me when I showed up Monday morning. My elation was slightly tempered when I discovered when I showed up for my first class that I'd been given a key for Angelo 028, not Angelo 027, which required another midday trek across campus to Facilities, where Tony greeted me like a long-lost sister and told everyone else in the office that I was from Georgia. Everyone else agreed that they'd never met anyone from far-off, exotic Georgia, and commented on my lack of accent.

Keys sorted, and, by Wednesday, CubID acquired, things went comparatively smoothly for the rest of the week, and the following week as well. The only disruption was Madison, who continued to chatter manically or fall asleep during class.

It took me until Friday of the second full week to catch her on her way out. I had been plotting it for days, but on top of her habit of sliding out of class first, I had been hampered by my lack of a place to meet with her. In the end I decided the classroom was as good as anywhere, and I would bide my time until the moment arrived.

The moment arrived when she, seeming on a fairly even keel for the first time since I'd met her, came up to me after class and asked if I needed any help with any "computer stuff."

"I think I'm okay, but thank you for asking," I told her. "How are you doing? I've noticed you've been having some problems staying awake in class. Are you getting enough sleep?"

"You know how it is," she said, fidgeting and picking at her sleeve.

"I do," I agreed. "But you must be having a really rough time, to be falling asleep so much."

"I'm sorry, Professor H!" she said, looking stricken. "I'll...I'll fix it, I promise! This is my favorite class. All the others are total wastes of time."

"How are you going to fix it?" I asked.

"Um...I have to get my meds sorted?"

"Your meds—like cocaine?"

There was an awkward pause.

"How'd you guess?" Madison asked eventually, looking guilty and awed at the same time.

"I've seen it before. Have you tried treatment?"

"Yeah. This summer. I spent all summer in a rehab clinic. And last winter too."

"And?"

"And as soon as I came back here I couldn't take it another minute, and..."

"I understand."

"You do? So...you've done it too?"

"Not cocaine," I said. "But I understand about being unhappy and needing to kill the pain, and frankly I can understand why you feel like that here."

"So"—Madison gave me a look of guilty defiance—"what are you going to do about it? Tell my dad?"

"Doesn't he already know?"

"Yeah."

"In that case I don't see the point. Have you spoken with counseling services here?"

"Yeah. Total waste."

"I'm sure," I said.

"So what're you going to do?"

"I'm going to ask you not to come to class hungover or high."

"That's it?"

"Would doing anything else help you? Would there be something else I could do that would help you?"

"I'm not going to quit! I can't quit!"

"That I can believe," I said. "It's called addiction for a reason. And seriously, Madison, I have no doubt that Campus Wellness can't help you, and that your dad has tried everything he can already"—she snorted—"and the rehab clinic this summer didn't help you either, but *someone* can help you."

"Oh yeah? Who's that? You?"

"No. You."

Madison scrubbed her skinny arms together, and said, her voice barely above a whisper, "I don't think so."

"Well, I do. And you're a grownup and I'm going to treat you like one, so I'm not going to report you, as long as you stop coming to my class strung out or high. Okay?"

"So, what: I should just show up to my other classes high, then?"

"That's up to you. I don't control you: you do."

"That's not what my dad would say."

"Well, does he control you?"

She flashed a grin. "Hell no. Not in this."

"I didn't think so. I'm sure I don't have to tell you how dangerous cocaine is, Madison, or how a drug charge could affect your life. You're a smart girl and you must know all this already and you do it anyway, so it must give you something worth that risk to you, and I'm not going to be able to compete with that, so I'm just asking you not to come to my classes high as a kite or too down to function, because frankly it's annoying and disruptive, and it irritates me to see a promising student like you performing so much less well than she could."

"You think I'm promising?" she asked, perking up.

"I think you could be a very promising student if you showed up to class sober."

"Oh." She shuffled her feet a little. "You ever know any others like me, Professor H?" she asked. "Like, as friends or something?"

"A lot of my friends have done a little recreational coke. That's...whatever. When they had addictions that came before everything else, that tended to ruin the friendship."

"Oh." She shuffled her feet a little more. "Sounds like you've got some sad stories of your own, Professor H. Did you have a boyfriend leave you for cocaine, or something?"

"It wasn't cocaine," I said. "It was adrenaline and idealism. But the effect was similar."

"I didn't know you could, like, take adrenaline as, like, a drug."

"He didn't shoot it up, if that's what you mean. He just went into dangerous places. Places he couldn't help but drag me into too, and then he'd get upset that I was there. But he couldn't quit doing it, even though he wanted me to quit for the both of us."

"Oh. So, like, a sad story."

"Something like that. So I know how little influence I have over others in this situation. It has to come from you, Madison: you have to want it. Just...don't come to class all spaced out, okay? And if you do decide you want more help, my parents work at an addiction counseling center. They would have ideas where you could find good help. So just ask if the time comes."

"Oh." She shuffled her feet some more. "You're not, like, mad at me, Professor H?"

"Not yet. I'll only be mad if you keep coming to class high."

"Most people get mad at me. My dad gets really mad at me." She shuddered. "Really mad."

"It's harder for close friends and family to stay calm in these situations."

"But you don't give a crap, right, Professor H?"

"I give a crap. But I'm your professor, not your parent. I'm a little more okay with treating you like an adult, a little more accepting of the fact that you might make mistakes."

"Oh. Well...I won't come to class high, I promise. I just wanted...I just wanted to make sure I did my best, you know?"

"Yeah. But I think your best might be when you're sober, not when you're high."

"Maybe," said Madison, not sounding at all convinced. "I'll give it a shot, I guess. Well, have a good weekend, Professor H, and, uh, thanks for not reporting me."

After Madison left, I told myself that I had done the right thing. Technically, I probably was supposed to report Madison as a "Student at risk." But everything I had seen of university administration in general, and TLASC's in particular, did not convince me that turning her over to their clutches would be the right thing. The Wellness Website had lots of fulsome language—I had checked—about helping students in times of crisis, and special hotlines to call, but my guess was that either they would do nothing, or they would have Madison arrested or committed, when she'd already admitted that two stints in rehab had done nothing for her. Taking that step was unlikely to make things better for her, and would very likely make things worse.

I had subtly (I hoped) felt out Kate about the issue, and she had said she had in fact reported a student as being "at risk" last year, and the only thing that had happened was that the student's dorm room had been raided and the student had been hauled in for mandatory counseling, which had so enraged the student that they had quit and

Kate had gotten into a fair amount of hot water over it with the department, even though she had supposedly done the right thing according to the department's own rules, and all for nothing.

No doubt something similar would happen if I reported Madison. And I sincerely doubted that getting the Provost's daughter brought up on a drug charge was likely to make things better for me, either. I just had to hope that Madison wouldn't have an overdose while I was here. With that encouraging thought, I went home.

18

The next week Madison did appear to be holding to our agreement and coming to class reasonably sober, but she could have shown up on campus wearing nothing but a flaming bra and panties and it still would have been only the second topic of conversation and concern in the adjunct office, because the Job Information List had been released.

"More jobs will be posted," Kate kept saying, as all four of us in the adjunct office crowded around her computer, looking at the listings and counting them. "They do rolling updates now, and more jobs will be posted."

"Yeah," I said encouragingly, while Alex said, "A few. Mainly temporary positions." He groaned. "Fuck it! I don't want to move to Beirut. Or Kentucky. Or Alabama." He put on a fake smile. "Why yes, I'd *love* to move to Bumfuck, Georgia—sorry, Rowena—or Asswipe, North Dakota! Spending the rest of my life in the Midwest is my dream opportunity! And as it happens, I *do* also speak French and would be happy to keep the French program going as well." He stalked off, muttering "Fuck, fuck, fucking Beirut," under his breath.

"I...I can't even argue," said Kate, looking like she might burst into tears. "But"—her lips trembled, but she carried on bravely—"look at this, Emma: there's a nice position in Chinese at Amherst."

"Yeah, and two hundred people applying for it," said Emma, and stalked off too.

"Ummm..." said Kate, and went back to looking at the German offerings. "Well, this one's in Muncie, Indiana—you lived in Indiana, right, Rowena? What's it like?"

"Midwestern," I said.

"Yeah, I guess so. And, um, Waco, TX—wasn't that where that shootout was? But it's probably fine now. I'm not a Baptist, and it says they can consider a candidate's religious affiliation since it's a religious college, but...what do you think? I guess I should go ahead and apply. And this one's at a Catholic school—how Catholic do you think you have to be?"

"I think I'd worry about that if I got an interview," I said.

"So are you just going to apply for all of them?"

"Pretty much." I had already gotten a form rejection letter for my application to the resident program director position, which was more response than I had been expecting, and was waiting with equally little hope for word on a similar position I'd applied to in St. Petersburg. In the meanwhile, I was, as I'd told Kate, going to apply to all the teaching jobs I was qualified for. It would only cost me time, money for postage and having the recommendations submitted at $6 a pop, and self-respect, and while I was short on all three, I could probably scrape up a little more. Or so I told myself.

The next couple of weeks were ones of gloom and despondency, followed by feverish activity, as all of us attempted to get out the applications due by October 1st, many of which required not just a CV, cover letter, statement of teaching philosophy, sample syllabi, copies of teaching evaluations, three letters of recommendation (some asked for four), and 25-page writing sample, but in the case of the postdocs, individually tailored research proposals with specific examples of how your research project fit into the program theme and/or how access to the university's library would be essential to the completion of your project, along with individually tailored course proposals for the university's First Year Seminar or Great Books or Introduction to the Humanities or whatever program. To make things more fun and fair, several of the postdocs had application fees. I couldn't help but wonder what Americans would say if they heard about something like that in Russia. But since it was in America, we told each other it was for the free market and "academic rigor."

Consumed with worry that I wouldn't get all my documentation submitted in time, or would submit something with a typo, or would send in a hard-copy application (still a requirement at some places) bound by a paperclip instead of by a staple as stated in the application instructions, I barely had any attention to spare for my students, even Madison, whom I was unintentionally punishing for her good behavior by ignoring her obvious semi-sobriety. So it wasn't until the second time she mentioned it that I realized that Mackenzie was trying to bring my attention to the fact that she wasn't getting my emails.

With the adjunct office having been colonized by Alex, who had spent the past week sleeping there at night and eating microwaved instant meals in order not to waste time on the drive back to his parents' house in Pennsylvania, I had moved my weekly meetings with Mackenzie to The Caff, where it was still warm enough, although just barely, to meet outdoors in the middle of the day. Mackenzie didn't show up to our first meeting and then sent me a profusely apologetic note, saying somehow she'd missed my email to meet at The Caff, which was so unlike her.

When it happened again the next week, she came running up to me fifteen minutes late, almost crying from mortification, and saying that she didn't know what was wrong, she had certainly checked her email, but hadn't gotten anything from me, and she didn't know what was wrong.

"Don't worry about it," I told her. "It's probably a glitch in the email system; goodness knows it's buggy enough. Let's ask Linda and see if she knows what's going on."

"Oh, thank you, Professor, thank you, I'm so sorry, you have to believe me, this independent study is so important to me..."

"Don't worry about it. I know how these things can happen. Come on. Let's go ask Linda."

When we showed up in the department office, Linda was, as was the case more often than not, out, but John Greene was sitting uneasily at her desk.

"Oh *hello* Rowena!" he said when he saw us. "I was just doing a little paperwork—well, I suppose it's not *paperwork* anymore, is it?—at Linda's computer, since my own is down. Can I help you with anything?"

"I just had a question for Linda, although maybe you've experienced this too. Have you had any problem with emails not being sent or received? Mackenzie hasn't been getting my emails. We were wondering if there was a glitch in the system."

John Greene frowned. "Are you *sure* you've been checking your emails regularly?" he said to Mackenzie. "You know that all university correspondence *must* be conducted on Cubmail, and students *are* responsible for checking their university email accounts regularly—at least once a day—and responding in a timely fashion. Faculty too, but you're very good about that, aren't you, Rowena?"

"I've been checking my email regularly," Mackenzie said, sounding once again like she might burst into tears. "I check it every hour, pretty much. And I'm *sure*, I'm *sure* that I never got those emails!"

"It's not a big deal," I said. "But it would be good to know if something's wrong with the system. Maybe I haven't been sending them properly."

"Have you been getting complaints from other students that they haven't been receiving your emails, Rowena?" said John Greene, drawing his bushy brows together till they formed a single sententious line.

"No. But perhaps they're just not telling me. I know at least some of the emails are getting through, but perhaps there's a problem with the server, or with Mackenzie's address."

John Greene frowned even more bushily, and picked up the phone and dialed an on-campus number. "Jason? Who is this? Get me Jason. Hello, Jason? This is Dr. Greene, the chair of the Department of Modern Languages. We're having a little problem with a student who's been missing department emails. No, not emails on the department listserv; individually sent emails from our faculty. Can you confirm that she's been receiving them? What's your name?" He fixed Mackenzie with a stern look.

"Um...Mackenzie D'Annunziato."

"Mackenzie D'Annunziato. What year are you, Mackenzie?"

"Um...a junior? I started in 2012. My email address is dannma12@tlasc.edu."

"What? No, it's dannma2012@tlasc.edu. Did you get that, Jason? Dannma2012@tlasc.edu. Can you see if there are any emails in that account from Dr. Halley? There are? Have they been opened? They have? Can you tell me what the emails say? Confirming a meeting on Wednesday. I see. Thank you *so* much for your time and assistance, Jason."

John Greene hung up the phone and gave Mackenzie a look more appropriate to a serial killer than a nervous college student. "You see? You *have* been getting Dr. Halley's emails, you just haven't been keeping track of your appointments. You really *must* learn to keep up with your inbox and your calendar, Mackenzie; it's an important part of preparing to be an adult and in the workplace. And if you're caught in a transgression, you shouldn't try to lie your way out of it. You see how easily you got caught. Wouldn't you agree, Dr. Halley?"

"Could you have two inboxes?" I asked Mackenzie. "You said your email was dannma12@tlasc.edu, but the one that was, um, just checked was dannma2012@tlasc.edu, which I'm pretty sure is where I've been sending at least some of my emails. Maybe IT created a second account for you by mistake."

Mackenzie shook her head. "Just...just the one email account, Professor Halley, I'm sure of it! My year was the last year to have email addresses with two digits instead of four. We had '12' added to our names, but the next year they started adding the full year, so 2013, 2014. But my email address just has 12 in it, I'm sure! I've been using it for more than two years!"

"They must have accidentally created a dummy account for you when they changed the system," I said. "Good thing you got it figured out now. I'd go and ask them to deactivate it, if I were you, to save confusion."

"Oh. Um, I guess you're right, Professor Halley. Can I go do it right now?"

"Sure, if you want to. Let me know when you get it straightened out, okay, and we'll set up a meeting for next week?"

"Sure thing!" Mackenzie gave me a look of gratitude, John Greene a look of deep fear and loathing, and speed-walked out of the office as fast as her overstuffed backpack would allow her.

"You shouldn't have been so easy on her, Rowena," said John Greene, as soon as she was gone. "I know you want to make a good impression on the students, and of course you *should,* especially given the importance of course evaluations to your, ah, situation, but you're not doing them any favors by being *too* nice to them. It doesn't even make them like you better. Students respect a teacher who keeps them in their place, don't you agree?"

"I doubt I have a lot to worry about with Mackenzie," I said, with the most noncommittal smile I could summon up.

"You'd be surprised, Rowena, you'd be surprised. It's the most innocent-looking who cause the most trouble, sometimes. And I know you want to be their big sister, but you're not a student any more, you know: you're an authority figure. You have to act like it. And you have to hold them accountable for their actions. Actions have consequences, you know: it's our job to teach that to them."

"Mmm," I said.

"Of course, it's harder for young women, I *understand* that, but this is the problem, you see: women never learn to be assertive enough to be good teachers, so they just end up perpetuating the cycle of student entitlement. Oh! Hello, Linda! As you see, I was just borrowing your computer for a moment. I knew you wouldn't mind. I'm afraid mine has turned into a pumpkin and I had to call the good folks at The Bear Cave to come take a look at it, but I had *pressing* business that had to be taken care of right away...I'll get out of your way now, though."

John Greene, with a distinct lack of masculine assertiveness, beat a hasty retreat in the face of Linda's silent disapproval.

"What's with him?" she whispered, once he was back in the chair's office and had shut the door behind him.

"I don't know. He was just..." But I didn't know what to say about what he had just done, and I was afraid that if I did bring it up, I would either be accused of lying, or accused of being complicit in a blatant student privacy violation, so instead I said, "You look like you've had a hard day."

"End-of-the month reconciliations," she said, taking off her cats-eye glasses and pinching the bridge of her nose. "I have to check each item manually, since the system tends to mess up on its own."

"That sounds tedious."

"Yes, well, this is why they have me do this kind of thing, and not the faculty. Have a good weekend, Rowena." She turned away, already rummaging through her receipts envelope before I was out the door.

19

The end of September brought with it my first paycheck, which all immediately disappeared into paying for health insurance and next month's rent, leaving me wondering how I was going to buy a plane ticket to San Antonio for the conference in mid-November, which was only a month and a half away. Which reminded me that I hadn't actually written my paper for it. But that would have to wait, because I still had at least fifteen applications to turn in between now and then.

The end of the month also brought the news that there had been two rapes on campus, which was pretty much par for the course, and also the murder of one of the janitors, which was less par for the course. While students getting raped or dying from car crashes and drug overdoses was the expected norm, employees being randomly murdered was less common, although perhaps that was just the way things were here in Jersey. Certainly the local news was full of reports of brutal murders over trivialities.

My 101 students were avidly discussing the murder when I showed up to class Monday morning.

"Did you hear, Prof?" said Danila, sounding more gleeful than anything. "It was right outside Angelo Hall! Right outside where we are now! It was a student who found the body."

"Poor thing," I said. "That must have been a shock."

"Yeah," said Danila, not very sympathetically. "I wonder what it would be like to find a dead body!"

"My dad said you get used to them," volunteered Vitya. "You see enough of them and you stop caring."

"Your dad's seen loads of dead bodies, has he?"

"Yeah. In Afghanistan."

"I thought your dad was Russian," said Morgan-the-girl (as opposed to Morgan-the-boy), one of the non-heritage speakers. "What was he doing in Afghanistan?"

"Belarusian. He was serving there. During the war."

"Belarusians are in the war in Afghanistan?"

"The Soviet war in Afghanistan, yeah."

"There was a Soviet war in Afghanistan? Really? When?"

Vitya shrugged. "Before I was born, I guess."

"1979 to 1989," I supplied.

All the students, heritage and non-heritage alike, stared at me with round eyes. "Whoa, Professor Halley!" said Jordan-the-boy (as opposed to Jordan-the-girl). "You, like, didn't even have to look that up on Wikipedia! How'd you *know* that?!"

"Knowing the basic outlines of Russian history is part of the job," I said.

"Yeah, but...you just *knew*. Just right off the top of your head!"

"Yes," I said. "It's part of being a professor. You're expected to know things."

"My father was in Afghanistan too," volunteered Ira, coming out of her pout for a moment. "He...it isn't good to talk to him about it." She hunched down as if trying to hide behind her pathetic little plastic desk.

"My father was in...what do you call it? It's like Czech but not," said Danila.

"Chechnya?" I suggested.

"Yeah! Wow, Prof, you knew that too! I guess there was like a war there too or something." He grinned. "Do you know when that war was too, Prof?"

"The first modern Chechen war went from 1994 to 1996. The second broke out in 1999 and went on till around 2008-9 or so, although the region is still plagued with violence."

Everyone stared at me as if I had just become the Oracle of Delphi. "How do you *know* all this stuff, Professor?" asked Megan.

"Well, in this case, because I was actually living in Russia during part of that time."

"*Really*??!" Now everyone's eyes were bugging out. "Did it, like, affect you?"

"Kind of like the war in Afghanistan affects you," I said. "Even though Chechnya's part of Russia, it's far away from where I was, so while there was some terrorist activity in Moscow, it was mainly something I read about in the news. But just like you might have friends and family in Afghanistan, lots of people had and have friends and family in Chechnya."

The non-Russians looked confused at that. Active-duty service members were not a major feature of these students' lives.

"So did *you* know anyone who was there, Professor?" asked Morgan-the-boy, his face filled with the bloodlust of the terminally bored and sheltered.

"Yes," I said. I must have said it more curtly than I had meant to, because everyone looked awkward and let me steer the conversation back to the genitive case, which they were not enjoying at all.

After class, though, I heard Danila and Vitya discussing the murder with morbid enthusiasm, and telling each other as we all went out the building door that maybe it had been *right here,* because the body had been discovered by an entrance to Angelo Hall.

"It wasn't right here," said Ira, pushing past all of us with the air of someone who just couldn't have the time for such foolish mortals. "It was in the back. Where there are no security cameras."

"How'd you find that out?" demanded Danila.

"My mom works here."

"Really? How come you've never said anything about it. Is she a professor? Why isn't she teaching Russian instead of Professor Halley?"

"It was in the back. There's a back entrance for staff," said Ira, not answering Danila's question. "It was by there."

"Show us, Irochka! Come on, Professor H—wanna see?"

"This hardly seems appropriate," I said.

"It's just around the corner," said Ira.

"Come on, Professor H! It's just around the corner!"

"It's on the way to the library," said Ira, and since I was going there anyway to meet with Mackenzie, I ended up going along with them to the back entrance to Angelo, which looked like any other back entrance to any other building, with no sign of a murder whatsoever, much to Danila and Vitya's disappointment.

"Did your mother know the person?" I asked Ira.

She shrugged.

"This must be tough for her," I said, which earned me another shrug, so I left the students to their ghoulish speculations and hurried off for my next appointment.

20

"Ah, Rowena, *just* the person I was looking for," said John Greene, cornering me as I was trying to sneak past the department office on my way from my meeting with Mackenzie to my 201 class. "I wanted to speak to you—to all of my LCTL instructors, actually—about the International Education Night coming up. I assume you got Provost Johnson's email? Or...actually, I think it might have just gone out to permanent faculty"—he laughed a high-pitched, false little laugh that was particularly irritating in such a big, bear-like man—"you know, it's hard to keep track sometimes, isn't it? We're all like one happy family here, that's what I like to say, with no difference between tenured and non-tenured faculty, or permanent and contingent faculty—but anyway, Provost Johnson is, as you *must* be aware, very keen to promote our TLASC Abroad initiative, and so we're really pushing the boat out, so to speak, on our upcoming International Education Night, so the Spanish program and the French program are both putting together tables, well, more than tables, very fancy booths really, and we—*I*—thought it would be nice have a booth for the LCTLs as well, since, while each individual LCTL program is too tiny to really be called a program"—he laughed another high-pitched little laugh at the thought—"you *can* join forces, and—oh! Kate! *Just* the person I was looking for. I was *just* talking to Rowena about putting together a LCTL booth for our International Education Night, and even though German isn't technically a LCTL, well, here at TLASC it *is*, isn't it, and so I thought you could all join forces, and...I think Rowena should be in charge of it, since she *is* the VAP—which reminds me, Rowena: have we talked about making you advisor to the Russian minor? It's part of the duties of your position but I don't know if anyone's talked to you about it yet. Advising week is coming up, so if anyone *should* want to declare a Russian minor, well, you'd be the person they'd talk to...but anyway, I think Rowena should be in charge of our little LCTL booth"—another ear-grating laugh—"but I'm *sure* she'd be very appreciative of your help, Kate, and I know how keen you are to participate in department activities and show your TLASC spirit."

"Um, I guess," said Kate. "What about Alex? Arabic's by far the biggest of the LCTL programs."

"Oh, well, Alex...you know, he's *so* busy, he has *so* many students, and with his long commute...and then his father has been complaining to me that he's never around—we're old friends, you know—and they're having a soiree that evening, so I *promised* I wouldn't keep Alex around late on Friday. But interest in German and especially Russian is *so* low; well, it's a major area of concern, you know, Provost Johnson was just talking to me about it, so, anyway...and has the Provost's office gotten in touch with you about that meeting yet? I'm sure it's been scheduled...anyway, International Education Night. Why don't you talk to Linda about it: she has all the details. And Professor Hernandez is in charge of the Spanish booth—I wish I could participate more; it sounds like just the kind of fun, creative thing that we administrators don't get to do enough of—so you really should talk to her, because she has *such* good ideas about decorations and things to attract student interest, so...Oh! Excuse me! You! Yes, you!" He rushed off in the direction of the Dreme Hall cleaning lady, who was pushing her cleaning cart out of the men's bathroom.

"I guess we could go talk to Linda about it now. You don't have class for another half an hour, right?" said Kate, with a distinct lack of enthusiasm.

"Let's do it now," I said. "The sooner you go to jail, the sooner you get out."

She gave me a look.

"It's a Russian saying. Like, you know, the sooner you get it over with, the, um, sooner you get it over with. Russian has a lot of jokes and such about jail."

"Oh." She tried to come up with something nice to say about that, but only managed a feeble, "Russian culture is very, uh, *different*, I guess."

"Sort of. Although it's American culture that thinks prison rape is a hilarious topic for comedy."

"Um, okay. Uh, Linda?" Kate poked her head into the department office.

"She's out," the work-study, who was a different work-study than the one we'd seen the week before, told us.

"Oh. Do you, um, know when she'll be back?"

The work-study shook her head wordlessly.

"When is International Education Night?" I asked. "How much time do we have to set up?"

"Friday, I think," the work-study told us with a frown of concentration at being asked such a difficult question.

"That's less than a week away!" exclaimed Kate in dismay. "We don't even have the weekend to prepare for it. And...I have a date!" She blushed. "With a man! I actually met someone, a *man*, who isn't an academic! And he asked me on a date! I can't...what time is the event?"

"Six to eight, I think," said the work-study.

Kate groaned.

"You go on your date," I told her.

"I can't leave you to man the booth on your own!"

"I'm not going to 'man' anything," I said dryly. "I'll be 'staffing' it. And I think I can handle it. It'll just be standing at a table and handing out brochures to anyone who stops by, right?"

"Professor Hernandez is planning to bring homemade empanadas," the work-study volunteered. "She says food always brings them in. And I think she's going to wear a flamenco dress, and maybe perform a flamenco dance."

"Good for her," I said. "Well, if the spirit moves me, maybe I'll recite some chastushki or dance a lezginka, but I think standing there and handing out brochures will be good enough. If they'd wanted something better, they'd have told us earlier."

Kate laughed hollowly.

"You know what I mean. Do we have any brochures for our programs?"

A quick perusal of the office failed to reveal any brochures for the Russian, German, Arabic, or Chinese programs, and the work-study said she didn't know about any, and couldn't authorize us to print any of our own, so I said I would email Linda about it and left to go to class.

John Greene was still in the corridor when I went by, berating the cleaning lady, whose name, I knew, was Darla, and who had a cousin in Atlanta. She was the only black person routinely seen in Dreme Hall, which seemed to me like a public relations disaster waiting to happen, as did John Greene's hectoring tone, but he appeared to be untroubled by such considerations. As I walked by I heard him say, his fleshy cheeks quivering under their scruffy beard, "This is the second time someone's gotten into my computer!"

The cliché in such moments is for the powerful, sassy black woman to give the over-entitled white man a piece of her mind, but the reality is that Darla, her eyes lowered like someone who needed to keep her job, was saying, "I'm sorry, sir, I don't know nothin' 'bout it, I don't know nothin' 'bout computers..."

"I don't know who *else* it could be. Someone is coming in when I'm not here and accessing my computer, or so I infer from the fact that my work emails are being accessed without my authorization, and *you're* the one with the key and access to the building after hours. That email account is *of course* password protected, just like all the accounts here at TLASC, but you can access it via my work computer without re-entering the password. So it *must* have been accessed via this computer, and you're the one most likely to have done it. Now, since this is your first offense, I'm just going to ask that you be reassigned to a different part of campus, but this will go on your record, make no mistake."

"Couldn't it have been accessed remotely?" I found myself saying.

John Greene whirled around.

"Couldn't the account have been accessed remotely?" I repeated. "I mean, either way, whoever did it must have hacked your password." It was hard to fire someone who was already on a short-term contract. So what did I have to lose? "It seems like they most likely got help from IT," I said. And then, unable to stop myself, I found myself adding, "You know, like you did with Mackenzie's email?"

His mouth opened, closed, and opened again, but before he could say whatever it was he was going to say, I said, "I have to get to class," and scurried off.

21

I expected some kind of explosion from John Greene, but instead he spent the rest of the week avoiding me, although Riva reported that when she dropped by the department to ask about the requirements for minoring in Russian, he came bustling out of his back office and harangued her about her irresponsibility in not asking me first, thus wasting the valuable time of the administrative employees, when it was my *duty* to advise students on declaring a minor in the first place, and why hadn't I been available for my advisees when it was my job, and so on and so forth, until Linda had told him I was currently teaching 101, which had made him retreat back into his office in a huff.

"I really didn't know," said Riva, sounding stricken. "I didn't mean to bother anyone or get anyone in trouble, I just thought I'd drop by and see if anyone could talk to me about it. But he was...are all professors that mean? He made it sound like I was doing something wrong by asking about declaring a minor for his department!"

"Only the ones who've been doing it too long," I told her. "Don't worry about it. I'll send you a link to the procedure for declaring a minor, which I don't think you can do until next year anyway. If you take 201 and 202 this year you should be well on your way. Have you thought about study abroad?"

She nodded. "My family keeps telling me I should go to St. Petersburg next summer. My grandmother's so excited about this! My cousins have all stopped speaking Russian entirely. People can be really mean about it, did you know that? My cousins had to start telling the other kids at Hebrew school that we're German, because apparently that's better than being Russian, and now they're ashamed of being Russian, even though half my family was killed by Germans, and my great-grandfather died fighting the Nazis at Stalingrad. My grandmother's the only one left from the older generations; everyone else was wiped out. She almost starved to death during the Siege of Leningrad, but she made it because her mother gave her double rations of bread and starved to death herself. She said they used to add sawdust to it, did you know that? She says that's why she's so short. Anyway, she's very proud of being from Leningrad—St. Petersburg—and she wants me to go back. She says it's the most cultured city in Europe."

"You could certainly argue that that's the case. I'll also send you some links to programs there."

"Will I have to talk to *him* again?" Riva asked with a little shudder.

"Probably not, or not very much," I assured her.

"Talk to who?" asked Madison, who had just come sliding into class at the last minute. At least she was holding to our agreement and staying semi-sober.

"The department chair—what's his name? John Greene," said Riva, with another little shudder. "He was really mean to me when I went to ask about declaring a Russian minor! It's like he hates the Russian program!"

"Oh, him," said Madison. "He's always nice enough to me, although all the other work-studies complain about him. I think he just hates everyone."

"I wouldn't worry about him," I said, with more certainty than I felt. Perhaps John Greene wasn't specifically targeting my students for harassment, but I couldn't help but notice that he had been jerky to the point of verging on illegal to Mackenzie and now Riva, both of whom were poster children for good student behavior, and was a bully towards the silent Darla and submissive Kate, while Madison, who, although I had a perverse fondness for her, was a drug addict with bad manners and questionable personal hygiene, got a free pass, presumably because she was the Provost's daughter.

John Greene continued to avoid me the rest of the week. I was worried he was going to cause some kind of a scene at International Education Night, but I needn't have wasted the emotional energy, because he never showed up at all.

"Oh, he never comes to these things," Professor Hernandez, who turned out to be the necklace-wearing woman and this evening was indeed kitted out in full flamenco costume as well as a full set of Central American jewelry, and had brought a tableful of homemade Spanish and Mexican delicacies, told me. "Have an empanada. Or a sopapilla."

"Thanks." I accepted a sopapilla. "Here's some, um, Mishka in the North candy." I had briefly considered handmaking several dozen pirozhki (stuffed pies), but discarded the idea after I had discovered that the department had no brochures for any of the LCTL programs. I'd had to create them all from scratch, with a reasonable amount of help from Kate and minimal contributions from Emma. Alex had written up a paragraph for Arabic, and told me morosely as he sent it to me that he almost wished he could come, but that his father had insisted on his appearance at the soiree thing at the same time.

"Well of course Alex isn't going to help," Kate had told me when I'd mentioned it. "Don't you know? His father used to be a dean at

Temple, back when John Greene used to work there. That's how Alex got the job here."

"Oh," I'd said, not sure whether to rail against this example of nepotism or against the fact that the academic job market was so bad that the best nepotism could bring Alex was two adjunct jobs at second-rate state institutions in not very nice parts of New Jersey.

"Alex was telling me his father is friends with someone who might be able to help set up an interview," Kate had gone on, fighting to keep the envy that was gnawing at her from exploding out for all to see. "For the position in Beirut. That's nice, isn't it?"

"He didn't seem very enthused about it when it was posted," I'd said.

"Yes, but it's a tenure-track job!" She'd sighed. "*I'd* move to Beirut for a tenure-track job, wouldn't you?"

"Maybe," I'd said. The truth was that yes, I probably would. I could mentally criticize Madison all I wanted for her cocaine habit, but at least she maybe got some joy out of it. I was at least as desperately addicted to my search for employment in my chosen profession, and it was making me a lot less happy than taking cocaine seemed to make her.

The end result of my addiction to employment or achievement or whatever sick compulsion it was that was driving me to keep at this instead of just giving up and working as a—what? What would I work as, after getting a PhD in Russian?—was that after spending Monday, Tuesday, and Wednesday evenings creating the brochures, I had gone out on Thursday evening to the nearest foreign food market (one thing this part of Jersey had in abundance, so at least it had that going for it) and bought, with my own money because the department funds had stretched very reluctantly to printing off the brochures in color and absolutely no further, a couple of pounds of Russian and Polish candy, which I was now trying to give away with minimal success.

Professor Hernandez made a face. "No thanks. I've heard that Russian chocolate isn't very good."

"Oh. Well, *I* like it." But she shuddered and turned away from the colorful wrappers I was proffering in her direction, and did an impromptu little flamenco dance instead.

"Hello, Rowena. Here by yourself?"

I started. While I had been watching Professor Hernandez, my first visitor of the evening had come up to the booth. It was Provost Johnson.

"Yes," I said.

"Why isn't anyone else here supporting you?" he asked. He was still wearing a $100 haircut and a different $1000 suit, but this evening his expensively groomed face appeared to be in almost a good mood, maybe because of the absence of John Greene.

"It just happened that way," I said, with a vague half-smile. "Would you like a Mishka in the North candy?"

He picked up a candy and examined the wrapper. "Cute," he said. "Did you get these yourself?"

"Um, yes."

"Very nice." He unwrapped it and popped it into his mouth. "Tasty," he said when he was done. "I wasn't expecting Russian chocolate to be so good."

"Lots of Westerners think it's an acquired taste."

"Well, maybe it's a taste I want to acquire." He examined the wrapper again before slipping it tidily in his pocket. "Madison tells me she's really enjoying your class."

"That's nice," I said, unable to come up with anything better to say.

"It seems to be having a beneficial effect on her," he said. He was giving me an intense look, as if trying to see into my soul and grasp the essence of my influence over his daughter. Or maybe he was just imagining me naked. It was hard to tell.

"I'm glad," I said, not adding how surprised I was. It was true that Madison had continued to show up to class semi-sober, making it a solid three weeks of comparative good behavior in Russian class, but I doubted that was extending to the rest of her life, or that I had had that much to do with it. As I had told her, the only person who could make her go clean was herself, and I doubted that things had changed so much for her in the past month that she would suddenly do so. I was just grateful that she was keeping her drug habit under the radar enough that I could get away with not reporting her.

"So how'd you do it, Rowena?" he asked. "Straighten my daughter out? Because"—he gave a tight little grimace that was probably supposed to be a smile—"no one else has been able to."

"I doubt it was me," I said.

"Well, I don't know who else it could have been, and *she* says it was you."

I shrugged. "I'm just...nice to her."

He frowned. "Everyone's nice to Madison, and it never seems to do her any good."

"I just...treat her like a grownup."

"You mean like high expectations and consequences."

"No," I said. "High expectations and consequences are how we treat children and convicts. And look how that turns out." Then I thought I shouldn't have said that, but it was too late to take the words back, so I said quickly, "I like her. She can tell."

He frowned some more. "Everyone's nice to Madison," he repeated.

"Yeah, but I *like* her."

He smiled bitterly. "Well, I guess that's more than her mother can boast of," he said, and then looked like he wished he could take back his words, too.

"Oh, Provost Johnson!" Professor Hernandez had spotted him and came fluttering over in her flamenco gear. "Here to support the troops? How school-spirited of you! We've had so much interest in the Spanish booth! And Rowena was so enterprising to get that candy, don't you think? I hope some students come to her booth and try it."

"Yes," said Provost Johnson, giving her a similar look of masked impatience to the one he'd given John Greene.

"I—all of us in the department—wanted to thank you, Provost, for your initiative to increase the number of classes available for language instructions. *Three* more classrooms in Angelo! Did you hear, Rowena? Well, how could you have: it was at a meeting just for permanent faculty. But we're hoping to increase our language offerings by twenty-five, maybe fifty percent over the next couple of years, and hire some new people as well. Who knows: maybe we can create another Russian position! Maybe even a renewable lectureship!"

"We're certainly considering it very seriously," said Provost Johnson. He gave me another intense look. "If we do, I sincerely hope that Rowena can apply."

"Um, thanks," I said.

"And we might be able to open up *two*—wasn't it?—tenure-line appointments for Spanish! There's so much interest in Spanish, you know! Oh, speaking of which, those students look like they're heading my way." Professor Hernandez rustled off in her flamenco dress.

Provost Johnson permitted himself a tiny smile at her departing back. It wasn't a very benevolent smile. "Thanks for the candy, Rowena," he said. "And for whatever you're doing for Madison, too. Whatever it is, keep up the good work. I look forward to our meeting in December." He took another piece of candy, and, slipping it into his pocket, left.

22

Other than Provost Johnson, the only people to come to my booth during International Education Night, which was lightly attended all around, were a couple whom I strongly suspected of being stoned, who took handfuls of the candy and stumbled off, giggling madly when I tried to get them to take some brochures. Well, more candy for me. After buying it my total available funds had shrunk to $413, with almost a month until my next tiny paycheck, and the problem of buying my ticket to San Antonio growing ever more pressing, so I was seriously considering eating the candy as my main food source that weekend.

Sober reflection the next day warned me what a diet consisting entirely of chocolate, even not very sweet Russian chocolate, would do to my blood sugar, so I took myself off to the dollar store down the street and tried to guess which of the items for sale there were actually edible, and which would have to be thrown out uneaten. Shopping at the dollar store was about all I could afford, but as with most experiences relating to poverty, it was more expensive than one might expect, as a lot of the food available at prices I could afford was already spoiled by the time I bought it.

While there I ran into Darla, who was on the hunt for similarly low-priced edibles. At first she didn't recognize me, and when she did, she couldn't understand why I was there.

"This is what I can afford," I told her.

"But you're a professor!" she protested.

"A lot of us make about the same as people on minimum wage,"
I told her. "A lot of professors are on food stamps, or have to turn
to other work like bagging groceries or becoming an escort to make
ends meet."

"But you got them fancy degrees!"

"I know," I said. "But a lot of fancy degrees mainly cost money,
not make money. My brother has a bachelor's, my father has a
master's, my mother has an MD, and I have a PhD, and none of us
make much money. My brother makes the most money, as an officer,
but even officers don't make a ton of money. My parents work in an
addiction clinic in Atlanta, but even for doctors, treating homeless
drug addicts doesn't pay well at all."

"They should work at one o' them places for rich people," said
Darla.

"Maybe. But it's not rich people who need them." I thought of
Madison, who could easily end up dead despite having a father who
spent more on suits than I spent on food. "Well, rich people still
need help. But poor people need it more."

"They're doin' the Lord's work, child." Darla patted my arm.
From her it seemed just friendly, not creepy the way it would have
from most of my colleagues. "And I'll be prayin' for you."

"Um, thanks."

"But not for that John Greene fellow. Is *he* poor?" She looked
around theatrically. "I don't see *him* here."

"No," I said. "I don't think he's particularly poor."

"I didn't think so." She looked around again, this time to see if
anyone was listening to us, and then said, lowering her voice, "I knew
he had to be rich, the way he was goin' on like that! Well, you heard
him! Sayin' I'd gotten into his computer! I told him, I *told* him, I
don't know nothin' 'bout computers! And it's true! My niece, the

one who lives in Atlanta, now *she's* real smart with computers, and my grandbaby—I shown you pictures o' my grandbaby yet?"

I shook my head. Darla whipped out a battered and elderly but still serviceable smartphone, and showed me a picture of a smiling girl of about ten, posing for a professional picture in a lacy white dress.

"She's very pretty," I said.

"She sure is, ain't she? And smart! Lord! That girl is so smart! The things she knows how to do with computers! We're tryin' to get together some money to get her one of her own, that's why I'm shoppin' here, you know; we've opened an account special for her and everythin', but anyway, if anyone was to get into someone else's computer it'd be her, but she knows better than that, she sure does! Ain't no one in *my* family who'd go snoopin' through someone else's computer without permission, you better believe it!"

"I'm sure," I said.

"'Cause I'd smack the daylights out of 'em just as soon as I found out, and as for what my mother'd do to 'em...So when that John Greene came at me with his accusations, at first I didn't know *what* to say, and then I was so mad, you know what I mean, I couldn't say nothin' at all, 'cause I was afraid if I opened my mouth somethin' downright unchristian would come out, and, well, *he* may not be a Christian, but I am!"

"Sometimes that's all you can do," I said. "Hold onto your own principles, and not worry about how other people are breaking them."

"You said it, girl! Anyway, he kept goin' on and on about how someone'd been breakin' into his computer, he said he had proof, and he kept goin' on about how he knew it was me makin' those demands on him and how dare I, and he was goin' to have me fired, but nothin's come of it." She snorted, but it was a snort that had a tinge of fear in it. "They just transferred me out o' Dreme Hall to

Angelo and that side o' campus, and good riddance, I say. You and Kate and a few o' the others over there was always nice to me, but some of those professors..."

"Yeah," I said. "Some of them aren't very nice to anyone. I don't think they know how to be. Um...do you know what kind of demands John Greene was talking about? Was someone trying to blackmail him?"

She shrugged. "Sounds like it, don't it? Makes you wonder what kind o' nasty little secrets a man like that'd have, don't it? Lord! I wouldn't read his emails for *nothing*!" She shuddered at the thought of finding out John Greene's intimate secrets, a distaste I shared.

"Anyway, I'll be prayin' for you, baby girl," she said, with another pat on my arm. "Prayin' you get a job where you'll be the rich one, and folks like *him* will be having to do what *you* say."

"Thanks," I said. "And, um, same here. Maybe if you were running things, there wouldn't be so many problems."

She grinned. "You and me, baby girl, we'd sure set those folks to rights, wouldn't we?"

"Yeah, absolutely."

"You and me, baby girl...Jimmy!"

I turned around. Mike and Jimmy were coming over, each pushing a shopping cart full of TV dinners.

"Darla! And if it ain't our favorite professor! What you doin' here, baby girl? Why ain't you in the nice stores 'stead o' hangin' out with us garbage men?"

"She shops here, same as us," Darla informed them. "'Cause they don't pay her nothin', do they, honey?"

"Pretty much," I agreed.

There was a lengthy discussion of what the point was of getting a doctoral degree if you were still going to have to shop at the dollar store, I question I couldn't really answer to either their or my satisfaction, and some talk of the annoying behavior of some of the other professors, and some gossip about the reason behind Darla's transfer from cleaning Dreme Hall to cleaning Angelo Hall, and what those secrets could possibly be that someone had apparently extracted from John Greene's computer—the speculation ranged from international spying to child porn—and the general agreement that education was overrated and it was the school of life that really taught you all you needed to know, and then Mike said his TV dinners were melting and he had to get out of there, so we all left.

23

The rest of the weekend was spent trying to figure out fresh ways to say "I would be delighted," so that my cover letters wouldn't sound quite so annoyingly repetitive to my own ears. I knew that most of the time no one would be reading my cover letters but me, which was sort of depressing, since I had put so much work into them, and sort of reassuring, since looking at them made me slightly queasy, like the way I imagined watching an unauthorized sex tape of myself would make me feel.

After two hours of that fun, I ended up with an "I would welcome the opportunity" in the fourth paragraph in place of a second "I would be delighted," which I decided was good enough, and I sent out the applications I should have sent out the previous week but that had gotten pushed aside in the press to get everything ready for International Education Night.

After the September 30/October 1 deadline for some of the most competitive postdocs, October 15, which was now less than a week away, was the deadline for several of the first, biggest, tenure-track jobs, the jobs I certainly wasn't going to get but that I *might* get an interview for, now that I had successfully defended and even had a visiting position in a school in the Mid-Atlantic, and an interview was an opportunity to network and make connections, in case they had, say, a two-year renewable position open up in the spring, and who knows, sometimes miracles did happen, so I had to submit these applications or I would feel like a failure who was letting myself and my PhD program down, just like I had to go to San Antonio on my own dime and give a talk to an empty room, because if I didn't, I would be letting down the other people on my panel, and who knows, I *might* get one of these highly coveted November first-round interviews, and so this trip *could* change my life in some major, fundamental way for the better, if only I could scrape together the cash for it, and anyway, sitting at home was the kind of thing that losers did, those losers who wanted to find a job in a place where they could tolerate living and create something called "work-life balance" and maybe do something like have a family or at least the opportunity to go out on dates or just out to the movies from time to time.

Thinking all that made me so mad I spent Sunday night tweaking my non-academic resume and then applying for a job as an editor at an academic press, which I was in no way qualified for and even if I were, I wouldn't get, but at least it made me feel as if I were trying to find a job outside of academia, which I was, I just didn't know what that job might be or how to convince people that I should be allowed to do it, let alone be paid money for it. People tended to hear things like "Russian" and "PhD" and shut down in shock before you could even get the rest out, but "NGO" and "Human Rights" didn't go over much better.

I even finished off my evening by doing a search for "Open Source Officer" and sifting through the results until I found the one I was looking for on the fourth page (they deliberately make it hard to find) and looking into the application procedure. But it was so time-consuming that even if I started it now, and even if I passed all the steps successfully, I wouldn't start working for another year at least, so I tabled it for the moment and went back to hunting around on HERC and the JIL in case some miracle job for the spring had magically popped up. It hadn't.

24

Monday morning I ran into a new cleaner in the women's restroom in Dreme Hall. She looked familiar, but I couldn't place her until she grabbed me by the sleeve and said in a heavy Russian accent, "You—Professor Khalli, yes?"

"Yes," I said. "Shall we speak Russian?"

Her previously dour face lit up, and she poured out a flood of enthusiastic and educated Russian, from which I gathered that she thought she knew me, or at least knew about me, and eventually realized that she was Ira's mother.

"Ira is a very good student," I said, only somewhat mendaciously. "She speaks Russian very well."

"Yes, but her writing—so bad! She refused to learn when she was a little girl, and now she can't write her own name! Well, now she can. Because you taught her. Why she had to learn from a professor and a foreigner and not from her own mother or grandmother, I don't understand, but that's young people for you. She wanted to learn from 'a real professor,' even though both I and my mother are doctors—medical doctors, you know, but still educated members of the intelligentsia, so she had to go to university and study with foreigners—you're a foreigner, aren't you? Your Russian is so good! Where did you learn?"

"Russia, mainly."

"Oh, you lived there, did you? Where?"

"Mostly in Moscow."

Ira's mother sighed. "Moscow! I miss Moscow so much!"

"Me too," I said.

"My family are real Muscovites, you know, from even before the Revolution, an intellectual family from the intelligentsia, but we thought we could do better in America after the fall of the Soviet Union, so...and it's true, you *can* do well for yourself here, but you have to have connections, money, things we didn't have. I used to be a doctor, work in a polyclinic, and now I clean toilets. Of course, doctors in Russia don't make a lot of money, not like your doctors here. But I have to get my certificate to practice medicine here, and that costs money, money we don't have because it's all going to Ira's education. You know who's done well for themselves?"

"Who?" I asked.

"That Danila's family. You know? He's in your class with my Ira. From"—her nose wrinkled—"Odessa. Well, what do you expect? We all know what kind of people come from Odessa, don't we? Criminals. Even their Jews are criminals, not doctors like they are in Moscow. Anyway, that Danila—you know what his father does?" She folded her arms over her impressive bosom. "Mafia, that's what. Of course, I shouldn't complain. He got me the job here. And he helped Ira get in, and helped her get a scholarship because I work here. He's a clever one, that Vova. He got in with the Italians as soon as he arrived here—you're not Italian, are you, sweetheart?"

"No. Not Italian at all."

"What kind of a name is Khalli anyway? Is it Central Asian? Middle Eastern?" She squinted at me. "You don't *look* like an Arab or a Tatar, although you do have lovely dark hair."

"It's British," I told her. "My family is from the British Isles. I look Celtic. Kind of 'Black Irish.'"

"The Irish aren't black. Although they sort of are, aren't they?"

"That's a complicated question," I said, in my best academic-evading-a-complicated-question voice. "But a lot of people from there have dark hair and pale skin, like me."

"So not Russian at all?"

"No, unfortunately not. But I did live there for a while."

"Of course you did, darling. You're practically one of us, now, aren't you?" She squinted at me again. "You don't have any Italian heritage, do you?"

"None at all."

"Good! Those Italians, they're all mafiosi, worse than Odessans...you know who is Italian?"

"Who?"

"That student of yours! Mak-ken-zi." She sounded out the name carefully.

"Mackenzie? Well, yes, I suppose she is of Italian heritage."

"No, not just of Italian heritage! Her father is mafioso!"

"Um," I said, trying to imagine Mackenzie as the daughter of a don or a godfather.

"He is!" Ira's mother insisted. "He's in business with Danila's father!"

"Um...what kind of business?"

"Construction. And you know what that means!"

"Not everyone who does construction is a criminal," I said.

Ira's mother gave me a look as if I were too stupid to be allowed outside unsupervised. "They are in New Jersey!"

"Well...maybe you're right. There certainly is a lot of crime and corruption here."

"I know! We came to America to get away from corruption, and what did we find here? More corruption! Of course," she said reflectively, "maybe it's from all the immigrants."

My tongue struggled between the instinct, drilled into it by years amongst liberal intellectuals, to insist that immigrants weren't criminals, and the knowledge, drilled into it by years of personal observation, that in fact many immigrants *were* criminals, in part because it was impossible to survive as an immigrant without breaking some law or other, often accidentally. I'd certainly broken plenty of my own when I'd been living abroad.

"It can be hard to be an immigrant," I said as a compromise.

"Especially when the natives are so corrupt themselves!" said Ira's mother. "Did you know that that Mak-ken-zi's father—"

Hay-hair woman, whose name I could never remember, came into the bathroom.

"Excuse me," said Ira's mother to me in Russian, and "Sorri," to hay-hair in English, before pushing her cart out of the restroom, giving me a significant wink and not looking hay-hair professor in the eye as she did so.

"Were you speaking Russian?" asked hay-hair.

"Yes. It turns out she's the mother of one of my students."

Hay-hair looked doubly taken aback at that, as if she couldn't believe that the child of a janitor could be a student here, and also that I could be talking to said janitor.

"Well," she said uncomfortably, "how, uh, nice for you. Are you, uh, having a good semester? Settling in nicely?"

"As well as can be expected," I said. Hay-hair must have realized that had been a stupid question, for after a short awkward pause, she said, "Of course, I suppose Tom will be coming back next semester, won't he?"

"Tom?"

"Oh! Professor Cahill. You know, our, uh, permanent Russian lecturer."

"So he's just a lecturer, then? Not tenured?"

Hay-hair looked even more awkward. "A lecturer, yes," she confirmed. "But in a renewable position. And maybe he's getting paid leave this semester? No, I suppose it's unpaid leave. Only

tenure-stream faculty get paid sabbaticals. Well, he's not really on a
sabbatical, is he? It's more administrative leave. Which I suppose is
generous after what happened."

"What happened?" I asked.

"You mean they didn't tell you? It was all about that boy, you
know, the one who"—she dropped her voice to a whisper—"killed
himself. That's why Tom was asked to step aside for a semester, so that
they could investigate the affair."

"What's to investigate? Do they normally do that for a student
suicide?"

"Well, no, but in his suicide note"—hay-hair's voice dropped
even lower, so that I could hardly make it out—"they say he
mentioned the Russian program."

"What!"

She looked around nervously, but no SWAT teams burst in on
us and dragged us away. That was only for students, not faculty
gossiping in the women's restroom. We just got fired. "It's all very
hush-hush," she said, still whispering. "But a friend of mine was on
the investigation committee, and *she* said that the boy left a note
saying that he'd been driven to it by his Russian class."

"What! How? Was Professor Cahill known for bullying? And
why aren't the police investigating this?"

"You know, it's funny, because Tom was always very popular with
the students as far as the rest of us could tell. It's not like he was
John...I mean, some professors have very rigorous standards that can
make them unpopular, you know? While Tom was always very laid
back. It made some of the faculty feel like he was being too easy on
the students, to be honest, and not upholding the standards of the
department."

She stopped and looked at me expectantly. I refrained from
saying what I was thinking, which was that if you taught Russian,
you didn't have create artificial rigor because there was plenty of real

rigor built right into the subject, and instead smiled what I hoped was a sympathetic and conciliatory smile.

It must have worked, for she went on, now speaking more loudly, "I mean, Tom was more like the students' friend than he was a professor, you know what I mean, and they all loved him for it, so, well, it created some ill feeling in the department, since Russian enrollments were rising when enrollments in other languages were dropping, but then there was the...*incident*, and the note, which said something like 'I thought I had friends in the Russian program, but those bitches turned on me.'"

The door opened and Professor Hernandez, sporting another gaudy Central American necklace, came in. She gave us a suspicious look, like there could be no good reason for a tenured professor to be talking to contingent faculty, and she couldn't bear the idea of peeing in the same bathroom as me. Hay-hair looked guilty, like maybe she was being stricken with the same thoughts, and scurried out of the bathroom before I could ask if she knew anything more.

25

The latter part of October brought a profusion of fall colors, which were, I had to admit, spectacular, especially in the chained-off parts of campus where students and faculty were not allowed to tread. It also brought a stunning display of Halloween decorations. Apparently no one in New Jersey was troubled by worries that Halloween might be a Satanic holiday, or at least a Catholic one, probably because most of them were Catholics.

Nor were they troubled by thoughts that decorating a tree by hanging it with a bunch of fake dead bodies made of black cloth might be inappropriate. The first time I saw what appeared to be a mass lynching, I almost drove off the road, and did in fact stall out. When I came across the second one a couple of blocks later, I realized it must be a Halloween decoration, although one that to a Southerner seemed like a stunning display of tastelessness. When I saw that there was one at either side of the campus entrance, I was nonplussed once again. Either my colleagues were completely tone-deaf, or we truly were living in a post-racial society.

I would have liked to have thought the latter, but having just driven through several miles of grim urban poverty in all-black neighborhoods, only to be dumped out into the all-white enclave that was TLASC, I suspected it was more the former. I would have felt a little better if only TLASC had truly been a haven of wealth and happiness, because at least that way *someone* would have been better off, but instead it was another ghetto of misery and exploitation, just one where people had paler skin and used words like "cultural appropriation" and "heteronormative" in everyday speech.

I almost brought up the lynching trees in my first class, just to confirm that I was the only one who saw a tree full of dead bodies and immediately thought "lynching," or that I was the only one who didn't think that fake lynchings were an acceptable form of holiday decoration, and maybe also to share with my students the fun fact that "to lynch" had been borrowed by Russian through the use of the -ova/-eva suffix, which we were just learning, but I was sidetracked by Vitya's black eye.

"What happened?" I asked, expecting to hear a tale of a skateboarding trick gone tragically wrong. But instead he only shrank down into his seat and mumbled something incoherent in some interlanguage halfway between English and Russian.

"A girl punched him!" Danila informed the rest of the class with glee.

"Um..." I said. "Why?"

Vitya muttered something in Russian about fucking American whores.

"We were at a frat party," Danila told me.

"Ah."

"No, no, it wasn't like that! Frat parties aren't like that!"

"Uh-huh," I said.

"No, really, everyone's very well-behaved! Only this girl, she was drunk, you know? She didn't understand what was going on, and she thought...well, there was no need to punch him. Vitya wasn't doing anything wrong! But she thought...she was such a bitch! And you know how it is, if you're Russian—"

"Belarusian!" interjected Vitya, coming out of his sulk for an instant.

"Yeah, right, whatever, man. Technically I'm Ukrainian but everyone thinks I'm Russian and really I am, you know what I mean? I mean, like, everyone in my family speaks Russian and half my family's in Rostov and places like that. And it's the same for you. Do you even speak any Belarusian?"

"No," said Vitya sullenly. "But it's because it's suppressed!"

"Yeah, whatever, man. Your last name is Ivanov, not like...something actually Belarusian. Your family's one of the oppressors, you know what I'm saying?"

Vitya elbowed Danila hard in the ribs before going back to his sulk.

"Anyway, so, like, this chick, she like, she was like all over him, all, you know"—Danila's voice took on the breathy falsetto that most men used to imitate women, the one that marked the person being imitated as an idiot—"'Oh, you're so cute! You must *work out*! You have such a cute accent! Where did you say you were from?' But when he told her, she got all angry, started talking about the Euromaidan and Russian aggression, and wanted to storm off, and, well..."

"Mmmm," I said.

"It's not fair!" Danila burst out. "People are constantly calling me an aggressor, an invader, and I've never even been in Russia! I lived in Odessa when I was a little kid, and I've been in Jersey for the past ten years! I have dual citizenship! I have an American passport! But as soon as you say 'Russian' people are all like that bitch who punched Vitya!"

"Mmmm," I said again. "You could tell them you're Ukrainian. Your last name *is* Petrenko."

"Yeah, but, I mean, like, I kind of am, but really my family's Russian, like I said. I don't give a shit about the Euromaidan! And you know it was Nazis! There were neo-Nazis doing the fighting! For the side that says it's all about 'democracy!' But there were a bunch of people wearing swastikas and shit on the side the Americans are supporting! My grandmother was Jewish, you know what I'm saying? Her family was fuckin' almost wiped out by the fuckin' Nazis—oops, sorry, Professor."

"That's okay," I said. "The offensive word in that sentence was 'Nazis,' not 'fucking.'"

Everyone tittered at the sound of their professor dropping an F-bomb, and Danila grinned appreciatively.

"So anyway, I fuckin' hate the fuckin' Nazis and so does the rest of my family. Like *hate* them. Like more than any fuckin' American can possibly understand. I mean, my grandmother's cousin, she was, like, *taken away*, you know what I'm saying? Like she was a little girl and she was, like, dragged away and taken to Dachau or some shit like that and thrown into the oven! Like, they came and got a little girl and threw her into the oven! So I see a swastika, and I, like...and my dad...and Vitya...well, he kind of flipped out, didn't you, Vitya?"

"Yeah," said Vitya. "But I didn't hurt her! I wasn't going to hurt her! She was the one who hurt me."

"Yeah! It's not right! Like, she just started on at us about all the bad things the Russians are doing, and when we started telling her about the swastikas, she told us we were liars and tried to run off all mad and shit, and so Vitya, he, well, he grabbed her. And, okay, so maybe he...kind of ripped her sleeve a little bit. But he wasn't going to hurt her! He just wanted to tell her his side of the story! But she *punched* him and now he's afraid he's going to get, like, accused of assault, when she was the one who assaulted him!"

"Uh-huh," I said. "I'm sure that was very upsetting. But grabbing women who don't want to be grabbed can seem very threatening to them. You really have to assume that anyone who does that is going to hurt you."

"That's not fair!"

"No," I agreed. "But it's rather more unfair to women than it is to men."

"But he wasn't going to hurt her!"

"But he grabbed her," I said. "How would you feel if someone you didn't know grabbed you and started shouting at you?"

"But that's what *she* was doing!"

"But how likely was she to commit some horrible sexual assault?"

"But...but...it's not fair! And, I mean, like, the fact that it was at a frat...everyone immediately assumes that it was something bad, just because it was at a frat!"

"And rightfully so," I said. "An unkind person might be tempted to say that by being at a frat party, you were 'asking for' an assault charge, and you should have known better and stayed away if you really didn't want one."

Seeing the boys' sullen, stricken faces, I said, more gently, "I know you didn't mean any harm, and it must be very frustrating to have people constantly throwing the Russian thing in your faces. I get it, I really do. If I had a dollar for every time some non-American brought up Iraq, I could take myself out to dinner. But you also have to understand that that was a very high-risk environment for any girl. It's like being in a combat zone or something, where you have to shoot first so they don't shoot you. My boyfriend..." I trailed off, not wanting to spill any more than I'd already spilled.

"What about your boyfriend, Prof?" asked Danila, his eyes avid, former offense forgotten. "Was he, like, in a war or something?"

"Yes," I said. "And in those situations, he always said it's better to shoot someone else who didn't deserve it than to get shot yourself by someone you thought wasn't dangerous."

"Yeah, but..."

"Is your boyfriend Russian, Professor Halley?" asked Ira, interrupting Danila's objection at being labeled an enemy combatant.

"Yes," I said, not wanting to get into the fact that he wasn't really my boyfriend anymore. "So I know a thing or two about Russian men, okay? And one of the things I know is you have to keep them in their place, or else they'll get totally out of hand."

Ira snickered. Danila and Vitya shot her irate glares that turned into rueful grins. "Yeah, you may have a point, Prof," said Danila. "So, um, I guess we should be a little cooler at frats, right?"

"Right," I said. "You always want to be the perfect gentleman, because most other men won't be."

"Does your boyfriend act like a gentleman, Professor?" asked Ira, looking more animated than she had the entire semester. "Or is he a jerk like those two?" She pointed her chin at Danila and Vitya, who both gave her the finger.

"He makes a point of acting like a gentleman around women," I said. "Really, with Russian men, that's the way it is: either real gentlemen, or rapists. So"—I gave Danila and Vitya a stern look—"you want to make sure you not only fall into the first category, but everyone knows you fall into the first category. Besides, women like gentlemen."

"Women like bad boys," said Danila skeptically.

"Everyone thinks so, but really, the men I know with the most dates are normally the really nice ones. So bear that in mind."

Danila argued some more for the benefits of being a bad boy, but Ira told him to shut up, he didn't know what he was talking about, as witnessed by the fact that he didn't have a girlfriend and had just gotten into an altercation in which a woman had punched his friend in the face for physically assaulting her, and for a moment I thought there was going to be a repeat of that scene and I was going to have to use my self-defense training on the boys, but eventually everyone settled down and tried, with very mixed success, to focus on the conjugation of -ova/-eva verbs.

26

I was half afraid that Vitya would be brought up on assault charges, which would have been unpleasant, not because he didn't deserve it, which he probably did, but because it would further tarnish the reputation of the Russian program. With the war going on in the Donbass, anti-Russian sentiment, inasmuch as most Americans thought about Russia at all, was high, as Danila and Vitya could testify. Rather than encouraging people to study Russian and maybe avoid making more of the egregious errors that Americans had made in the past, most people who thought about it at all seemed to think that studying Russian would somehow infect them with pro-Russian sentiment (quite possibly true—it's terrible how getting to know people tends to make you like them more), and that unclouded judgment could only be the result of a completely ignorant mind. So not only were students not signing up for Russian classes all over the country, oftentimes because they were actively discouraged by their parents, but whenever I said the word "Russian" to my colleagues here, they tended to make little faces and edge away, as if I smelled bad.

But, to my relief, Danila confided a week later that they had "straightened everything out in a left-handed way," and Vitya came slinking into class just like always, if a touch more sulky and argumentative. Which allowed me to worry less about whether one of my students was going to be brought up on assault charges, and more about why a student who had never been mine had killed himself over something that had happened in the program that was currently my responsibility. The story hay-hair had told me seemed so fantastical that I couldn't stop myself from worrying at it, both because I was afraid I was going to be suddenly called on the carpet over something that had nothing to do with me, and because I was curious, and because worrying over someone else's suicide was more fun than worrying over my own lack of job prospects.

We had Thursday and Friday off in the end of October for fall break, which I spent at home sending out job applications. It was ridiculous, as Alex and I agreed during a moment of mutual commiseration on the day before the break, that such a poor market would require so much time and effort on job applications.

"My advisor was telling me he applied for twenty-five jobs," Alex said from where he was lying on his mattress, trying to get in a little rest before heading off to his other job. All his stuff was gathered around him in preparation to be hauled back to his parents' house, since Dreme Hall was going to be closed to faculty and students during fall break, so that campus police could use it for active shooter drills.

"Yeah, so did mine."

"And he got a tenure-track job straight out of grad school! After only twenty-five applications and one year on the market! While I've submitted—I counted—two hundred applications in the past two years, and I'm still working this fucking job, and I have to kiss John Greene's ass in order to keep it! He thinks he's doing me such a big favor by giving me this piece of shit job, and you know what the worst thing is? He's right."

"Yeah," I said.

"I should have stayed in the fucking Navy, I really should have," said Alex. "But I was all like: 'Oh, I can't stand to take any more orders, I can't stand to go around licking the senior officers' boots, so I'm going to find *freedom* and *self-determination* and all that shit by going back to school and getting my PhD, which will also make my dad happy, and I'll be sure to find a job, because the demand for Arabic speakers is sky-high.' Ha! Haha-fucking-ha! And you know what? I was half-right. There *are* plenty of jobs for Arabic speakers. They just all pay six to nine thousand dollars a semester, no benefits. Who the fuck is supposed to be doing these jobs, that's what I want to know?"

"Women," I said.

"Didn't Kate say something about how you were a feminist scholar?" Alex lifted his head up from where it was propped on his arms folded behind his head, and looked at me intently. "Maybe you should be leading our revolution. You look like a revolutionary to me."

"I don't know about that," I said. "And you can't really be a feminist scholar in Slavic studies. It just isn't done. God forbid that you might say something that suggests that Gogol or someone was sexist. Plus, everyone has to be a generalist, anyway. You have to be ready to teach all levels of the language, plus survey literature and culture courses, plus individual author courses, plus First Year Seminars, plus specialized courses for grad students."

"Yeah." Alex flung his head back down onto his folded arms and stared up at the ceiling. "Same in all the LCTLs, I think. You got any good prospects for next semester?"

"Not yet." I was trying not to panic about it. This semester was already half over and I didn't have anything lined up yet for next semester. I hadn't even seen any jobs advertised for next semester. I tried to tell myself I would be okay with taking John up on his offer and spending the next semester hanging out rent-free and unemployed in his apartment at Camp Lejeune. That would totally not be a humiliating and boring experience. Maybe it would be a great opportunity for me and Masha to try out our backup plan of becoming strippers. Would anyone, even drunk Marines, pay money to watch 35-year-olds with permanent eye strain from poring over pre-Revolutionary texts shimmy off their clothes? And could I even shimmy?

"What do you think?" I asked Alex. "Could I make it as a stripper in a military town? My friend Masha and I keep talking about it. It started out as a joke, but it's rapidly becoming a lot less funny."

He lifted his head up to give me a brief piercing look, as his mind temporarily returned to where his body was. "Fuck yeah," he said when he was done. "You're way hotter than most of the strippers I've seen." He paused for a moment, possibly from embarrassment, before asking, "Do you have a specific town in mind?"

"Jacksonville?"

"Like, Florida? Like, undergrads?" He looked aghast.

"No, Jacksonville, North Carolina."

"Oh God! Not Marines! Have some self-respect, Rowena! At least hold out for sailors." He paused for a moment, once again, I thought, from embarrassment, while contemplating the ceiling morosely. "Maybe *I* should join you," he said once he'd recovered himself. "What do you think? Is there room in your act for an Arabist? Maybe you two could do some kind of act as those nesting dolls, and I could...dance around in nothing but a fez or something."

He stared some more at the ceiling. "Hustling my ass sounds a lot less degrading right now than hanging around here waiting for them to convert my position to a full-time renewable lectureship. Have they been feeding you that line? Because they've been telling me since my first semester here that they're really, really interested in expanding the Arabic program, and there's *definitely* going to be money coming into the department for Arabic, and they're *definitely* going to have a full-time, long-term position opening up any day now, and when they do, I would be *welcome* to apply to it. FUCK!

I'd have to fight off about a hundred and fifty bright-eyed little grads, and people with two books to their names, and people who'd get down on their knees and suck John Greene's dick just for the chance to interview for the job, and...whatever. They're never going to do it anyway. They've been talking and talking about it, but it's just a way to yank my chain, keep me compliant. Have they been feeding you that BS?"

"Some," I said.

"Yeah, I'm not surprised. Of course, Russian already has a renewable lectureship, but...I'm surprised they didn't cut it after what happened last semester."

"What *did* happen last semester?" I asked. "I keep hearing hints, but I can't figure out what really went on."

Alex rolled up to sitting in a single lithe movement and looked straight at me. "Well, you know that kid—Brandy—killed himself, right?"

I nodded.

"And he said something about the Russian program in his notebook?"

"You mean it wasn't an actual suicide note?"

Alex shrugged. "They're saying it was, but from what I heard, it was just the last thing he wrote in his notebook. But it was about how he couldn't take what those bitches in the Russian program were doing to him anymore, so it sure sounds like a suicide note."

I nodded again.

"And you know he was gay, right? Not just gay, but, like, the president of the Student Lambda Club and stuff?"

I nodded a third time.

"So, the thing is, he was, like, dating a student of mine. You didn't hear that from me. My student isn't out. Only you know how it is: you're the tiniest bit nice to these kids and they're in your office, or in our case, following us around campus because we don't have a private office, confessing all their sins and blurting out all their secrets, because they don't have anyone else to talk to about it. They're looking for an adult to talk to, someone they can trust, someone they respect, about stuff that they're scared about and looking for help with, and they can't go to their parents and they sure as shit can't go to anyone with tenure or those motherfuckers in Student Wellness or whatever the fuck it's called because, like I said, they're looking for someone they respect. But me, and probably you too, well, we've been around, right? Were you ever in the service?"

"No," I said. "My brother enlisted, but I took the other route. I spent several years working for an NGO in Moscow, observing elections and documenting human rights abuses, interviewing torture and hazing victims, stuff like that."

"No shit?" He gave me another look of intense interest. "What made you quit?"

"Basically I got to a position where the only way I could advance was by becoming a better fundraiser than I wanted to become. It didn't pay very much and I thought I needed something a little more remunerative and stable, and I thought going into higher education would provide that."

"Yeah, same here, pretty much. Why didn't anyone *tell* us?"

We both shared a moment of silence for our youthful naivety.

"Anyway," said Alex, shaking himself out of his depressing musings on the follies of youth. "We've done stuff that's *cool*. Or that sounds cool, anyway. These kids, they don't want to be professors, or most of them don't, and rightly so, but they *love* thinking about being in the service, or doing some idealistic shit in Russia or somewhere dangerous, somewhere things actually *happen*, they *love* thinking about that as they get their little degrees in accounting or business management or whatever and go on to their lives that they don't want and are so boring and meaningless they're probably going to drink themselves to death or something just to get out of it, and anyway...when they've got secrets to tell, bad stuff, shit that's really real for once in their super-boring little lives, they're going to come to us, aren't they?"

"Um, yeah," I agreed. "I guess so, sometimes."

"So, anyway, my student-who-isn't-out-except-to-me came to me and told me he was seeing this Brandy kid on the sly and he didn't know what to do, Brandy was pressuring him to come out publicly. My kid's in the sports program, so...I mean, the college says a lot of shit about supporting their gay athletes, but we both know how much that means, right? So anyway, Brandy was coming down on him really hard"—Alex paused to snort at his double entendre—"to come out, and my kid was saying no, no, his teammates'd kill him, his parents would kill him, and Brandy was threatening to make some of their texts and emails public if he didn't come out, and I told him that wasn't how someone who cared about you treated you, you know what I mean? I mean, I know gay rights were important to this Brandy kid, and that's cool as far as it goes, but you don't blackmail your boyfriend, right? Especially when it might literally get him killed. I mean, my kid was genuinely scared, the real deal. For once in his life something real was happening, and he was finding out what we all find out, which is that real trouble isn't nearly as much fun as we think it's going to be. His dad is, like, a bit mafia, or more than a bit, and maybe would have actually killed him if he stepped out of the upper-middle-class line his dad had drawn for him.

"So anyway, yeah, this Brandy was basically blackmailing him, and my kid was genuinely thinking about running away or killing himself or something, and I was like, 'Oh shit, they do *not* pay me enough to deal with this shit, but no one else is going to help this kid if I don't, so here we go, let's try and get together after class man, you want me try to talk some sense into this Brandy kid, threaten him back, or what?' I mean, I'm basically a wimp and I know it, although I do climb a mean wall when I get the chance, but as soon as you say something like, 'ex-Navy, active duty deployment in the Middle East,' even I can get some respect. Little as I deserve it. I mean, I sure as hell am no Chris Kyle. But whatever. That's the first thing that everyone thinks of now, so sometimes it works out for me."

"And so did you? Threaten him?"

"Nah." Alex shook his head. "It never came to that. My kid came to me the day before we were supposed to meet with Brandy and told me it had all been straightened out. Brandy had apologized to him, told him someone was blackmailing *him* and it was a shitty thing to do, he saw that now, and he could really use a friend, really use someone to stand by him and watch his back now, because some bad shit might be about to come out, and he was really sorry for even thinking about doing to his boyfriend what people were doing to him, yada yada yada, and then...they found him two days later. Actually, it was my student who found him."

"Poor kid," I said.

"Yeah, he's still well and truly fucked in the head. I thought he was going to drop out or at least take a semester off, but he couldn't tell his parents why he needed to do that, so...he sits in the back of class and snivels when he thinks no one can see him."

"Poor thing."

"Yeah. Hey, you want to talk to him?" Alex eyed me speculatively. "You might be better at it than me."

"Um, okay. If you think it would be helpful."

"I'll ask him, okay? After break. Because you're, like, an expert at talking to people who've had bad shit happen to them, right?"

"Um," I said. "Not really. But I'm happy to talk to him if you think it would help."

"Why not? I really am worried about him. I'll be in touch after break, all right?"

"All right," I agreed. "Have a good break."

"Ha!" said Alex, and, jumping to his feet with athletic lightness, gathered up his three bags of supplies and took off with a surprisingly springy step.

27

Five job applications in four days later, and fall break was over. When I looked at my spreadsheet, I had the warm glow of knowing I was at least a couple of weeks ahead of desperate last-minute scrambles to get applications in by the deadline. So, with the ASEEES convention less than a month away, I really needed to take a week off from applying for jobs and write the paper I was supposed to present there.

If, of course, I could afford to go. Despite grocery shopping at the dollar store and only eating in the evenings—that dissertation weight was definitely gone, to the point that if I could have afforded it, I should have bought a new pair of pants, or at least started eating lunch again—my total available funds, including what was left on my credit card limit, were down to below $300. I would get my next paycheck at the end of October, only a week away, but most of it would get sucked up by rent and health insurance, and the tiny dregs that were left would have to go to food and gas.

And if by some miracle I could scrape together a couple of hundred dollars extra, they should really, really be spent on getting my car looked at. Second gear was almost nonexistent by this point, involving some pretty comical (to onlookers) moments at intersections as I revved up the engine as much as I dared in first, slammed it into second with a nasty grinding noise—when, that is, I didn't stall out—and then sprinted into the safety of third. So basically my transmission was not long for this world, and even if I could afford to get it looked at, I almost certainly couldn't afford to get it fixed.

I was contemplating the shame of pulling out of a conference at the last minute, when, two days before Halloween, an email showed up in both my personal and TLASC inboxes, inviting me to an interview. For a tenure-track job, one of the ones I had been so certain I didn't have a chance at. At ASEEES. Which was in San Antonio.

I reread the email. There was no mention of any option of doing the interview via Skype. I was of course within my rights to request a Skype interview, but, but...if you were invited to an interview for a tenure-track job at a conference, you forked out the $1,000-2,000 and damn well went, or gave up and resigned yourself to a career at the local supermarket. Which right now was sounding pretty good.

No, no, no, you can't quit now, I told myself, and emailed back, saying I would be *delighted* to interview with the search committee, and that other than my two panels, one as presenter and one as chair, Thursday afternoon, I would be entirely at the committee's disposal.

I got back an email within an hour from the department admin, telling me I had been scheduled for 9:00am Friday morning. Well, at least I wouldn't have to sit around all day fretting about it. I emailed promptly back confirming the appointment and saying how much I looked forward to speaking to the search committee. Then I stared at my phone in indecision, wondering which of my relatives to call and beg for money.

Just as I was composing a Skype text to John, saying I was sorry to bother him when I knew he must have a million things to do, what with the imminent withdrawal from Camp Leatherneck, but I really, really needed money, my phone rang, startling me. I so rarely got actual phone calls.

"Hello, Grandma," I said.

"Darling! Rowena! How *are* you? How's the new job? We're all *so proud* of you, darling. I just can't believe we have a real professor in the family! I was just telling all the ladies in my book club about it. Of course, we always knew you were a smart one; it was just a matter of time. I was *so worried* when you went off to Russia for that awful job, but then you came back, and now you're doing what you've always been meant to do!"

"Uh-huh," I said. "How have you been?"

"Oh, so busy, darling. We've decorated the house and the front garden for Halloween, of course, and it's just so delightfully spooky! I wish you could come see it, but we'll have to take it down before you come for Thanksgiving."

"Um," I said. "I don't think I'm going to be able to make it to Thanksgiving."

"Oh, but darling..."

"I'll only have a couple of days off, so I won't have time to drive down. And my car is having trouble, anyway. It wouldn't be safe."

"Well, why don't you get it fixed?"

"I will when I can."

"Of course, of course, I'm sure you're *so busy*, with your new job as a professor...but why don't you just fly down, darling? You could fly down to Atlanta, your parents could pick you up, and you could all drive over to Macon together."

"I can't afford to fly," I said. "Actually, I can't afford to drive, either."

There was a pause at the other end of the line.

"But darling," said my grandmother, once she'd recovered enough to speak. "You're not a grad student any more. You're a professor."

"Yes, but I'm even poorer as a professor than I was as a grad student."

"But you're teaching more!"

"Yes, but I get paid less per credit hour, and I don't get health insurance anymore. I can't afford to come to Macon for Thanksgiving. I can barely afford to buy groceries. Actually, I can't really afford even to do that."

"Oh. Oh. Well, do you have any better job prospects?"

"Actually, I was just invited to a first-round interview for a tenure-track job."

"Darling! That's wonderful. When is this interview?"

"The week before Thanksgiving. In San Antonio."

"Oh. Well, are they flying you down there themselves?"

"No. I'm supposed to fly myself down."

"But...darling...can you afford it?"

"No," I said. "Actually, I was literally writing to John for money when you called."

"Oh." There was such a long pause at the other end of the line that I thought we'd gotten cut off. "Well," said my grandmother, just as I was about to start the "can you hear me" routine, "what if *I* gave you the money, darling? As an early Christmas present."

"It would be a lot of money," I warned her. "At least a thousand dollars."

"*Two* thousand dollars, darling, so that you could fly straight back down to Atlanta for Thanksgiving."

"Um," I said. "Okay."

"Are you crying, darling?"

"Maybe a little bit."

"Darling, we have to get you away from that place. New Jersey! Is it as bad as it is on TV?"

"Not in the same way," I said, wiping my nose on my sleeve like Madison. "But it's not very nice, either."

"Darling, I'm not surprised at all, to be honest. I was so glad when you got the job because it was a job, and your mother was telling me how competitive it is right now, but...New Jersey? It's so far away. Where's this job you're interviewing for?"

"Charlotte," I told her.

"North Carolina?" asked my grandmother, perking up.

"Yep."

"Oh darling, that's *much* better. Charlotte's a lovely city, and you could drive down to visit us on weekends. Is it a good job? A good school?"

"It's okay," I said. "Better than where I am now, at least. It's a little concerning that they've just shut down the PhD program at Chapel Hill, so everyone's surprised that they're hiring in Charlotte, but it would at least be a job. *If* it turns into anything."

"Oh, of course, darling, but I'll have all my fingers and toes crossed for you, and surely, darling"—she lowered her voice as if the search committee, or maybe the other candidates, could hear us—"you *must* have an edge, being a Southerner. You know how snooty some of those Northerners can be, not even wanting to consider a job anywhere below the Mason-Dixon. Being from Georgia is probably a real advantage for you."

"You're probably right." And she was. A lot of people from the Mid-Atlantic, where I had the privilege of living and working right now, could hardly bring themselves to even consider a job in the South or the Midwest, which did in fact give me a major edge for those jobs. "But a tenure-track job is likely to have more than a hundred candidates, even one in Charlotte," I warned.

"But how many get invited for an interview?"

"Normally ten for a first-round interview, which is what this is, and then three for a campus interview."

"So you're already in the top ten! Darling, just charm the socks off them like I know you can! Do Macon proud!"

"I will," I promised.

"And I'll send the check out today, darling. Overnight mail."

"Thank you," I said.

"Now, don't go crying again, darling! You don't want to spoil your appearance for that big interview—or for Thanksgiving dinner! Let me know as soon as you get your tickets. I know we all want to see you very much, darling."

"I'll let you know," I said. "And thanks again, Grandma."

"Thank me by coming and bringing your appetite," said my grandmother sternly, hanging up and leaving me with the thought that sometimes heroes didn't wear capes and carry laser-guns. Sometimes they were little old checkbook-wielding ladies from Macon, Georgia.

28

The news of my upcoming interview filled the adjunct warehouse chatter the next day, with Kate and Emma both agreeing that one could get used to the idea of living in a remote hinterland like Charlotte if it came with a twelve-month appointment and full benefits.

Things got even more animated when Alex came in from class and announced that he, too, had gotten an interview invitation for a tenure-track position.

"Wow!" cried Emma, trying and failing to suppress her naked envy. "For where?"

"Beirut," said Alex.

"Oh," we all said at once.

"But...Beirut could be nice, right?" said Kate. "I mean...it's not like it used to be, right? It's a nice place to live now, right?"

Alex shrugged and threw himself down onto his mattress, which he was no longer bothering to roll up and place against the wall, especially since Emma was also using it almost every day too. I had been speculating to myself over whether they sometimes shared the mattress simultaneously and in a non-Platonic fashion, because that was the way my mind ran, but if they were, they were keeping it well under wraps. Emma always seemed resentful of Alex's comparative success and Alex always seemed like he could barely stand to be in the same building as Emma, and anyway, both of them seemed too frazzled to have the time or energy for any hanky-panky. More likely, Alex was enough of a gentleman under his stubbly, prickly exterior to offer his mattress to a lady in need, no strings attached, even a lady he disliked.

"It's far away from my parents," he said to the ceiling. He sat up. "Hey! That's right! It's like a solid fifteen-hour flight from Pennsylvania." He grinned for the first time since I'd met him. "What's the occasional car bombing compared with living with my dad at the age of thirty-seven? What?" He looked at our shocked faces. "I don't look thirty-seven, right? I don't look a day over twenty-seven, am I right? But really I'm pushing forty. It must be the magic elixir of academia. Or maybe the infantilizing effect of living with my dad while I pay off my student loans. I paid for undergrad by swearing myself over body and soul to Uncle Sam and letting him send me to bad places where people would kill you if only they could find you down in the depths of the supply closet where you get to sit out your war writing reports, and I'm paying for grad school by living at home with my dad and letting him lecture me about how I need to make something of myself. I'd feel a tiny bit better about it if it were actually rent-free, but he even makes me pay rent, so that I can 'Act like an adult' and 'Learn some responsibility.' I mean, Jesus Christ. Going into academia was *his* idea as much as mine. Maybe he should foot a little more of the bill for it."

"Surely he can't be that bad!" protested Kate. "He was a dean at Temple! He must be very supportive of your career!" She sighed. I knew that her parents kept harassing her to give up on academia and join the family real estate business. Some days that sounded like a pretty good deal to both of us, but these days the chances of making a living in real estate seemed pretty slim too, so, we agreed, why bother going through the trouble of switching careers only to end up broke and desperate all over again?

"Yeah," said Alex, lying back down and going back to looking at the ceiling. "He's supportive all right. He was so fucking supportive of it that he wouldn't speak to me the whole time I was in the Navy. No 'Thanks for making the world safe for democracy, son,' or even a 'Thanks for getting an all-expenses-paid trip to college, son.' No, he'd decided I was going to study business management and get an MBA and then a PhD in something administration-friendly like education and take up deaning like him, so when I said I wanted to study Arabic, well...and when I joined up because he refused to pay for college unless I chose the major he wanted...there's no temper tantrum like an academic temper tantrum, you know what I'm saying? He gave me the silent treatment until I got into a PhD program, and even then he was still in a snit because it was Arabic. And he's hardly the only one. It's like dealing with toddlers but with advanced degrees and power over your future."

We all nodded in silent agreement.

"Anyway, Beirut isn't sounding so bad anymore. And so what if I end up working with, like, someone from Hezbollah or something? At least they're comparatively honest about their terrorism. There could be worse things in the world."

"Yeah," said Emma. "Like unemployment and desperate poverty. Speaking of which"—she checked her phone—"I have to get to my other job."

"Yeah, me too," said Kate, and they both rushed off.

"Congratulations on the interview," I told Alex. "I know it's not the job you wanted, but an interview is an interview."

"Yeah. You too. Oh, and I haven't forgotten about getting you to talk to that student of mine. You still up for it? Because he's still really fucked in the head. I'm starting to worry he's not going to make it through finals."

"Sure," I said. "When and where shall we meet?"

We both contemplated this complicated problem. "You good with meeting in the evening?" Alex asked eventually.

"Sure."

"It's just that the easiest thing for me would be if we met here, in the evening. The kid doesn't have a car, and I don't think this is really a conversation for the campus Starbucks, you know what I'm saying? And we can't meet here during the day, but I doubt anyone's going to be here in the evening."

"Evening is good for me," I said. "I'm normally free."

"No hot dates or anything?"

"No," I said.

"Yeah, me neither. Even if I could find a woman who'd put up with me, when would I find the time?"

"Yeah, I know what you mean."

"I fucking *hate* saving the world! And the pay is shit, too!"

"Is that why you're doing this?" I asked. "To save the world?"

He shrugged. "Isn't that why you're doing it?" He sat back up. His body, which most of the time looked almost boneless, took on that lithe intensity I saw only when it was just the two of us, and suddenly, I felt at a visceral level, the real Alex was in the room.

"It's not like you go into Russian or Arabic or something like that for the money or because it's safe and easy," he said, now looking straight at me. His eyes were a pleasant hazel that went nicely with his dark blond hair and beard, which he kept trimmed to a uniform length. It was all innocuous, except for the intensity radiating off of him. "You go into it because you like the darkness and the danger. And you go into teaching it because you want to jump into that darkness and danger and pull other people down into it with your bare hands. You know, you got it all wrong at that little booth of yours with your candy and your cutesy brochures. Not that I blame you. I know that's what the university wants. They'd never let us do the right thing. Because the right thing would be to stand up and say, 'Hey kids! Want to do something that will make all your friends go, 'Whoa, I wish that was me?' Want to leave behind your carefully micromanaged misery that you've been brainwashed into believing is happiness, and come walk on the wild side with us? Want to stand face-to-face with the dark side, and realize that you'll never be more alive than when you're dancing with death? Want to stop fucking around with empanadas and flamenco skirts and shit and get out and get your hands dirty and your minds dirty and live a little? Want to actually get out of college what you came to college to get, which is to go through something that will turn you from a little kid into a real man—or real woman?'"

"Um, I guess," I said.

"You guess right. You used to work getting interviews with torture victims, right, go toe-to-toe with the Russian government over human rights?"

"Um, yeah. Among other things. Although I don't think it could really be described as 'going toe-to-toe.' More like flying under the radar."

"Uh-huh. And now that you've given that up you spend all your extra time on people like that Mackenzie girl, prepping her to follow in your saintly footsteps no matter how much her parents want her to become an accountant or whatever and wash their dirty business clean and become a respectable upper-middle-class WASP who'll never lift a finger to make the world a better place because it might mess up her hair, or that Madison kid, who has to take drugs because she can't even get her own parents to love her. Admit it. You're staying because of them, am I right? Every day you're like, 'I should get the fuck out of here before it sucks me down into its quagmire,' and every day you're like, 'But Madison! But Mackenzie! But all those kids who need me and don't have anyone else!' Because you care about them when their blood relatives and the people who are actually getting paid to care about them don't give a shit. Because

face it, universities go on and on about how much they care about
their students, but so do slaughterhouses. I mean, they go on and
on about how much they care about their hogs. The university cares
about its students and its faculty like a slaughterhouse does about its
hogs—they might not want to be cruel just for fun, but they make
money out of processing us all through as quickly as possible, so they
shock us and gas us and slit our throats and send us on down the line
just as fast as they can. And we let them do it, even though we could
walk away any time."

"You make it sound so pathetic," I said.

"Because it is! Actually, I don't know if it's more pathetic or
really fucking evil. Because the administration—they're holding us
hostage, aren't they? I mean, they're holding our students hostage.
They *know* we won't leave them, they *know* that we know that we're
the only people who actually give a shit about them, so they can pay
us shit and treat us like dirt and we won't walk away because we *can't*,
because we're fucking addicted to saving the fucking world, one sad,
suicidal, overprivileged kid at a time. They're like Shamil goddamn
Basayev, holding the maternity ward hostage, and we're letting them
do it, even though those aren't even really our kids, we're just such
saps we treat them like they are. Isn't that something your feminist
theory talks about? How feeling responsible for those who depend
on us makes us vulnerable to manipulation and exploitation and
every other bad thing? As soon as you start to care about people who
need you and don't have anyone else, the vultures start to descend
and begin sucking your blood before you're even dead, and you'll
let them, because better you than whoever you're acting as a human
shield for."

"Weren't we making arrangements for an after-hours meeting to
talk to one of *your* students because you're afraid he's too fucked in
the head to make it through finals?" I asked.

Alex grinned for a second time. "Don't tell anyone," he said. "But I'm doing it for them. And because I spent ten years learning Arabic and I have no intention of forgetting it any fucking time soon. I'll email you when I set something up, all right?"

"Sounds good," I said.

"Great. Oh shit!" He looked at his phone. "I have to go to my other job too. You know, saving the world two campuses at a time."

29

Halloween brought with it showers of candy for the students, and, even more excitingly, showers of money for the faculty. Or at least a tiny drizzle. Between my paycheck and the check from my grandmother, I was able to pay my rent, pay for my health insurance, buy my tickets to San Antonio and Atlanta—I tried to work up some enthusiasm for traveling during Thanksgiving on what was sure to be a stressful and exhausting trip, right on the heels of another stressful and exhausting trip, at the tail end of a stressful and exhausting semester—and even buy some groceries.

The money didn't stretch far enough for me to take my car to get looked at, so I had taken to saying little prayers to whatever benevolent deities might be listening whenever I set off to or from campus, which was the only place I drove to these days. Shopping was strictly done via on-foot expeditions to the dollar store and the foreign food store, as a way of avoiding getting stuck in a stalled-out car in the neighborhoods around my apartment. Simply walking seemed safer, since it made me look less like a victim and more like someone who lived there, even if my skin was about six shades too pale to fit in on most blocks.

The week following Halloween Alex emailed me to say that his student would be available Wednesday evening, and was I still up for a meeting.

I don't know how much good it will do, he said in his email. *But the kid is now saying that someone from the Russian program is giving him problems and he really needs your help because he doesn't know where else to turn, so it might do him some good to vent or share dirty secrets or whatever.*

Consider me there, I wrote back. *At the very least because it will be a nice distraction from my other woes.*

It was true that I would have appreciated a distraction, and a reason to feel good about myself. The other faculty, I was becoming ever more convinced, were deliberately avoiding me in the hallway, or giving me weird looks. I had originally thought it was because I was a newcomer, or because they didn't want to catch my contingency cooties, or because they held me personally responsible for Russia's annexation of the Crimea earlier in the year and were afraid I was suddenly going to reveal myself as one of the "polite people" or "little green men" who had carried out the operation.

Which was an amusing mistake I wished I could share with someone who would understand. Like Dima, for example. He was probably the only one who would get the joke, and laugh about it with me. The desire to share it with him was so strong that I almost broke down on at least two separate occasions and wrote to him. But then I read his latest dispatches from the war zone, and thought he probably would consider what I was doing to be trivial and cowardly, and he didn't have time for my jokes, and maybe his sense of humor was gone for good, and we weren't speaking anyway, so I should just suck it up and keep my thoughts to myself.

But I couldn't laugh it off when John Greene stopped me in the hallway and started talking about how registration week had just happened and the enrollments for Russian next semester were lower than expected, because it was only continuing students, and not even all of them, but no new students at all, and it was my job to be attracting new students and raise enrollments, and so on and so forth.

"I thought next semester we were just offering 102 and 202," I said. "We can't really expect to get a lot of new students in those, since they have prerequisites."

"Yes, but, Rowena, we also have our Introduction to Russian Literature course, you know, one of the cross-listed CLIT courses. You were there at the meeting! You should have remembered."

"Oh, I remember CLIT," I said, keeping my face, I hoped, absolutely immobile. The very thought of sharing a sexual innuendo with John Greene was enough to send me screaming to the nearest shower.

"Yes, well, if you'd been paying attention, you *would* have remembered that this semester—I mean, the spring semester—we'll be offering a cross-listed FORL/CLIT course in Russian. It has a cap of twenty-five, but so far only eight students have enrolled, all current Russian students. Now, what do you think we should do to raise enrollments? I don't have to say that the Dean's office is not happy with the low enrollments in Russian next semester, not happy at all, and especially after the big push from the Office of the Provost to enhance our language and culture offerings, especially for the LCTLs, well...it doesn't look good."

"I'm sure," I said. "Perhaps we should put up some posters for the course?"

"Yes, but really, Rowena, you should have been postering for it *prior* to registration week."

"Mmmm-hmmm," I said, carefully not saying that I had never been sent the schedule for next semester, which, since I would not be there next semester, was not surprising.

"And it's especially important to emphasize that this course fulfills the Diversity requirement, which is something that CDIF has been pushing very hard as well! Send me your poster when it's ready, so I can make sure you've included all the necessary information. Really, Rowena, I expected more from you! Everyone had such high hopes of you when you arrived."

"Mmmm-hmmm," I said again. John Greene's fleshy cheeks and thinning hair, I couldn't help but think, made him look like an overgrown toddler, despite his height. One that, unlike with an actual toddler, I had an almost overwhelming urge to give a good hard spanking to and send to bed without any supper, except that there was no way my hand was ever going to come within six feet of John Greene's nasty ass. He didn't deserve a spanking. But I'd be more than happy to send him to bed without any dinner, which, judging by the way his jowls quivered, would only do him good.

"I'll get the poster to you this week," I said.

"Today, Rowena, today! The Provost was *just* on the phone with me, talking about his plans to expand our language and culture offerings, and we need to show to him that we're doing our part!"

"Mmmm-hmmm," I said for a third time. "I'll get it to you after class." I made my escape before I could say anything I regretted. Not that they could do anything to me right now, other than make my last few weeks here at TLASC miserable, since the position they kept hinting at had as of yet failed to materialize, but my own pride wanted me to avoid doing anything I considered beneath me, like sinking to their level, and my advisor's practical voice in my head kept advising me never to poke a snake unless I was wearing snake boots.

I did, as promised, throw together a poster, using the description from the course bulletin, after class, and send it to John Greene and Linda, both of whom responded almost immediately with snippy requests for improvements based on information I did not, in fact, have, which resulted, after the second time this happened, with me reminding them that I was not, in fact, teaching this course next semester, and that therefore I could not provide an enticing list of texts and exciting student-centered activities. A picture of Pushkin and the meeting times was as good as it was going to get.

This caused John Greene to send me a hotly-worded email about my attitude and how I was being irresponsible and lacking in motivation and drive and commitment to the school and my profession and really, early-career scholars like me should be better at accepting feedback from their mentors if they wanted to advance.

Hunting him down and trying out those chokeholds Dima and John kept insisting you practice will hurt you more than it does him, I reminded myself. Instead of replying, which would be pointless since the whole point of the exchange had been for John Greene to vent at someone who couldn't vent back, I shut down my laptop and set off again for campus, where I was scheduled to meet Alex and his student at 7:00pm.

30

The days had grown short enough that it was already as full dark as it was going to get in urban New Jersey, and there was a dank chill in the air. I drove through the fluorescent strip-mall lighting of the pawn shops and payday loan places, the police station, the school, and True Grit, before descending into the deeper darkness of the really bad neighborhood, and then making my way out into the gradually gentrifying largely residential neighborhoods, still with their lynching trees up, that surrounded campus.

Campus at night was a much more student-centered place than during the day. Most of the faculty were gone, with only a few sad night-class teachers about. At Research 1 institutions there would also have been the all-night researchers, but TLASC was far from an R1 institution, so no faculty members were up burning the midnight oil at their carrels and lab benches. Instead of moving in defensive packs, the students wandered in groups of two or three, talking and laughing and avoiding me when they realized I was probably faculty.

Dreme Hall was a shadowy half-lit place when I arrived, without so much as the cleaning staff around. I expected to find the front door locked—at TLASC even the front doors of classroom buildings were locked at night, in marked contrast to every other US campus I had ever been on—but it was open, probably because Alex had already unlocked it.

And when I showed up at the adjunct warehouse, Alex and his student were there, going over homework.

"Oh, hey, come on in," said Alex, looking up as I stepped through the door. He was wearing that expression of serious focus he occasionally directed my way. "Justin, this is Dr. Halley, our Russian professor."

"Nice to meet you, Professor," said Justin, with a nervous little duck of his head.

"Nice to meet you too, Justin," I said, taking a seat on the remaining chair.

"Justin and I were just going over one of his essays," Alex explained. "He's been making a lot of progress this semester, but he still had some questions after the last test."

"Yeah," said Justin, swallowing nervously. "Professor Miller's been really helpful. With homework and...everything."

"I'm sure," I said, giving Justin what I hoped was a sympathetic smile. He squirmed uncomfortably in his seat, and swallowed again. On closer inspection he had a shy smile and faintly unexpected features, that on third glance resolved into the realization that he was multiracial, with full lips, dark golden freckles scattered over light golden skin, and tightly ringleted golden-brown hair. It all came together to make him almost painfully good-looking. If his sports career tanked, maybe he could make a living as a model. No doubt TLASC was trumpeting his presence to the rafters, and putting him in every publicity photo they could manage. If he came out as gay as well, the entire administration would probably go into a group orgasm at the thought of the positive publicity it would generate, his personal privacy or basic safety be damned.

"Why don't you tell Professor Halley what you were telling me, Justin," Alex said. He was still wearing that expression of serious focus, and he radiated caring trustworthiness. For the first time I could see that he must have been a good officer in the Navy, and he was a good professor now. His working two jobs and sleeping in the office suddenly appeared to me in a different light, as a sign of drive and single-minded devotion. No wonder the department was keeping him stashed away in the adjunct warehouse. John Greene & Co. would probably give their right hands to have their students look at them the way Justin was looking at Alex, but not, unfortunately, their egos, which was the one sacrifice that would get them the respect and admiration they craved.

"Um, okay." Justin swallowed nervously again, and looked at me uncertainly from his big brown eyes.

"It's okay." Alex gave him a fond smile. "She's cool. She used to interview torture victims, right, Rowena?"

"Right," I said. "Among other people. So really, Justin, anything you want to say to me—it won't shock me. And I won't judge you for anything you might have done." That last was a bit of a fib, but I wouldn't *tell* him I was judging him.

"Really?" said Justin, perking up at the mention of my dark past. "How'd you, like, get a job like that? What kind of things did you, like, used to hear?"

"I used to work for an NGO that documented election violations and human rights abuses," I told him. "I used to go around gathering people's stories."

"In Russian?" asked Justin, looking impressed.

"Normally."

"Whoa! That's, like, amazing. I can't *imagine* my Arabic ever being good enough to, like, do something like *that* with it."

"You'd be surprised," said Alex dryly. "Uncle Sam doesn't always expect your Arabic to be that good before it sends you over to where you have to use it."

"Oh. Really? So, like, I could be like over there somewhere using it right now?"

"It would be better if you learned a bit more first. But yes. Don't worry," Alex told him. "You'd get really good, really fast."

"Oh." Justin focused back on me. "Is that what happened to you, Professor Halley? Did you have to get really good, really fast?"

"Pretty much," I said.

"Oh. That'd be...that'd be cool, actually. To be over there doing something important, building your skills...that's what"—he swallowed twice before continuing—"Brandy and I used to talk about doing. Not just sitting around here, but going somewhere, somewhere important and exciting, and *doing* something with our skills, with our lives."

"He sounds like he was a very brave and idealistic young man," I said.

"Yeah! Way braver than me. Well, about some things. I mean"—Justin half-smiled at a bittersweet memory—"if he cut his finger or something, he'd whine like a bi—like a baby for hours. He'd never make it in sports. I mean, I play tennis, which isn't, like, a super-macho sport or anything, but you still have to be tough enough, you know what I'm saying? But Brandy couldn't even play tennis, not even for fun. But he was super-brave about other things. Like the political stuff."

"It sounds like he was very active in that sphere," I said.

"Yeah! I mean, he was president of the campus Lambda group, and he actually had them out there doing stuff, I mean, public stuff, getting publicity, getting students to get out there and speak out publicly, come out of the closet, raise awareness...that's how I met him, actually. I'd been dragged into something for OSOC—that's the Organization for Students of Color," he explained. "It's a thing started by CDIF to make it seem like they'd be more welcoming of people from the neighborhood next door to come study here, and it's for, like, everyone who isn't a WASP, basically. So there's, like, the three of us who have, like, a black grandparent or something, and then the four Indian kids, subcontinental Indian, I mean, and some kid who's like one-quarter Cherokee or something like that, and that's about it, really. And somehow we're all supposed to be in a club or a lobbying group or something, and do...I don't know. Whine to each other about how oppressed we are, I guess. Which would be cool except the one time we did that, the black-ish kids like me started whining at the Indians for taking all the jobs, and the immigrants started whining about American privilege, and the Cherokee kid started whining at the rest of us for stealing Native American land, and the girls started accusing the boys of being sexist pigs, and the sad thing was that everything they said was kinda true...like, I guess I could have whined at the others for being a bunch of homo-haters, 'cause they kept saying stuff like 'That's so *gay*' when they meant 'bad' or 'stupid,' but I didn't want anyone to know about me, so I kept my mouth shut, and we never did anything like that again, thank God."

"That's pretty much how those things go, in my experience," I said

"Really, Professor? I thought...I guess I thought people would be nicer. Better. Like, we've all had to deal with shit—oops, sorry, Professor, I meant 'bad stuff'—in our lives, other people putting us down or treating us like we don't belong, so I thought we'd not do that, uh, stuff to each other, but we just jumped right into it."

"The problem with minorities, or immigrants, or women, or gays, or anyone like that, in my experience, is that they're people too," I said. "With all the failings and frailties that entails."

It took Justin a moment to translate that into English that he could understand, but once he had, he nodded vigorously. "Exactly, Professor! Like, first I joined OSOC, and then I started hanging out with Brandy and his friends over at Lambda, and every time I kept thinking, 'Now I've found my people, now I've found people who aren't going to give me shit—oops, sorry Professor—like everyone else does, but it was still all the same old shit all over again. Sorry. Really sorry about swearing, Professor. I'm just..."

"It's okay," I said. "It's nothing I haven't heard before."

"Yeah, that's what Professor Miller always says, but it seems wrong somehow. Swearing in front of a professor. Although Professor Miller says he swears too, sometimes." Justin eyed us both speculatively. Alex and I suppressed grins.

"Swearing is hardly the worst sin in the world," I said.

"That's not what my grandma says," said Justin. "She's always threatening to take a belt to me if I don't stop it."

"I can see that's worked out really well," I said.

"Haha, yeah. It's like, the more she threatens me, the more I want to do it. I don't know what she'd do if she found out...if I came out. She loves me, but church is the most important thing in her life, you know what I mean? Right now I'm someone she can brag about to her church-lady friends, her white grandson going to a white college on a tennis scholarship—it doesn't get much whiter than that, does it? It's funny: she always likes to talk about how white she is and how she feels more comfortable around white people, even though she looks and acts, well, black as black. But she's super-proud of me for being here. But coming out as gay—that'd be a little too white for her, I think."

"Grandmothers can be like that," I said.

"Yeah. So, anyway, OSOC was doing a thing for Student Engagement Day, where all the clubs had booths out and tried to get more members to sign up, and they put us right in between the Campus Feminists and Lambda, I guess 'cause they thought they might as well put all the dykes and queers and troublemakers together, and Brandy and I got to talking, and afterwards we started hanging out, and..."

"Was he your first boyfriend?" I asked softly, once it became clear that Justin wasn't going to say any more.

He gave a tiny nod. "I...before that I wasn't sure...I thought there was something wrong with me, or maybe everyone was like this, but Brandy, he...anyway."

"It must have been really tough to lose him."

"Yeah. He was, like...for a little while he was everything for me, you know? Like he showed me all kinds of stuff, stuff I couldn't even imagine, and made me feel like I was okay for being...who I was. Only...only after a couple months, he started in on me about coming out. I wasn't okay just the way I was, it turned out."

"That must have been difficult."

"Yeah. I mean, I get it. Brandy wanted us to be together, you know, like a regular couple, and he wanted me to be proud of who I was, but, I mean, I'm on a sports scholarship, you know what I mean? Some of my teammates, they'd be cool about it, but some of them...and then there's my family. My dad..." Justin shivered. "He *definitely* wouldn't be cool about it. He wasn't even cool about me playing tennis. He wanted me to play football, he kept going on and on about how it was only queers who played tennis." Justin smiled wryly. "Guess he was right about that. But Brandy just wouldn't understand. His family had been all excited and supportive when he came out, and he couldn't understand that not everyone's family is like that. Not everyone has a family who'll love 'em, no matter what."

"Unfortunately not," I agreed.

"So anyway, this was going on all last fall and over winter break and got really bad at the beginning of the spring semester. Like, I thought we were going to break up or something, and I...I would have done anything to keep Brandy, but, like, keeping him wouldn't do either of us any good if my dad did something, would it? But he just wouldn't understand. By February he was threatening to put out stuff I'd sent him in emails and texts, you know...stuff that made it clear we were in a relationship. He kept threatening to blog about it, and, well, no one reads the Lambda blog, but if he put out something really juicy instead of the political stuff he kept putting out, well, that'd probably change. No doubt if he posted my emails, that'd be the day the blog went from two hits to two hundred, or two thousand."

"No doubt," I said.

"And he kept going on and on about how I was ashamed of him, and I kept telling him I wasn't ashamed of him, but it just *wasn't safe*, and he wouldn't get that, and we started fighting really badly, like, it makes me sick to think of some of the stuff we said to each other, and I *did* start to feel ashamed of him, 'cause he was being such an asshole, and so was I, and anyway, some of that stuff he was threatening to publish, it was, like, you know"—he dropped his voice—"sexy stuff. Like, I mean, you know how it is. Sometimes you say stuff to your boyfriend or whatever that's just for him, right? Right?"

Justin was looking at me, his eyes wide with desperation. He'd probably never gotten to confide in anyone else who'd had a boyfriend before, and he was looking as much as anything for validation that this was how it went, this was how relationships with men went, or relationships at all.

"Right," I said. "That's kind of the point of having a boyfriend."

He smiled a little at that. "That's what I kept telling him. Like, I would tell him stuff that...I mean, you wouldn't want to share that kind of thing with the world, gay or straight, you know what I'm saying? Like it was private, special, just for us two. Not because it was gay, but because it was just for us two. I wouldn't want him to spill it out to the world if he'd been a girl, either."

"Of course not," I agreed.

"Right. So, we were fighting about that, and I even...I even said I wanted to break up, if this was how he was going to be, but that only made him threaten me even more, and then...and then someone started to threaten him."

"And you think this someone was from the Russian program," I stated.

Justin nodded. "Yeah, he specifically said it was someone in the Russian program. Or anyways, he started going on about 'That bitch from Russian' and how she was going to cause him all kinds of trouble, telling the world about stuff that wasn't the world's business."

"Do you know who it was?" I asked.

He shook his head. "No, but I mean, how many people could it be? It was a girl in the Russian program. So, there're, like, three people to choose from. Mackenzie'd be my first guess, but I don't want to think she'd do something like that to me."

"You're sure it was Mackenzie?"

"No. He never said it was Mackenzie, and when I, you know, asked her about it, she said it wasn't her. Mackenzie is just the one we both knew best, who would have the best access to our secrets and stuff. And he was always talking about Mackenzie. It was always 'Mackenzie this' and 'Mackenzie that' and 'Next summer Mackenzie and I are going to Russia' and stuff like that, till I started telling him it sounded like he was in love with Mackenzie, not me."

"Blackmail doesn't really sound like Mackenzie's style," I said.

Justin shrugged. "I wouldn't think so either, but her dad..."

"What about her dad?"

He squirmed uneasily. "It could have been her dad," he said. "You know, trying to get something on my dad. They're kind of, um, business partners, I guess you'd say, but they don't like each other very much. So maybe it was about Mackenzie's dad getting at my dad, or Mackenzie getting revenge on me for something my dad had done to her dad. I wouldn't like to think so, but sometimes you never know with people."

"Do you think this was about getting at your dad?" I asked.

"Honestly, not really. I mean, that seems like the most likely thing, but Brandy never said anything about that, and I never heard anything about that. It was all about Brandy, as far as I could tell. Stuff that he wouldn't want to get out, that would ruin his chance at becoming student body president, or even maybe get him expelled."

I was trying to formulate the exact right choice of words that would get Justin to reveal to me what kind of terrible skeletons the nineteen-year-old overprivileged Brandy had had in his closet, when Justin burst out, "And it was...I found some of the stuff they had on him. You know...afterwards. I was helping go through his things, and I had his computer password and I went in to make sure, well, that there weren't any pictures, videos, stuff like that, stuff we wouldn't want found by anyone else, and I found some of the emails. I mean, the emails threatening him. They had some stuff on him, stuff he'd posted on a private chatroom or message or whatever, stuff that...stuff that...I mean, it was only sort of about me, but..." Justin started to sniffle.

Alex handed him a tissue from a box on the table. He must have stocked it specially beforehand for just such an eventuality, since normally our office didn't run to luxuries like boxes of tissues.

"It's very hurtful to find out someone you think cares about you doesn't care as much as you thought," I said.

"Yeah...it wasn't just that. I mean, it was, but not exactly. He said...he said..." Justin gave a big gulp and, straightening up, said all in a rush, "He said a bunch of stuff about how he didn't like...black guys. How he'd never date a black guy. All kinds of stuff about how ugly they were. And then a bunch of stuff about me, about how I wasn't as bad as he thought, even kind of cute, and since I was, you know, a, a virgin, maybe he could train me up, and anyway, I wasn't really black, only just enough to make it, you know, dirty enough to be exciting."

Justin gave a big sob and mashed his face with his tissue. Alex wordlessly handed him the entire box, which he clutched at and curled up around, his whole body shaking.

"I'm really sorry you had to find that out," I said. I wanted to put my arms around him, but the prohibition against touching students, pounded into me since day one of grad school, was too strong to overcome, even in the face of such pain.

"I thought he loved me," said Justin, once he had gone through a fistful of tissues and could speak again.

"Maybe he did, in his own way," I said.

"Yeah, but..."

"Falling in love doesn't immediately make you a better person all over," I said. "If you're a cocky little self-centered racist before, you'll still be a cocky little self-centered racist afterwards. At least at first."

"Yeah, I guess," said Justin, scrubbing off his face. "And, I mean, he did say some stuff in the emails about how that wasn't who he was anymore, and he really did seem really sorry, those last few days. Like he knew he'd done a bad thing, and wanted a second chance."

"Probably he did," I said.

"But then he had to go and kill himself! So now he'll never get that second chance! I'll never be able to forgive him!"

"You can still forgive him, even if he isn't here to accept your forgiveness," I said.

"It's not the same!"

"No, it isn't," I agreed.

"Anyway, anyway...I thought it was all over, I thought the nightmare would be over this semester, and I'd try to get on with my life, you know, really work on my game, on my studies, try to figure out what I wanted in my life, but...last week I got an email."

"From the blackmailer?" I asked.

"Uh-huh. With some of Brandy's old messages, and some of mine. They said unless I paid them a hundred dollars every week, they'd release the messages on the internet."

"A hundred dollars a week?"

"I know, right? Where am I going to get a hundred dollars a week?"

"Yeah," I said, not adding that a hundred dollars a week sounded like chump change to me. Or rather, I could sympathize all too well with Justin's inability to scrape together that much cash, but it seemed like a ridiculously paltry sum to bother blackmailing someone over.

"Do you think it's still the same person?" I asked.

"Who else could it be?"

"Do you still have those emails?"

"Yeah, of course."

"Could you, ah, send them to me?"

Justin hesitated. "I, uh, don't want you reading the stuff they sent. I mean, like I said, it's private. I really don't want a professor...it'd just be weird, you know what I mean, even if you're not my professor."

"Yeah. I understand. Could you just forward me the email address, and maybe the content of some of the emails? Not the stuff they're threatening you with, just what they themselves wrote."

"Um, okay. I guess."

"I mean, it almost certainly has to be one of my students. They could be doing something really stupid like using their own email address, in which case I'd recognize it right off the bat. At least it's a place to start."

"Yeah," said Justin. "And what happens if you figure out who it is?"

"Well, blackmail is a crime. You could go to the police."

"Nuh-uh." He shook his head vigorously.

"Or the college's Honor Court."

"Even worse!"

"Or I could just threaten to give them an F if they don't quit it."

"Yeah." He relaxed. "That sounds better."

"It might not work," I warned. "They might not care about getting an F."

"Yeah, but...please, Professor. Can you please try?"

"Sure," I said. "I can certainly try."

31

I half-hoped with a cowardly hope, because Justin's problems sounded like a sticky mess that was likely to drag me down into the murky world of Title IX, FERPA, and Honor Code violations, or at least cause me a major headache with one of my students, that he would chicken out and not send me the email address of the blackmailer, but by the time I'd gotten home from campus, I already had an email waiting for me from Alex.

> *Hey Rowena*, it said. *Thanks so much for talking to Justin. To be honest, I've been really worried about him, especially the past couple of weeks. But after talking to you he seems calmer than he has all semester. I guess I can see why you used to do what you did* ☺ *If it is this Mackenzie or one of the other students who's doing this to him, anything you could do to get her to back off would be really appreciated. Here's what Justin sent me:*
>
> *Address: dannma2012@tlasc.edu*
>
> *Message 1: Hey Justin, Look man, I'm really sorry about you losing your boyfriend and everything, but some of us are still alive and you've got to help out the living, you know what I mean? Can you loan me a couple hundred bucks, just to keep me going? Please* ☺ ☺ ☺

Message 2: Hey Justin, I know you say you don't have the money, but that's just not true. I know who your dad is and how much you must be getting for your scholarship and you've got to have at least a couple hundred lying around, no matter what you say. And I really need it! You know how it is. I'll pay you back as soon as I can, pinkie swear ☺ ☺ ☺

Message 3: Hey Justin, Look man, I really didn't want to do this, but you're forcing me into it, you know what I mean? Get me the money by next week or I'll post some of the stuff that Brandy wrote, you know what I'm talking about, on the OSOC Twitter feed. Boy, I bet that could go viral fast. People wouldn't be so nice about him if they knew what he was really like, would they? I bet everyone would be furious if they knew what a little racist he really was underneath. And they'd wonder about you and how you could be with him and write him those sexy notes you kept writing him. He was a racist who would have gotten expelled if the university had found out what he really thought, but you were in love with him anyway and let him fuck you. Some Black Pride! But if you leave $200 in cash, and then $100 every week for the rest of the semester, under the trash can in the library basement by the study desks, your secret is safe with me.

"Shit, shit, shit," I said. I recognized the address as Mackenzie's second email account, the one she had sworn at the beginning of the semester she didn't know anything about. Blackmailing a friend and a fellow Russian student, especially for a few hundred measly dollars, really didn't seem like Mackenzie's style, but people do all kinds of stuff when they're desperate. Mackenzie had made it clear more than once that she wasn't enthusiastic about her parents' choices of major and career, and that she was having trouble raising the money to go on another study abroad trip next summer, which she saw as her last chance to do something that she wanted to do before graduation. Maybe blackmailing someone for racist statements didn't seem so bad to her. After all, according to Justin, Brandy had said some genuinely nasty stuff.

And universities were cracking down on that kind of thing all over the country, often by expelling undergraduates who made inadvisable statements in private and were then outed by their so-called friends. Which some of us, like those of us who knew our Soviet history, considered to be a very disturbing trend. Who needed Big Brother when you had friends who would do One State's dirty work? Plus, it seemed kind of harsh to expel nineteen-year-olds for a few ill-chosen words uttered in private, when universities were raking in millions of dollars and then keeping their mainly-black cleaning crews on private contracts in order to pay them strictly minimum wage and no benefits. But maybe that was my radical socialist perspective. I probably *had* been infected by Marxism after living in Russia for so long.

I wrestled with what to do about the situation the rest of the evening. The following morning I, struck with a moment of cunning, and reminding myself that the sooner you go to jail, the sooner you get out, sent an email at the dannma12@tlasc.edu address to Mackenzie.

Hi Mackenzie!

> *I just wanted to check in with you and set up a meeting to make sure everything is on track for your Russian minor. I'm sure it is, I'm just meeting with all the Russian minors this week to make sure they've registered for the courses they need. And we can also talk about study abroad options. The Critical Language Scholarship application is due really soon: are you still thinking about applying? Let's set up a*

time to meet sometime in the next week and we can discuss all this.

Best,

Professor Halley

Within an hour I had gotten a reply.

Hi Professor Halley!

Yes, I'm still very interested in applying for the CLS. In fact, I'm mostly finished with my application. Is it still okay if I put you down as a recommender? Can we meet tomorrow?

Best,

Mackenzie

A couple of hours of emailing later, I had secured the adjunct office, which seemed like the only place to hold a meeting like this, for my personal, private use the next day at noon, and set up a meeting with Mackenzie.

32

She came bouncing into the office the next day at 11:55. "Thanks so much for meeting with me, Professor!" she said. "I'm really excited about the CLS! I know you said it's super-competitive, but I might as well apply, just like you said, right? And it would be awesome to go to Kazan! Have you been there?"

"Only briefly," I said. "It would be a good opportunity if you could get it. But I have a couple of questions for you."

"Of course, Professor! I brought my statement of purpose—do you think we could go over it? I'm kind of nervous about it."

"In a minute." Oh jeez. Mackenzie's big brown eyes were shining trustingly up at me, just like Justin's had, and her whole body seemed infused with energy, enthusiasm, and scholarly zeal at the very thought of applying for a study abroad program in Kazan. She certainly didn't look like a blackmailer. Or if she was one, she didn't look like someone who should have their dreams crushed and their future taken away. Of course, if she was the blackmailer, then she had tried to do exactly that to someone else, someone who was her friend. Someone who had been a complete jerk to *his* friend, and tried to blackmail him. And none of them were old enough to buy a beer.

"You remember your other email?" I started.

Mackenzie frowned.

"Your other email address," I clarified. "The one that was getting my emails at the beginning of the semester."

"Oh, that one!" She put her hand over her mouth. "Have I been missing some of your emails, Professor? I'm *so* sorry! It just never even occurred to me to check it. I went to The Bear Cave and told them about it, and I thought it had been shut down. I didn't realize..."

"It's not that," I said. "But other people have been getting emails from that address.

She frowned some more. "Really, Professor? I'm sure it's not me. Unless the system is sending them out from my email address? I mean, my real address, the one I usually use. Maybe the system has them both together and when you send from one, it shows up as being from the other, you know what I mean?"

"Uh-huh," I said. "It's certainly possible. Have you been emailing Justin?"

"Justin?" she repeated. "Which Justin?"

"Brandy's, um, friend?"

"Yeah, of course. But when I email him I use my Gmail account."

"So you haven't been emailing him from your TLASC account?" I pressed.

She shook her head. "No, I'm sure of it, Professor. Why?"

"Someone's been sending him emails. From your email address. The dannma2012 email address."

"Whoa, really? That's weird. I know he mentioned something about getting funny emails, but I already told him it wasn't from me. And I don't even know how to get into that email account. Here, I'll show you." She opened up her laptop and angled it to show me that she was bringing up Cubmail. She signed out and then signed back in, showing me that she was signing in for the dannma12 address.

"See, that's my email," she said. "I don't know how to get into the other one. Has someone been sending him mean emails, or something, from it?"

"Something like that," I said.

She put her hand over her mouth again. "But that's *terrible!*" she said. "That's so mean! Was it stuff about Brandy?"

I nodded.

"That's just *awful*! Who would do something like that! Poor guy! It's really tough for him to be in the closet—you know, right? I know he told Professor Miller, so I don't think he'd mind you knowing too, but other than that it was just me. Although I think his brother might have figured it out. Anyway, I can't say I blame him for keeping it quiet, and then after what happened with Brandy, well, you know...and then to get mean emails about it...that's just *terrible!*"

"Yes," I said. "He thinks so too. And he thinks it's someone from the Russian program, and, well, it was obviously your email address..."

"But...it *wasn't*. I mean, I don't know how to prove it to you, Professor, I know it looks bad, but it *wasn't*. I'd never do something like that! Especially not to Justin!"

"That's what I thought," I said, truthfully. "It seemed very strange to me. But I thought you might have some idea who it might be, or who might have access to your other email address."

"Not with that email address, Professor: I told you. I don't know anything about it and I already asked to have it shut down, just like you told me to. And who would do it...is he *sure* it's someone from the Russian program?"

"It's his best guess. He thought someone from the Russian program was sending Brandy, um, mean emails last semester, and now it looks like the same person is doing the same to him."

"Oh no! Do you think...do you think"—she dropped her voice to a whisper—"that's why Brandy...did what he did?"

"It's possible."

"But that's...I mean, that's, like, like, *murder*."

"It's not good," I said. "And you can't think of anyone who might be doing that?"

She shook her head. "I can't *imagine* anyone in the Russian program doing something like that, Professor! Everyone's always so nice."

"Yes," I said. "That's what I thought."

"It must be someone else," she said. "Someone from, well, Justin's dad, he isn't...very nice, you know? It's probably something to do with that."

"Probably," I said. "I'm sure you're right. I'll tell Justin to go to the police."

"I don't know that the police will be very much help, Professor, even if Justin does go to them," Mackenzie said doubtfully.

"Well, I'll start by suggesting it. And it would be good if you didn't talk about this, of course. It could really hurt Justin if the story got out."

"Not to mention the Russian program, right, Professor? Don't worry: I know how to keep a secret. My lips are sealed." She made a lip-zipping gesture and mimed throwing away the key.

"That's great," I said. "I really appreciate it. So why don't we talk about your application?"

33

I was afraid Madison would elude me after class, but I managed to say, with surprising normalcy, "Hey, Madison, can we chat for a couple of minutes after class? I'm checking in on all the Russian minors and potential minors to make sure they're on track with their credits," and Madison said chirpily, "Sure, Professor H!" and waited for me after the class was over. Inconveniently, so did Riva and Adam, so I had to make appointments to meet with them the following week as if I really were on a mission to meet with potential Russian minors, before I could dismiss them.

"Let's just talk here, if you don't mind," I told Madison, sitting down in one of the classroom chairs. It was quite uncomfortable, just as my students had been complaining all semester. "The next class doesn't meet on Fridays."

"Sure, Professor H!" Madison took a seat facing me. "So, what do I need to do to make sure I get my Russian minor? And have you noticed? I haven't come in high once all month!" She flashed me a genuine, not-on-drugs grin.

"Yes," I said, biting back a groan. If anything, this was even worse than talking to Mackenzie. "I've noticed. That's great. Has it been difficult?"

"Not as hard as I thought it would be!"

"That's great," I repeated.

"So anyway, what do I need to do?" she asked, wiping her nose with her sleeve. "I've already signed up for 202; is there something else I should be taking next semester?"

"Well, we are offering a literature survey course that would count towards your arts and literature requirement and your diversity requirement, if you haven't fulfilled that already, and also fulfill three of your nine required elective hours. If you did that and 202 and a study abroad program this summer, you would have your minor." *I'm not actually advising her!* I reminded myself, but really I was. Remind her of all the other things, the things she could be doing, if she weren't taking drugs and blackmailing people, and maybe she would be a little more cooperative.

"Really? That's awesome! I'll definitely do that. Well, 202 and the other course—what's it called?"

"FORL/CLIT 101. Introduction to Russian Literature in Translation."

"I'll check and see if it fits in with my schedule, but if I can work it in, I'll take it. Professor Cahill will be teaching it, right?"

"That's right."

"I'm glad he'll be coming back, but do you have to leave us?" she asked plaintively. "Couldn't you both stay? Couldn't you stay and offer advanced courses so we could have a proper Russian program?"

"The program doesn't have the money for that, unfortunately."

"Huh!" She snorted and wiped her nose again. "My dad's always talking about bringing in more money for all the programs, but it's never enough! It's never enough to have any cool programs. Just more STEM crap. I mean, I'm, like, a computer science major, and that's cool too, but what's the point without the other stuff? Like, you can't make good games, or even good apps, without languages and cultural stuff and stuff like that, can you?"

"Not really," I said. "But I have a question for you, Madison. Do you remember how you helped me get into my email when I first arrived?"

"Of course, Professor H!"

"Well, is that something anyone could do? Or something you've done for other people?"

"Why?" She sat up a little straighter, starting to look wary.

"Because there have been problems. Some people have been having problems, problems with emails coming from their email accounts that they haven't been sending, or getting emails from fake accounts."

"Oh." She made a little circle on the table with her finger, but didn't say anything more.

"Do you know anything about that?" I asked. "Have you heard anything about that?"

She shook her head wordlessly.

"Or have you been doing it yourself?" I asked. "To get money for cocaine?"

She flashed me a look of deep astonishment, before staring shamefacedly down at the table, where she continued to trace a complex pattern with her index finger.

"It was you who sent those emails," I said. "The emails to Justin, from Mackenzie's second account, the one she didn't know about and then asked to have shut down."

She sat very still for a long moment, her shoulders hunched. Finally she said, in a tiny little-girl voice, "What are you going to do, Professor H?"

"I'm going to ask you to stop," I said. "Stop blackmailing people, and especially leave Justin alone."

"That's it?"

"I mean, if you stop, yeah. I don't want to punish you, Madison. You did it because you needed the money, right?"

She nodded tightly.

"Cocaine is expensive, and while you might have stopped coming to my class high, you haven't stopped taking it."

She nodded tightly again.

"Maybe your dad put you on a strict allowance in order to stop you from buying it, so you had to figure out things on your own. So first you went after Brandy, and then you went after Justin."

She stared at me, open-mouthed, and then said, "Brandy deserved it! The things he said!"

"The things about Justin?"

She nodded. "Justin was my friend too! Once he started hanging out with Brandy, he became my friend too. And Brandy was such an asshole to him! I mean, Brandy was my friend, but he was dick sometimes, you know what I mean? He liked to make fun of other people, say mean things about other people, when he thought he could get away with it. He was always getting on me and Mackenzie's case about being girls, and when we'd tell him off, he'd play the gay card, tell us he was one of the girls, we shouldn't be getting after him, we should be getting after guys who were still in the closet, like Justin, they were the real menace. Only Justin was always nice. So after a while I got pissed off, like really pissed off, for me and Mackenzie and Justin, and I started following what Brandy was writing, and I found...I mean, I guess in the grand scheme of things people have said worse stuff, but it was pretty mean, about black people and stuff and about Justin. He even"—Madison wrinkled up her nose in distaste as she wiped it on her sleeve—"used the N word. So I decided to stop him, but when I threatened to report him to CDIF he just laughed at me, told me not to be such a *girl*, and I needed the money, so I...I killed two birds with one stone. Only, only...then Brandy killed himself."

"You think Brandy killed himself because of you?" I asked, as gently as I could.

She shrugged and twisted back and forth in her seat. "I...I hope not. I don't think so. I had no idea he was thinking about doing it. He, I mean, he was a jerk sometimes, but he always seemed happy, he always had lots of plans. He and Mackenzie were talking about going to Russia last summer, he had a spot on the same program as her, he'd even bought plane tickets and everything."

"Did he do it right after you, uh, approached him?"

She shook her head. "I'd been, um, contacting him for more than a month when it happened. We even, like, had kind of a regular thing going. He'd even make jokes about it. The last couple of weeks he, like, stopped giving me money and just...he'd just invite me over to his room and we'd, like, you know, get high together. That was all that I wanted. That, and that he'd stop being such a jerk to Justin."

"Did anything change in the last few days?"

She gnawed at a fingernail. "He'd always treated what I was doing like a joke," she said eventually. "It was like he wasn't even mad about it. But the last couple of days—it was like he was mad, even scared."

"Because of you?"

She shook her head. "I don't think so. I mean, he asked me over one day, started shouting at me about how I'd told someone when I'd promised I hadn't, but I told him that wasn't true. And it wasn't! I hadn't told anyone. I'm not that kind of person! I just wanted him to, you know, help me out and stop being so mean to Justin, that was all."

"But someone else had found out?"

She shrugged. "I guess. But I don't know who, Professor H, I really don't!"

"I believe you," I said. And I did. Madison was smart, in her own way, but she'd never struck me as a sophisticated liar, and her voice had the desperate ring of outraged truth to it.

"So...what are you going to do? Are you going to turn me in?"

"Not if you stop," I told her. "Not if you delete all the stuff you have on Brandy and Justin, and tell Justin you're sorry and you won't do it anymore."

"Okay. No problem!"

She'd agreed much too easily. "Are you blackmailing John Greene as well?" I asked.

She jumped in her seat and yelped like a toy poodle whose tail had been stepped on. "How did you *know*?"

"Someone has been, I'm pretty sure. You seemed like a likely suspect."

"He deserves it too!"

"I have no doubt."

"He had an affair with a student! A boy!"

"Really?!"

"Well." She reconsidered her statement. "To be honest, I don't think they ever had sex. I don't think they ever even had a real relationship. It was just some, you know, some flirty stuff. It probably wasn't illegal. But if someone like my dad found it out, he could get in trouble."

"Yeah." After a brief but fierce struggle, I gave into temptation and banged my head on the classroom table.

"Are you okay, Professor H?!"

"I'm fine," I said. "But you've gotten yourself into quite a mess, haven't you, Madison? Are you using Mackenzie's email address to blackmail John Greene as well?"

She shook her head. "I thought he might recognize it, since she's a student in the department, so I used a different address, one of the dummy addresses for someone in the biology department that got set up when they changed the system."

"Well, that's good, at least."

"So are you going to make me stop with him, as well?"

"Yes," I said. "Mainly because I don't want you to get caught and get into trouble. You do know that blackmail is illegal, right?"

"Yeah, but I wasn't doing anything really *bad*. And they deserved it!"

"I know, but you could still get into big trouble for it, Madison. Maybe worse than the drugs. Although I don't know. You know that any kind of a drug offense automatically disqualifies you for federal financial aid?"

"Really?"

"Yes," I said. "You can be a rapist or a murderer and still plead your case, at least in theory, but not someone who got caught with a dime bag of weed at a party."

"Oh. That's not fair!"

"It's not. But it's how it is. So just...it's really, really important that you stop this, okay? You're hurting people. Including yourself, which is the thing I'm really concerned about, to be honest. Stop blackmailing people, and...if you want me to, I'll walk you over to the Student Wellness building right now, help you check into their addiction counseling services."

She shuddered. "My dad'd never forgive me. They'd know who I was, and..."

"Okay," I said. "I get that. But you have to get off the coke someday, Madison, and it might as well be today. I can put you in touch with other rehab services, if you want. Some are expensive, but it seems like your dad might pay for something like that."

She hunched her shoulders. "Maybe. He was pretty mad last time, kept going on about how expensive it was. I think he'd be even madder if he had to do it again."

"Well, it isn't going to get any cheaper," I said.

"Um, yeah, I guess so."

"And you've already proven you have at least a little control over it, right? You've been coming to Russian class sober for most of the semester, so you know you can do *that.* So you can get clean entirely and stay clean, if you really want to."

"Um, yeah," she said, sounding like she didn't believe it.

"So what are you going to do?"

"I'm, um, I'm going to email Justin, tell him I'm sorry and I won't be blackmailing him anymore. And I'll send him all the stuff I have—isn't that what you do?—and then delete my own copies of it. And, um, I guess I'll do the same thing with Professor Greene. Although I think he should sweat a little more," she added with a flash of defiance.

"We're not doing this for him," I told her. "We're doing it for you."

"Oh. Okay. Well, and then...could you, like, send me some info about some of those rehab places you were talking about? I don't think...I don't know...maybe that's something I could look into for winter break."

"Of course," I told her. "And I'm very proud of you, Madison."

"Normally when grownups say that, you can tell it's bullshit," she said. "But I think you mean it, Professor H."

"I do."

"Well then." She flashed me another grin. "Can I fire my real parents and hire you instead?"

"No," I told her. "But you can email me whenever you want to."

"As long as it's not blackmail, huh?"

"I'm having a hard time thinking of what someone might blackmail me about."

"'Cause you've never done anything bad, Professor H? Never broken any laws?"

"I've broken a lot of laws," I said. "But none that I was ashamed of."

"That's cool," she said, looking impressed. "I'll let you know when I send the email to Justin, okay?"

"Okay," I said, and watched her sling her backpack over her shoulder and set off with only one wipe of her nose on her sleeve, as jaunty as if I'd never accused her of a crime.

34

Over the weekend I got emails first from Madison and then from Justin confirming that Madison had apologized to Justin and promised not to blackmail him anymore. Madison also told me she had deleted all the screenshots she'd taken of the incriminating messages, which I hoped was the truth, but there wasn't a lot I could do about it either way.

She also claimed that she'd stopped her extortion of John Greene, which I decided to take on face value and not delve into that sordid story too deeply. I sent her a hearty thanks and a list of rehab clinics I knew my parents recommended to people of means, and hoped, rather than believed, that something good would come of it.

That little mess taken care of, I had to get serious about finishing my paper for the convention, which was only a week and a half away. My great good luck in having to only work one job, which was less due to luck and more due to the fact that Tom Cahill was still working the only other available job in the area, meant that I actually had the time to write papers and articles, but I'd frittered away that time writing individually tailored research proposals for postdocs I wasn't going to get—a casual guestimation suggested that if I'd worked on my research instead of applications, I'd have the better part of a book done by now—so between that and my extracurricular

student advising activities, I was behind on the paper front. And
there was the interview. Mustn't forget about that.

Some feverish writing over that weekend and the next got the
paper in semi-finished shape, and exactly the right length when read
aloud (very important). I also made copious notes about
UNC-Charlotte and its itsy-bitsy Russian program, *and* I got the
next round of applications in on time as well. So I was feeling as good
as I was going to feel as I set off for San Antonio.

The Texas warmth was a pleasant shock when I arrived
Wednesday night and checked into my hotel room that I was going
to share with three other people, starting the next day. Even split four
ways, no one else had wanted to spring for an extra night in the hotel,
but with my panel at the very first slot on the convention schedule, I
hadn't wanted to risk missing it, which was a common occurrence for
the Thursday afternoon panels, as everyone tried to get in Thursday
morning and then had flight delays or car accidents or whatever.

And in fact, when we convened at 1:00pm Thursday for the
panel, we were missing our chair, and our discussant came racing
in at the last minute, breathing heavily and apologizing, saying he'd
been caught in traffic on the way from the airport.

"I think the thronging hordes will forgive you," I said.

"Yeah," he agreed, surveying the room, which was a regular hotel
suite that had had its bed rolled out and a conference table rolled
in. Other than the three panelists and the discussant, there were
precisely two other people in attendance, both of whom appeared to
be asleep.

A third audience member did slip in when I was halfway through
reading my paper, and everyone woke up enough at the end to
criticize my translation of the poems I had written about (criticizing
translations was something of a national sport amongst language
and literature scholars). A spirited discussion almost broke out, but
then we all remembered the time and, so, after a few parting shots

suggesting improvements they were *sure* I would find helpful, improvements that would—oh funny thing!—make the paper's thesis much less subversive, we all rushed off to our next panels.

I was chair for a panel on Futurist poetry in the next session, which was attended by *four* people who were not directly related to the panel itself, so for a Thursday afternoon that was considered a smashing success. All of the audience members were pleasant and polite, probably because there was nothing in any of the papers that so much as whispered of feminist scholarship.

By the time we got out, the hotel lobby was heaving with people. It was funny how almost no one attended most of the panels at most conferences, but hundreds if not thousands of people showed up for the conferences themselves. Mainly to give papers to empty rooms themselves, or, at the big conferences, to go to interviews.

"Innochka! Innochka, over here!" Masha, my best friend from grad school, was standing in the middle of the lobby, bookbags and suitcases piled around her feet, and waving at me furiously.

I ran over and, negotiating the baggage in my way, hugged her. Russian women were hugging each other and speaking in a mix of English and Russian all over the lobby. For a moment it was almost pleasant.

"Innochka, you look great! Really great! *And* you have an interview tomorrow, right? For a tenure-track job! That's fantastic! Is it a good school?"

"An okay school," I said. "What about you?"

She made a face. "Nothing yet. But I haven't sent out very many applications. No point until I have a firm defense date set."

"Have you set one?"

"Not yet. Hopefully in March, but I don't want to set a date until I've finished a full draft."

"Yeah," I said. It was the eternal debate of the dissertating grad student: no search committee would take you seriously until you had a firm defense date set, but setting a date when you hadn't finished your dissertation yet was a dicey business. Aside from your own questionable ability to finish the project on time, the gods old and new alone knew what your advisor and your committee might get up to.

"Yeah, I know. Oh look, it's Sveta and Lena!"

Our other two roommates came over from where they had been checking in, and all four of us made our way up to the room, where we divvied up the beds—me and Masha in one bed, and Sveta and Lena in the other—and set off to explore the River Walk and find a place to eat that would be authentically TexMex but also not too hard on Russian stomachs, which had a strong aversion to anything spicy.

The evening was almost fun, almost the way it should be, with earnest conversations about pedagogical technique and great works of world literature and how we were going to enlighten the masses (in a non-coercive way), punctuated only every ten or fifteen minutes by worries about jobs, money, jobs, bullying, jobs, bad students, and jobs, jobs, jobs. When everyone else decided to hit a bar after dinner, I, pleading my morning interview, left them to go to bed early in order to be fresh and ready for what, I was trying very hard not to think, was probably one of the most important events of my life.

35

The interview, once I had wound my way through the hotel in search of it, was in another of those converted suites, except that it still had its bed in it. At least I wasn't asked to sit on it. The MLA had issued guidelines in recent years declaring it inappropriate to hold interviews in bedrooms, especially when the candidate had to sit on the bed, but female candidates were still warned, if they had caring advisors or committees or mentors, to dress in something that wouldn't ride up and flash the search committee if they had to climb on and off a bed, or sit on a bed with their legs straight out in front of them. Obviously sitting cross-legged was out of the question.

Wearing a thrift-shop pantsuit that had seen better days but was unlikely to reveal my panties, unless the semi-rotten stitches split at the seams—*no, don't think that!*—and boots that really should have been replaced last year, I sat down carefully on the chair that was offered to me, crossed my legs modestly at the ankle, tucking my feet back as far as possible in order to hide the scuffs on my shoes that no amount of cleaning was ever going to fix, and prepared to be grilled.

Things started off smoothly enough, with pleasantries about the weather exchanged and semi-innocuous questions about my current position asked. The chair of the search committee, a silver-haired man named Brent who on first glance seemed to be reasonably decent, said that he knew a little about TLASC and told the other members of the committee that it was outside of New Brunswick,

New Jersey. This elicited remarks from the rest of them on how impressive it was that I'd gotten a job in the Mid-Atlantic straight out of grad school. I smiled meekly and nodded.

Then the one Russian speaker on the committee asked me to explain my dissertation, in Russian. This was a standard question that everyone agreed was pointless, because your dissertation was the one thing you *didn't* talk about in Russian, even if, as in my case, your advisor and all your friends were Russian, because you wrote it in English. Even native Russian speakers had to study up for this question, because they had only ever used the technical terms in English.

But I had studied up for the question, so I answered it reasonably competently, which somehow led to getting asked, still in Russian, what literature courses I would teach if I had free rein, which somehow segued, still in Russian—the other committee members were fidgeting politely by this point—to a question about which was my favorite Dostoevsky novel, even though my dissertation had been about Marina Tsvetaeva, a 20th-century female poet, and Dostoevsky was a 19th-century male prose author, and I had never mentioned him at all. Which had been the problem: the interviewer had pounced on what she saw as my omission, and started quizzing me about Dostoevsky and which of his works I considered the best.

"*The Idiot*," I said.

"*The Idiot*?" repeated the interviewer, looking like I'd confessed to pedophilia. "Why not *Notes from Underground*? Everyone likes *Notes from Underground* best!"

"*Notes from Underground* is also a very interesting work, and easy to teach, since it's short," I agreed cautiously.

"Explain why you prefer *The Idiot*!"

I spent a couple of minutes trying to explain why I preferred *The Idiot*, which I had read once six years earlier, and had chosen because in my terror-befuddled state it was the only Dostoevsky work whose name I could remember in Russian, before Brent interrupted politely and steered the discussion back into English and into my ideas for growing the program, which as usual was under threat. At every interview I had ever been on, the committee had been looking for some bright young thing who would save a dying program from itself and the jackals and hyenas surrounding it, all for low pay, less power, and little expectation of permanent employment. This particular position was ostensibly tenure-track, but the basic story was still the same.

When I was done, everyone shook my hand warmly and thanked me for coming, and the Russian-speaking member of the committee told me she hoped we could discuss Dostoevsky some more, which I took to mean that she hadn't hated me as much as it might have seemed at first glance.

Immediately after returning to my hotel room, where Masha had been waiting in a state of agonized nervousness the entire time, I sat down and composed a flowery letter to Brent and the rest of the search committee, thanking them for taking the time to speak with me and telling them how much I enjoyed the experience and how interested I was in the job and how I was sure I would be a great fit for it, etc. etc., and then filled Masha in on what had happened.

"And I think I may have ruined everything by mentioning *The Idiot*!" I finished.

"They asked and you answered!" she said indignantly. "What, there's some kind of secret requirement for what Dostoevsky books you're allowed to like?"

We shared a dry smile. Of course there was.

"And I think I might have made a mistake in an ending while I was speaking!"

"I make mistakes all the time, and I'm a native speaker!" she said loyally.

"Yeah," I said. The truth was that there was a strong prejudice in favor of native speakers in Russian studies, fed by decades of insecure Russian immigrants clinging to the one thing that allowed them to lord their superiority over their new colleagues. And it was true that most Americans spoke abysmal Russian, even those who had studied it for years. Sadly, it was also true that fluency in the target language did not automatically translate into competence in teaching, which led to a lot of unhappy classroom experiences when people whose only skill set was their native language were hired to teach American college students. But the prejudice against non-native speakers was still strong enough that my name alone was enough to get my application tossed in the trash at least 50% of the time.

Besides, although this was not normally stated as a reason, it was easier to hire an immigrant for a crappy, low-paying job and then hold the threat of yanking their visa over their heads if they protested their mistreatment. American universities could fire me, but they couldn't deport me. And while American universities were, as Alex had said, kind of like slaughterhouses in the way they pushed you through and chopped you up, stripping you of all the money and self-respect they could get from you, they were only *kind* of like slaughterhouses. Most people associated with them might be poor and miserable, and many might kill themselves, and some might get shot down in a spectacular hail of bullets, but being a professor at an American university was still a dream job for people all over the world.

Masha and I spent a little while longer dissecting the interview and in particular the Dostoevsky question, and I fretted a bit over the possibility that I had somehow ruined my only chance at a tenure-track job, and thus a life of middle-class respectability, which had been the main point of this entire multi-year exercise, by blurting out *The Idiot* instead of *Notes from Underground* in reply to an off-the-cuff question about personal taste, and that I might have made a faux pas and used the accusative when it was technically correct but the genitive was more colloquial.

After an hour of that we were both in such a state of nerves and depression that I declared our worry session over and forbade us to discuss it any further, and I was free, free to run away and not worry about anything other than what panels to go to and how to stay awake during them until my flight home Sunday.

36

After a very bumpy flight back from San Antonio via Charlotte, which I shared, awkwardly, with two members of the search committee, I taught on Monday and Tuesday and then headed back to the Newark airport, whose third-world grime was becoming all too familiar, to fly down to Atlanta.

"Darling, you look...have you been working out a lot?" asked my mother as soon as she caught sight of me.

"A lot of running," I told her.

She sucked on her bottom lip. "Running is so hard on the knees," she said. "Especially on pavement. I take it you're running on sidewalks?"

"That's pretty much all there is where I live."

She sucked on her bottom lip some more. "Very hard on the knees," she said again. "You're already almost thirty-five. You really should look into something more low-impact. Have you considered cycling?"

"Cycling is expensive."

"Yes, but...well, what about yoga?"

"I also do yoga."

She cheered up. "Are you taking classes? Have you found a studio? Or how about hapkido? Do you still do that?"

"I do. I can't afford to take classes."

"Oh. Well...but it's important to make friends, darling, you know that."

"I'll almost certainly be leaving in a few weeks," I pointed out.

"So they haven't offered you a renewal yet? Any chance that they might?"

"They've hinted at it, but mainly just to yank my chain, as far as I can tell."

"Oh. But you had that interview! How did it go?"

"Okay, I think."

"Just okay? Do you think they'll invite you to a campus interview?"

"I don't know," I said. My mother must have guessed from my face that I didn't want to talk about it anymore, having exhausted the topic pretty thoroughly with Masha during the convention and then again with Kate and Alex and even the envious Emma on Monday and Tuesday, since she switched back to talking about how important it was to make friends.

"Luckily I have Fevronia," I said.

"Yes, of course...so you found a cat-sitter for her?"

"Uh-huh," I said. "Hopefully the cat-sitter is a brave woman."

"Yes, darling...Fevronia is a lovely cat, of course, but you can't have as your only friend a cat whose main hobby is biting the hand that feeds her. Surely there must be someone in your department you could make friends with. And this Alex...you've mentioned him several times..."

The rest of the car ride from the airport and then to my grandmother's house was spent fending off my parents' hints that maybe Alex and I should hook up. Maybe I should share the information about the office mattress with them. Maybe they were so desperate for me to find a boyfriend, an American boyfriend, one who would wipe out the dangerous memory of Dima, that they would cheer on sad liaisons on a dirty mattress in my shared office.

The rest of the non-holiday went pretty much the same way. My grandparents were delighted to see me, and everyone clustered around me and said, their faces and voices full of false encouragement, how *well* I was doing and how *proud* they were of me and how I was *certainly* going to get a great job soon, and incidentally how I needed to find a boyfriend and casual friends and do various other things that would cost me time and money I didn't have.

This was punctuated by a short Skype call from John, who was still in Afghanistan, where the drawdown was still dragging on. He managed to talk to us just long enough to wind our dad up about politics—John had once confessed to me that he routinely voted Democrat, but couldn't resist the thrill of telling our dad that he had converted to Republicanism while at The Citadel and had never converted back—before saying, maybe truthfully, that he had to go deal with stuff if he ever wanted to come home at all. This put a damper on our Thanksgiving, and my parents and grandparents spent a while talking in strained voices about how he was going to be home for Christmas for sure, until I couldn't take it anymore, and had to check my email in order to escape the room.

Although I didn't share the news with anyone else in case it gave them the wrong idea, one of the emails I got was from Alex, saying that he had dusted off his escape-and-evasion tactics in order to flee his parents' Thanksgiving celebrations. After a short stint of rock climbing he had met with Justin, who was similarly trying to avoid his family as much as possible, and that Justin remained untroubled by further threats of blackmail, and seemed almost cheerful for the first time this semester.

So thanks, he wrote. *I think we might all make it through finals. Hope your Thanksgiving is going okay.*

The usual, I wrote back. *Why don't you have money and fun and a family and all those things.*

Yeah, he replied almost immediately. *I know what you're talking about. Good questions all. Is it too late to switch over to retail? Any further plans with that friend of yours to open your own strip show? And if so, can I join?* ☺ ☺ ☺

We did in fact do a little research on it during the convention, I told him. *But we'd have to get work at some club or start our own business, and that seemed too exhausting to contemplate during the semester. And we might already be too far along the process of morphing into dragon-ladies. Or dragons, in your case. Someone tried to hassle me at the airport and I shut them down with extreme prejudice.*

Yeah, know what you mean. In a couple more years everyone will fear the very sound of our tread. If I do get this job in Beirut, I'm not going to have to worry about Hezbollah because they're going to be too scared of me to try anything.

When's your interview?

Monday. Skype.

Good luck! Break a leg, into the mouth of the wolf, etc. etc. I told him.

Thanks! You too. Don't let your family get you down!

You too!

*Too late for that. But it's only a couple more days, and then
I have the joy of coming into work AND a Skype interview.
By the way, can I have the office at 9:00am Monday? I know
Kate has class then and Emma will be off at Tech.*

Of course! No problem.

*Okay then. See you sometime after 10am on Monday.
Hopefully without any further student crises to defuse.*

It was a sad comment on my current state that I was half-hoping there would be a student crisis or two to deal with. It would be a pleasant distraction from my own problems.

37

No student crises greeted me upon my return, however. Everyone was too caught up in the pre-finals grind to have other problems. Mackenzie was in a state over getting her final project for the independent study done in time, having frittered away the first part of November putting together what she hoped was the perfect application for the Critical Language Scholarship for Kazan next summer. It required two separate meetings, plus multiple emails, to convince her that she could complete the project in a satisfactory manner, as well as her other papers and finals, and didn't need to try to swing a late drop or take an Incomplete for the independent study.

"You can't take an Incomplete," I pointed out to her. "I won't be here next semester."

"Oh, right." Her face fell. "But will you be around? Maybe at Rutgers or Princeton? Doesn't Princeton have a big Russian department? Maybe you could get a job there!"

Laughing at such earnest faith and naivety would be very wrong, I told myself sternly. "I'm afraid not," I said.

"Oh, but maybe..."

"I don't know where I'm going to be yet, but wherever I am, you can always email or Skype me."

"It won't be the same!"

"I know. But you can do a lot via email or Skype."

"Yeah, I guess," she said, unconvinced.

"So anyway, you should finish up this project now. Not just because I won't be here, but because if you don't, you'll have it hanging over your head all break. You can finish everything you need to finish in time, you really can."

"It doesn't feel like it. And Principles of Accounting is really kicking my butt!"

"Mmmm," I said. Mackenzie had been complaining about Principles of Accounting all semester as being both boring and difficult. It was unfortunate that her parents remained determined for her to major in either Accounting or Business Management. I debated advising her to just flunk out and solve the problem that way. Probably that was not the most graceful and mature method of dealing with the issue. Probably her parents routinely put her in positions where grace and maturity were hard to come by, and not very useful.

"You don't *have* to get an A in it," I said as a compromise.

"But if I don't get an A I won't be able to get into a good MBA program!"

"Do you *want* to get into a good MBA program?"

She shrugged and hunched her shoulders, looking rather like Madison as she did so. She was one, maybe two semesters away from picking up a nasty drug habit like Madison as well, I judged.

"Why don't you look into applying for a Boren Scholarship," I said instead of voicing my real thoughts.

"Isn't that the one where you have to agree to do government service afterwards?"

"Yep."

"I don't think my dad would like that," she said doubtfully. "Although...he has suggested I consider going into politics a few times." Her face cleared. "That's what I'll do! I'll tell him I want to be a county commissioner or something like that, and I need the political experience!"

"Why stop at county commissioner?" I said. "If you get a Boren, you could end up working in DC."

"DC! Wow! Yeah, my dad'd *love* that! Thanks for the idea, Professor!"

"No problem. So is your dad in politics, then?"

"What? No. My grandfather is in politics. My dad has a construction company."

"Oh."

"Yeah, actually, it was his company that got the contract on Angelo Hall, you know, that new building that just opened this semester?"

"So he wants you to go into the family business?" I asked. "That's why he wants you to study accounting and business."

"Yeah, but I don't care about construction at all. I want to do non-profit work, but he's always like, 'There's no profit in non-profits,' and starts talking about how his business paid for me to go to college, which is, like, kind of true, even though I'm on a full-ride scholarship, but it's like he thinks if he makes me do it enough, I'll get good at this stuff, and I just haven't yet. I get straight As in all my Russian classes, and I can barely get a B in my business classes, even though I work twice as hard on them, I swear."

"I believe you," I said. "If you're not interested in something, you'll never really learn it."

"Yeah," she said. "But my dad thinks he can *make* me be interested in his business. Oh! Professor Cahill!"

"Mackenzie! Look at you!" A slender man with a mane of white hair that screamed "Professor," and a beneficent look in his blue eyes, peered into the adjunct office.

"Professor Cahill, this is Professor Halley! She's been working with me on an independent study this semester."

"A pleasure to meet you." The man who must have been Tom Cahill stepped all the way into the office. "I can see my students have been in very capable hands in my absence."

"Professor Halley's been really helpful, but we all missed you, Professor Cahill!"

"I'm very flattered to hear that."

"And a bunch of us have signed up for that lit course in the spring!"

"I'm very flattered to hear that as well."

"Well, I have to go," announced Mackenzie, looking at her phone. "Thanks for the help Professor—um, Professor Halley—and good to see you, Professor Cahill!" She gathered up her laptop and her bookbag and her phone and rushed off.

"I'm sorry, I don't think I know your name," Professor Cahill said, once she was gone.

"Rowena."

"A lovely name, but it must present some difficulties for Russian-speakers. I'm Tom."

"Most of my Russian friends call me Inna or Innochka," I explained.

"An elegant solution. I was just dropping by to check on my old office, and move some things in preparation for the spring semester, but I see my office is occupied and unlikely to be vacated any time soon."

"Um...so do they have a plan for what to do with you?" I asked.

He shrugged, in an unusually supple and elegant movement for a man, especially one his age. "Not that I can ascertain. I may be joining you in—what do the adjuncts call it?—the 'adjunct warehouse' next semester."

"Oh. Well...it's not *that* bad. To be honest, the lack of chalk and markers is much more of a problem."

"Indeed. If you have a moment, Rowena, I'd love to grab a coffee with you and talk about the semester and the students. You can fill me in on all the wild and exciting developments that have taken place in my absence."

"Sure. I'm free now."

"Have you sampled the campus Starbucks?"

"A couple of times," I said. "It's not as good as a regular Starbucks, is it?"

He laughed. "No. No, it isn't. We used to have an independent coffee shop, called The Campus Grind, but there was a renovation of the library a couple of years ago, and somehow we ended up with this travesty of a Starbucks. I wouldn't mind so much if it were a *good* Starbucks, since to be frank The Campus Grind served only middling coffee and stale pastries. Now we still have only middling coffee and stale pastries, but with the money going back to Seattle instead of staying here in New Jersey. But if you have a serious coffee addiction like I do, you support your dealers no matter what. Shall we?"

We walked together over from Dreme Hall to the library. Going through the department was awkward, because several people stopped and stared without saying anything, but if it bothered Tom, he didn't show it.

Once out on the quad, he started asking me about myself, and expressed interest in Georgia, and mentioned several mutual acquaintances who were connected with the program at Indiana, and asked me about my research, and told me about his own interest in the poetry of Annensky, and generally behaved the way a colleague should, which was a refreshing change.

We got into Starbucks, and, after a long wait in line behind chattering undergrads, ordered and sat down on a rickety table that barely had room for both our cups. "So," he asked me, his bright blue eyes fixed on my face as he stirred his coffee, "how has Madison been this semester, Rowena?"

"Ummm...."

He laughed. "That good? She was always a handful. Is she still taking cocaine?"

I looked around. No one else appeared to be paying any attention to us. "Yes," I whispered. "She's stopped coming to class obviously strung out of her mind, but that's about as good as it's gotten."

"I'm not surprised. I didn't expect her latest stint in rehab to take. The first one certainly didn't." He stirred his coffee, his face now serious.

"People can only get clean if they want to," I said.

"And Maddie doesn't want to yet, does she? Not that I can blame her too much. You know about her life? Her mother left the family when Maddie was in high school and ran off with her ski instructor or some such jet-set cliché. Not that I can blame *her* too much either. You know Maddie's father is Provost Johnson, don't you? Imagine coming home to *him* every night!" Tom gave a delicate shudder.

"He doesn't seem that bad to me," I said. "But I don't know him that well. I don't mix much with provosts."

"And very wise of you, if I may say. Poor for the digestion, provosts, and even worse for the career, sometimes."

"Yeah," I said. "Poor Madison. It must be tough for her."

"Yes, although maybe not tough enough. Maybe if it got *really* tough, she'd pull herself together."

"Or maybe she'd fall apart completely," I said. "Most people do, under pressure."

"Too true." He stirred his coffee some more. "I had hoped that Maddie was made of sterner stuff, however. After the whole thing with Brandy last semester..." He gave another delicate shudder, this one less theatrical and more heartfelt.

"That must have been really tough," I said. "To lose a student like that."

"Yes. It is. Especially when it's a student you like so much." He made a small frown that he couldn't quite turn into a smile. "You know, Brandy reminded me a lot of myself at that age. Not because he was a particularly good kid, because he wasn't, but because he was so...I don't know. Full of everything. Full of life. Full of himself. Full of shit." This time he managed a smile. "Brandy wasn't a good kid, you know."

"Yeah. I heard from Justin about the stuff that he wrote, the stuff that almost came out."

"Yeah." Tom picked up his coffee, thought about taking a sip, and then put it down untasted. "He came and talked to me about it, a few days before...well, you know. He confessed to everything, asked me what to do."

"I'm sorry," I said, when it became apparent that Tom wasn't going to say anything more.

"For what? Brandy did what he did. It had little to do with me, and even less to do with you."

"Yeah, but I'm sorry even so. That must have been a hard thing to deal with."

He gave me a sharp look. "Were you a counselor in a previous career, dear Rowena?"

"Not exactly, but sort of. Enough to know how to empathize with people."

"No, my dear. Counselors only learn how to sympathize. Empathizing is something you've learned on your own. And all credit to you. Because you're right: it was hard."

"I'm sure," I said.

"Especially since it was all so stupid! I'm not defending what Brandy did, because it was puerile and hurtful, both the things he wrote and the way he treated Justin, who really *is* a good kid, but it certainly wasn't worth dying for. It wasn't even worth getting expelled for. A little community service or, much as it pains me to have the phrase even cross my lips, 'sensitivity training,' would more than suffice, it seems to me."

"I agree," I said. "Especially since..." I trailed off.

"Especially since the university keeps adjuncts on starvation pay and employs privately contracted cleaning staff at minimum wage with no benefits, is that what you were going to say? And—it's *so funny* how this happens, isn't it—75% or so of the adjuncts and contingent faculty are women, and 75% or so of the janitorial staff are black? And the rest are immigrants? Isn't it funny how that works out? To be honest, I don't know who's the more exploited here. Both of you are being paid less than enough to live off of, for what should be more than full-time jobs. But after all, most people who go into teaching these days are idealistic young women from the middle and upper classes—like you, my dear. No doubt most of you think that this is a great career for you, one where you can live the life of the mind and make the world a better place and also be treated with respect and make a decent living. But there's no need to pay women of that social class a living wage, is there? Because they are expected to make their real money through blow jobs and brow wipes, something their oh-so-enlightened poorer, darker sisters are only too happy to rub in their faces, while they pat themselves on the back with both hands for their third-wave feminism, or whatever stage we've reached now.

"And then the poor women who clean the toilets and take out the trash—why should they get a living wage? If they really wanted one, they'd go back to school and get an education, the way white middle-class girls do. Funny how you just can't win, isn't it? Whichever way you turn, you're back to begging for scraps in exchange for blow jobs, literal or metaphorical. But what is that in comparison with a nineteen-year-old mouthing off in a private message forum? The former is just good business, while the latter is a serious crime."

"I know," I said.

"But I really shouldn't be saying this, my dear, as you know all too well. After all, I'm grateful to be let off with nothing but a one-semester administrative suspension without pay to let the stink around the Russian program dissipate a little, and to show that they're taking the matter seriously and punishing *someone* for what Brandy did, and I have every intention of slinking back obediently in January and being a good little boy. So forgive an old Marxist who doesn't have the courage of his convictions."

"Um, yeah," I said.

"But *you*, my dear, are free. Free to starve to death, you might object, and you would be correct to do so, but still—free. You won't be slinking back next semester, so you might as well stride out in a blaze of glory." He gave me another bright look. "Have they been feeding you some line about expanding the program, creating a permanent position for you? Because they've been feeding that line to Alex for two years, and—once again it's *so funny*, isn't it?—the coveted position has as of yet failed to materialize."

"Yeah," I said. "I know about Alex. And yeah, there have been hints, half-suggested promises, that kind of thing, but my contract expires next week and so far no one's put their money where their mouth is."

"Your contract expires next week? But finals are in two weeks."

"I know. But they started my contract on September 1 and ended it on December 15, even though my actual work period goes from August 25 to December 19 or 20."

Tom burst out laughing. "Ah, Lib State!" he said when he had recovered. "Will your avarice ever cease to amaze me? Truly, you are a wonder! And you didn't protest it, my dear?"

"I tried," I said. "But they obviously didn't give a crap in HR—I mean, they'd done it on purpose—so I saw real fast it wasn't going to do any good, so I figured I'd just...I don't know. It wasn't like they were going to pay me any more in any case."

"Too true. Well, I wouldn't slave away too hard over exams, my dear. In fact, if you want a hand, let me know."

"Surely you have your own exams coming up? Aren't you working at Rutgers?"

"Yes, but I'm always working at Rutgers. There wouldn't be anything unusual about me putting in double duty. In fact, I'm rather pining for it. And for my students."

"They all remember you fondly."

"Do they? That's lovely to hear. And how *is* Mackenzie? Did her summer in Russia do her good?"

"I think so. Her conversational ability is quite developed at this point. And she's thinking about going back, if she can. That's what she was talking to me about when you showed up."

"Well, good for her. Although I can't see her father agreeing."

"That's what she says. But it's her life, not his."

"True. But Mack D'Annunziato rarely sees it that way, about his daughter or anyone else. And neither, to be frank, does his father-in-law Vinnie Angelo, former mayor of our fair city. After whom, in case you haven't guessed, Angelo Hall is named."

"Wow," I said. "I didn't realize Mackenzie's family was so rich."

"They are somewhat rich in money, and much richer in connections and influence. So while I'm sure Mack D'Annunziato loves his daughter in his own way, she would be wise not to cross him—as would you, my dear."

"I thought you said I had nothing to fear," I said. "After all, I'm going to be riding out of here in a blaze of glory no matter what."

"True. But until that moment, I wouldn't get on Mackenzie's father's bad side."

"Is that what happened to you?" I asked. "Is that why they sent you away?"

"Maybe," he said. "A little. In truth, Brandy's death was just an excuse to get me out of the way. I'd made some...unwise statements about the new building, you see, at faculty meetings. Protesting the expense, the use—misuse, as I saw it—of Superstorm Sandy money that was earmarked for rebuilding after the storm to build a brand-new, obscenely expensive, state-of-the-art building that would serve more to stroke egos than to benefit the campus community. Oh, I know we needed more classrooms," he said, seeing by my face that I was about to object. "That I don't argue with. But that building has hardly any classrooms. Have you looked at the plan? Have you been in it?"

"101 is in the basement."

"You see? The basement. All the classrooms are in the basement, except for a couple for show right at the front doors. The rest is just offices and recreational space—but mainly offices for people who do...what? Not teach, that's certain, nor research either, as far as I can tell. I was just wandering around there before I bumped into you. Most enlightening. Most of the office space seems to be dedicated to people with only a tenuous affiliation with the university. Meanwhile, you and I have to beg for keys to get into our own classrooms at the beginning of every semester."

"Yeah," I said. "That *is* weird."

"Only because you're from a more honest society than ours, my dear. But I may get to experience the joys of Angelo Hall in greater depth soon. Apparently I, too, will be teaching in the basement next semester."

"I hope it goes well," I said, for lack of anything better to say.

"So do I, my dear. I'll look over my rosters and ask if there's anyone I have questions about. I'm glad to hear that Mackenzie has benefited so much from her summer abroad, and that Madison has managed to show up to class with her brain more or less in the same space as her body from time to time. Anyone else I should know about?"

"Riva Goldshteyn is very strong," I said. "I jumped her straight into 201. And I think there might be a romance brewing between her and Adam."

"Lovely! Adam is an excellent student. Perhaps they will go forth and multiply and provide us with more diligent little students. Anyone else?"

"The heritage speakers in 101 are all trouble," I said. "Ira wouldn't be a bad student if she didn't have such a big chip on her shoulder over being a heritage speaker who can't read or write, but she does. And I can't really blame her: her mother is a medical doctor by training who's now one of those women cleaning the toilets and taking out the trash for minimum wage."

Tom shook his head in stagey sorrow. "The future of us all, no doubt. And the others?"

"Danila and Vitya are handfuls. They're not bad—exactly. But when they're not cutting up, they're strolling out during the middle of class for smoke breaks."

"And you don't stop this?"

"Frankly I figured we could all use the break from their presence."

Tom smiled. "Probably wise."

"And I wanted to stay on their good side, since they're the ones who go on supply-stealing raids."

"Ah. I take it the classrooms in Angelo are no better supplied than the ones elsewhere?"

"Nope."

"Oh *good*. I'm glad Lib State is being so cost-conscious. We wouldn't want to have to raise tuition yet *again* for the fifth straight year, now would we? Where is this Danila and this Vitya from?"

"Danila—Danila Petrenko—is from Odessa, and Vitya—Viktor Ivanov—is from Minsk. Ira is from Moscow. So there's a certain amount of tension over that."

"I'm sure. Is Danila from the Moscow Mafiya, as it's called now?"

"Maybe? Given some of the things he's let drop, I wouldn't be surprised if there were mafia connections."

"Well." Tom sighed. "It's good to see that Russian is keeping up its reputation for being the safe, clean, crime-free subject it's always been. Thank you so much for catching me up to speed, my dear, and now I'll let you go. There's more poking around I want to do. Don't hesitate to give me a call if you decide you do need help with finals." He stood up from the table, gave me a courtly half-bow, and left.

38

The second week of December brought the last week of classes, and also the news via The Wiki that invitations for campus visits for the UNC-Charlotte job had already gone out. I was not one of the lucky three. Maybe my preference for *The Idiot* had been just as fatal as I had thought, or my imagined ending errors had been too egregious, or there had been an inside candidate, or, most likely of all, there had been too many qualified applicants and they had had to make a choice by tossing a dart at the applications and hoping for the best.

I wasn't that surprised, and in a perfect world I wouldn't have been super excited about the job anyway, but with no other prospects on hand either for next semester or next year, any job at all sounded great. Maybe Ira's mother or the Moscow Mafiya could hook me up with the janitorial staff.

Alex, on the other hand, was having slightly better luck. Although he claimed that his Skype interview for the job in Beirut was "a complete piece of shit," he came into the office on the last week of class, a dazed look in his eyes, and announced that he'd been invited for a campus interview.

"They're going to fly you all the way out to Beirut?" we all asked, stunned.

"Yes. They got some kind of cut-rate flight, and are going to put me up in someone's house." He groaned. "Because that won't be awkward at all!"

"It could still be fun," said Kate encouragingly. "An all-expenses-paid trip to Beirut!"

"I've already had my all-expenses-paid trip to the Middle East," Alex said. "I wasn't really looking for another one."

"Maybe you shouldn't have gone into Arabic, then," said Emma, with a snideness probably generated by the fact that no one was offering her a cut-rate flight to Beijing and someone's couch to sleep on while she was grilled and paraded and generally put up for auction.

"I wanted to learn something different and hardcore and save the world. And also to hang out in cool places like Marrakesh and smoke dope," said Alex. "Instead they keep sending me into fucking war zones."

"Beirut isn't a war zone anymore!" Kate pointed out.

"As good as," said Alex, but then he burst into a grin. "But it's a fifteen-hour flight from home—actually, a twenty-five hour flight with the connections they've got for me—so hey, it's got that going for it! I'll be gone for the better part of a week, most of which will be spent in the air, but whatever."

"I'm sure you'll do great," said Kate.

"Yeah, whatever," said Alex, but he left the office still looking pleased.

The other exciting thing that happened that week was the long-scheduled meeting between the LCTL instructors and the Provost. Somehow the only time Provost Johnson had managed to find in his busy schedule all semester was the Friday afternoon of the last week of classes. It added another layer of stress around setting up pre-finals study sessions and trying to cajole Linda into giving us a few more copies over our limits so that we could print off the exams.

"You knew this was coming up!" she told me, Alex, Kate, and Emma when we all trooped in as a delegation. "You knew you'd have to print off your finals!"

"Yeah, but we also had to print off our last chapter tests," I said when no one else spoke up. Apparently I was taking Tom's advice and going out in a blaze of glory since I had nothing to lose. If one could call asking to have your final exams printed out by the department copy machine to be a "blaze of glory."

She emitted a sigh that was more of a groan of someone being tortured beyond their endurance, and agreed to print off our finals, since, as she told us, she knew we had to go to the meeting with the Provost in a few minutes and she didn't want us to be late for that after spending so much time and effort setting it up.

There was a raw nip in the dank wind that met us as we walked between the chains from Dreme Hall to Morrison, where the main administrative offices were located. Emma and Kate speculated nervously over what the meeting would be about, until Alex told them that it didn't matter because we were just there as window dressing anyway, and if our opinions did happen to be requested, the only weight they would have would be in our reappointment next year or lack thereof.

"For God's sake, don't make me any more nervous than I already am!" said Emma, giving him a punch on the shoulder that completely failed to rock him back.

He shrugged. "I'm just saying: the stakes are low."

"Not for me they're not! And maybe not for you either. After all, you still don't have that job in Beirut yet. Have you gotten any more interview invites?"

"Not a one," said Alex.

So we were in fine fettle when we trailed uncertainly behind Janey, the Provost's admin, into the conference room that had been set aside for the meeting. Provost Johnson "would be right with us,"

Janey told us, "just as soon as he got off an important conference call."

"Who the fuck has an important conference call at 3:30pm on the last Friday of the semester?" Alex whispered to me, but then shut up when someone opened the door.

Instead of Provost Johnson, though, the person who came in was Tom Cahill. He distributed hugs all around, and said, "I hope you don't mind that I'm here, Rowena. I got wind of this meeting and thought perhaps I should be in attendance as well."

"Of course," I said. "It only makes sense." Which it did. Whatever the Provost and the university had planned for the LCTL program, it didn't affect me. With only three more days left on my contract and no renewal in sight, I was already gone, in mind if not in body. If only I had had someplace to go to, I would have felt a lot better about it, but you can't have everything.

After some nervous chatter about finals and holiday plans, we all fell silent as Provost Johnson came striding into the room, only twenty minutes late.

"Sorry for the hold up," he said, sounding more indifferent than sorry. "Budget negotiations. Alex, Emma, nice to see you. Kate, thanks for coming: I know German isn't officially a LCTL, but at TLASC it is. Something that perhaps we could work to change. Rowena." Something warm in his eyes flared for an instant as he said my name. "Thank you for coming as well. I know it's your last week here, but the university appreciates everything you've done for the program—as do I personally, so it seems right to include you. Tom." Something flared in Provost Johnson's eyes again, but this time it was cold, not warm.

"Glad to be here," said Tom, inclining his head in a courtly half-bow and not coming across at all like an old Marxist who lacked the courage of his convictions.

"Yes, I'm sure." Provost Johnson bit his lip. I wondered how much his lip balm cost. Probably more than all my toiletries combined.

"Please, have a seat." He indicated the conference table, and we all sat down. "Janey! Do you have...oh, great."

Janey brought in a pile of printouts and handed them around. Maybe the Provost's office didn't have a 100-page limit per month. Maybe the Provost's office could print handouts whenever it wanted to. I looked at the first page. In color.

"I'll jump right in with the good news," said Provost Johnson. "The university has recently received a generous donation. We'd—I'd—like to use some of that money to develop the language program, specifically the LCTL program. As you no doubt know, TLASC is positioning itself as the premier selective liberal arts college in New Jersey, with an SLAC education at state school prices. We were very pleased with our position in this year's US News and World Report's rankings, which was three places higher than it had ever been before, but we need to rise higher. Our goal is to break the top twenty in the National Liberal Arts Colleges rankings by the end of the decade. We're moving in that direction, but we're not on track to hit that goal yet. One of the real areas of weakness we need to target is the lack of a decent LCTL program, along with the lack of research-focused faculty in that area. We're considering opening up tenure-line positions in all the LCTL languages, with research-intensive appointments."

There was a stunned silence from the rest of us, as we all wondered feverishly whether this were true or if it was just another example of the university dangling a carrot before hitting us with an even bigger stick.

"That's very commendable," said Tom eventually, flipping through the handout. "And it looks like the budgeting committee has done a thorough job of examining costs. Although the projected salary ranges look awfully low. $55,000 a year for a tenure-track position? In New Jersey? Where we have one of the highest costs of living in the nation?"

"With full benefits," said Provost Johnson.

"Yes, of course, but isn't the national average for professors more in the range of $80-$90,000 a year?"

"For professors in STEM subjects maybe. I think you'll find that for languages it's considerably lower. $55,000 is quite generous."

"I see," said Tom. Kate, Emma, and I all exchanged glances. Alex was sitting too close to me for me to catch his eye, but no doubt he was thinking the same thing the rest of us were. While I knew that $55,000 was pathetically paltry for a white-collar job that required a post-graduate degree, right now it sounded like unimaginable riches. With a $55,000—*plus* health insurance!—salary I could buy groceries at real grocery stores. I could replace my scuffed shoes that were splitting at the seams. I could take Fevronia to the vet to get her teeth cleaned. I could get my transmission fixed, or maybe even buy a whole new used car.

"Anyway, that's not what I brought you here to discuss. My hands are tied when it comes to faculty salaries: that's the budgeting committee's department," said Provost Johnson, throwing up his hands as if to show his helplessness before the might of the budgeting committee.

"Of course," murmured Tom. "But as an expert in the field I felt it was my duty to point out that you might have trouble attracting the *best* people in the field at that salary range."

"I think there are plenty of *best* people who would be happy to work for that salary," said Provost Johnson. "Isn't that right, Alex? Rowena?"

"Um, I guess," I said. Alex stared down at the handout in front of him without speaking. Anger lines were showing through the stubble around his mouth, and the arm next to mine was shaking visibly.

"Yes, of course," said Provost Johnson, giving me a fond look, as if I were his special teacher's pet, even though I had hardly given his plan a ringing endorsement. Still, it was more enthusiasm than anyone else had evinced. Kate and Emma both looked like they were about to burst into tears, Tom was staring at Provost Johnson with a level look that was just short of an open challenge, and Alex was surreptitiously clenching and unclenching his fist under the table.

"Anyway, this is not the subject of this meeting," Provost Johnson continued. "This is all entirely speculative in any case; we're still waiting for final approval. But it is looking *very* likely that it will be approved, and if it does, of course, it goes without saying that all of you would be considered seriously for these positions. You too, of course, Rowena," he added to me. "I know we were unable to renew your contract for the spring, which I'm sure the department considers a shame, and I know I do, but our obligations to Tom came first, as I'm sure you understand."

"Um," I said, when it became apparent that he was waiting for an answer. "Of course."

"But of course if a tenure-track position *were* to open up, we would strongly encourage you to apply. Naturally we're looking for young, up-and-coming scholars with fresh research agendas to fill these positions. Naturally we want to encourage such people, provide them with the opportunity to succeed and contribute to their discipline, and, of course, that will help us rise in the rankings as well. Our research productivity, or rather, lack thereof, is, frankly, holding us back, and that's something the university wants to address as soon as possible, since we know good research takes time to produce—and more importantly, to get published. I believe you already had an article published prior to graduation, and another under review? And plans to publish your dissertation? How is that going?"

"Um," I said. Emma and Kate were staring at me as if I had suddenly morphed into a venomous snake before their eyes. Not that I could blame them. Alex was still shaking with rage beside me. Only Tom was watching me with benign kindness, only slightly tinged with sadness. "Okay," I said. "My article was, um, accepted for publication earlier this semester."

"Of course it was! We wouldn't expect anything less from a talented, and most importantly, driven young scholar like yourself. Of course, I'm sure it helped that you were only teaching two classes, instead of having to take on an overload or extra teaching at another campus."

"Um," I said. *I did take on an overload!* I shouted inside my head. *I just didn't get any money for it!* "Yeah," I said out loud.

"Excellent. And that's the kind of support we want to provide to our up-and-coming scholars. There would also be other help as well; in fact, that's what I brought you here today to discuss. What kinds of ideas do you have to make this potential LCTL program dynamic and productive? How could we attract more students? How, most importantly, could we increase faculty output? Rowena, perhaps you'd care to start."

"Excuse me for a moment, if I may," Tom interjected. "I'm sure Rowena has excellent ideas on all those topics, and at another time I would love to hear them, but it hardly seems fair to put her on the spot when she's only been here one semester and, if you'll all pardon me for saying so, will be leaving us next week, since while all these plans are wonderful, in the here-and-now we can't even offer her a one-semester contract as an adjunct. Perhaps I, as the most senior of the instructors here, and the one with the most knowledge of TLASC and its strengths and weaknesses, should be the one to start."

"I think it would be best to hear first from someone with fresh new ideas," said Provost Johnson. "Someone who could push us in the direction we want to move in."

"Tom's right," I heard myself say. My mouth felt like it was being operated by some body that wasn't mine. I had to stop and clear my throat. Arguing against what Provost Johnson was saying was harder than it should have been. Not because I was afraid of losing this job that didn't exist yet and probably never would, but because he was Madison's father and because he liked me, I was sure of it. "I think someone with more experience with the program and the college should start," I found myself saying. "I'm sure Tom has lots of good ideas for how to develop the program and how the university could give it the support it needs in order to flourish, better than I do."

I felt something brush my knee, and looked down. Alex gave my knee a quick squeeze, and flashed me a tiny thumbs-up under the table.

Provost Johnson sat back. Instead of being angry, he seemed almost pleased, like I had proven something to him, something that made him like me more. I wished that gave me confidence that this would somehow turn out well for all of us.

"You make a compelling point, Rowena, although don't sell your own abilities short," he said, with a tiny half-smile. "So, Tom: why don't you start? What *are* your thoughts on how the program could be developed? I take it you've come up with some, over the years?"

"I have," said Tom. "But first, a question. Am I understanding the source of this funding correctly?" He pointed at something in the handout.

I leaned over and looked at what he was pointing at. A footnote on the bottom of the last page. I sat back and turned to the same page on my own handout. Alex quickly copied me. Emma and Kate continued to sit there in frozen horror.

At first I didn't understand what I was looking at. Then it made sense:

> *The funding for the proposed program expansion will come from the Angelo and D'Annunziato endowment.*

Next to me, Alex sucked in his breath.

"The Angelo and D'Annunziato families have decided to be very generous to the university," said Provost Johnson. "I trust those names are familiar to you?" he asked, turning to me and Alex.

I nodded. Next to me, Alex was nodding as well, looking incredulous.

"So I don't need to explain to you why they have taken a particular interest in the LCTL program?" Provost Johnson asked. "Or why your involvement in developing the program will be essential? I'm sure you've been told of the importance of networking: well, here you see its practical applications. Because of what you've done for the Angelo and D'Annunziato children, their families have made giving back specifically to your programs an especial target of interest."

"That's lovely," Tom said mildly. "It is always rewarding to know that our work has made an impression on our students. But is the university *sure* that, how shall I put this, the money is something we want to accept?"

Provost Johnson stiffened. His head turned slowly from where he had been contemplating me and Alex to focus on Tom. "Yes," he said slowly. "The university has vetted the source of these funds with all due diligence, as it always does with its donors and endowments."

"And this doesn't have anything to do with that fancy new building just on the other side of Morrison Hall?"

"Angelo Hall was, shall we say, a down payment on the endowment. An initial expression of interest, a test to see if the families could work with the university for mutual benefit."

"Is that so," said Tom. "And those people in those offices in the upper floors of Angelo, the ones where there are no classrooms, those people who work for Angelo Operations Ltd., or D'Annunziato & Co., is this an example of the kind of 'mutual benefit' the university is looking for?"

Provost Johnson stiffened even more. "What are you implying, Tom?" he demanded.

"Implying? Nothing. I'm asking why the university is renting out space in a campus building to a private enterprise, one that paid for said building. Or paid in part."

"If you're referring to the Superstorm Sandy money, everything has been cleared with the state. We were given a certain sum for damages, but how we chose to implement it was up to us. Instead of rebuilding that sad trailer park on the far side of the stadium that was blown away, we chose to invest the money in building a brand-new, state-of-the-art classroom building. The state agreed that was a legitimate use of the funds, one with greater long-term benefit for the state than mere replacement of the original structures, which, as I'm sure *you*, Tom, as the most senior person here in terms of years of service at TLASC, remember as a sorry collection of cheap prefab and mobile homes. What did you call it? I'm sure someone repeated your rather pithy statement about it to me when we were discussing what to do with it. Oh yes: 'Kansas trailer trash in dire need of its tornado.' Well, its tornado came, Tom, and we decided to take your implied advice and upgrade in its aftermath."

"And a sorely needed upgrade that was," said Tom. "But with Angelo money on the bargain?"

"Are you suggesting that our mayor's money isn't good enough for the college located in his own home town and constituency? Are you suggesting that he shouldn't be allowed to give back to the community he has served so long and faithfully?"

"You make him sound like a real public servant," said Tom, his mouth quirked in a wry smile.

"Because he is."

"Of sorts," said Tom, his mouth still quirked in that wry smile. "A Jersey-style public servant."

"Yes," said Provost Johnson. "Just like we are a Jersey-style public institution of higher education. Enough." He slapped the handout against the table for emphasis. "The money has already been accepted, so any discussion of its provenance is fruitless. And, may I remind you, some of it has been specifically earmarked for your program, the program that you, Tom, have been complaining for years is the 'red-headed stepchild,' if I recall your words correctly, of the college. Well, no longer. This is your chance to vault it from red-headed stepchild to first-born son, and all because of the Angelo and D'Annunziato families, who, need I remind you, are expressing their gratitude for services you"—he swept us all with his gaze—"you all personally have rendered them. If anyone should be worried about being seen as in their pocket, Tom, I would think it would be you. And Rowena and Alex as well. But you don't consider yourselves compromised, do you?" He fixed both me and Alex with a piercing look, demanding an answer.

"Um." Alex and I shared a glance. "Whatever I might have done for Mackenzie, it was nothing out of the ordinary," I said. "Nothing I wouldn't have done for any student. And I did it for her, because of her, not for her family or because of whoever they might be."

"Same here," said Alex. "Money can't buy love, you know what I mean?" He sat back and folded his arms. "As we get to prove every day."

"Indeed," said Provost Johnson. "You see? Nothing untoward there at all. And it's the same with the building, and the endowment." He looked us all each in the face once again. "*This is your chance*," he said. "Do you think I don't know what it's like? Do

you think I wasn't once in your shoes? I taught English, for God's
sake. What's being done to humanities programs across the country
is a crying shame, and we all know it. Well, instead of whining and
moaning and wringing our hands about it, we need to do something.
We're always talking about how our subjects have real-world
applications, and here you go, you've just proven that they do. You've
just proven that the kinds of connections, the kind of human
relations and human knowledge that we're all committed to
building, really *do* make the world a better place, really *do* make the
world go round. So, if you'll permit me to say it, *don't fuck this up.*
Take the money and be happy!"

There was a knock at the door. Janey stuck her head cautiously
in. "I'm sorry to disturb you, Provost, when you're engaged in such
an important discussion, but you did ask me to let you know when
your next appointment arrived."

Provost Johnson sighed. "Tell John Greene I'll be right with
him," he said, sounding even less enthused about meeting with John
Greene than I would have been.

"I'm sure John Greene will be full of ideas for how the Romance
Languages program can use its share of the endowment money," he
said, once Janey had withdrawn her head and shut the door again.
"And how he could use your share, too, if you don't want it. The
money *will* get used, one way or another; the question is how much
your program will benefit from it. So why don't you draw up a list of
requests and suggestions, and submit it to me, by, shall we say next
week? Tom, why don't you take point on this, and solicit everyone
else's suggestions and compile them. Does that sound good?"

There was a pause. "Very well," said Tom slowly. "Next week it is.
As soon as finals are over."

"Very good," said Provost Johnson, looking pleased. He stood
up, the rest of us copying him. "I think this has been a very
productive meeting. Thank you all for coming. Oh, Rowena." He

caught my arm as I started to file past him, his hand firm on my bicep. *Two* men touching me in one meeting. My lucky day. The sad thing was, I'd been alone for long enough now that it almost felt like it. "A word, please." He dropped my arm as Alex sidled past us, giving Provost Johnson's hand a sideways look as he did so.

"I just wanted to thank you for taking the time to work with Madison so much this semester," Provost Johnson said, loudly enough that everyone could hear. "I know she can be...challenging at times, but she's really blossomed under your instruction. She's mentioned several times how you've really taken a personal interest in her, and it's made all the difference for her."

"Um, it's nothing," I said. We were alone now.

"No, it's not," said Provost Johnson, stepping back and leaning a hip against the conference table. I guessed he wasn't worried about creasing his $1000 suit. Probably he had one for each day of the week, and a maid who gathered them up and took them in to be dry cleaned each weekend, cancer risk be damned. "Look, Rowena, can I be straight with you?"

"Of course."

"We both know about Madison's...little problem. I know, and I know that you know, because she came and told me that you've been pushing her to go back into rehab. You even sent her a list of programs and clinics, isn't that right, on top of insisting she sober up, at least for your classes."

"Um...yeah..."

"Oh don't worry, I'm not going to tell you off for not reporting her to the authorities. First of all, aside from the fact that I *am* the authorities, at least as far as this university is concerned, because as a father I appreciate not having to deal with all that legal crap, and second of all, because we both know it won't do her a damn bit of good, don't we?"

"I mean, it rarely does."

"Yeah. I won't say I haven't thought from time to time that a little stint in jail might do Madison some good, break through where nothing else will." He ran a hand over his face, looking for a moment less like the representative of the new, corporate face of higher education, and more like a father concerned for his willful, wayward, unhappy teenage daughter.

"But tempting a thought as that can be at times, I know it won't actually work," he said, once his face had emerged from behind his hand. "Jail would probably just introduce her to even more cokeheads, and maybe get her hooked on heroin or something in the bargain."

"Yeah. That's normally how it works."

"I've promised Madison a trip to anywhere in the world she wants to go next summer, if she goes back into rehab over winter break, and stays clean all spring," he told me. He smiled ruefully. "I'm not above bribery, and when it comes to Madison, never have been. She says she wants to do a study abroad program in Russia. I have to say I was impressed. I thought she'd want to go clubbing in Ibiza or something, waste her summer completely, but she wants to spend it studying. She was even talking about looking for an internship over there. Do they offer such things?"

"They do," I said. "I'll be happy to suggest some programs to her, if she's interested."

"That's great. Look, can we meet next week, after finals? You, me, and Madison. To talk about programs. Both kinds of programs. I've told her she has until the end of finals to pick out her rehab program, or I'm picking it out for her. That's the stick. And the carrot is letting her pick out what program she'll do afterwards. *If* she can manage to stay clean."

"She can do it."

"So sure of that?"

"Actually, no," I said. "I mean, I'm sure in theory. She's a smart girl and, in her own way, a brave girl, and I'm sure that if she really wants to, she can stay clean. The trick is getting her to really want to, and only she can do that. But giving her something to work towards, something she really wants, might help."

"Yeah, that's what I thought too." He blew out a breath. "I really am sorry we can't keep you, Rowena, and I really do want you to apply for the new Russian position if—*when*—it opens up. Do you have anything lined up for next semester yet? Next year?"

I shook my head.

"Well." He smiled slightly. "If you want to come and be Madison's full time minder and life coach, let me know."

"Um..."

"Actually, that's not a bad idea. I'm serious, Rowena: Madison doesn't have anyone else who will do that for her, and you've been more effective than anyone else thus far. Unless you've got some place you're going back to. You're not married, are you?"

I shook my head.

"Yeah, the good ones never are—don't have the time, am I right?"

"Um...something like that."

"Yeah. I really do remember what it was like, Rowena, although I'm sure you'd tell me that it's worse now than when I was coming through the system. And you'd probably be right, but it was bad enough then that I can make a pretty good guess of what it's like now. So seriously, Rowena, let me know. The offer will be open until Madison straightens out, and God alone knows when that will be."

"Um," I said. "Thank you."

"Yeah. So, next week? Next Friday? Can we meet...not here. Madison doesn't like it here, and to be honest I don't want to have this conversation in my own office. How about your office?"

"Well..." I began.

"Let me guess," he said. "You don't have your own office."

"Something like that."

"Well, let's let Angelo Hall earn its keep. Neutral territory, so to speak. Shall we say...do you have class there?"

"Yeah. Angelo 027. The basement."

"Well, don't turn in your key just yet. How about we meet in your classroom Friday afternoon. Or evening, if you're available. That would certainly work better for me, let me get all my meetings out of the way, and if all goes well, which I have a good feeling that it will, we can take Madison out for a celebratory dinner afterwards."

"Um," I said. "Okay. I should be free all evening."

"6:00pm work for you?"

"Sure."

"Great." He gave me a genuine smile. "See you next week, Rowena. 6:00pm, in the basement."

39

I hurried out into the early-evening twilight to catch up with the others. Tom was already halfway back across the quad, in earnest discussion with Emma and Kate, but Alex was loitering near the entrance to Morrison.

"Jesus Christ, what was that about?" he whispered as soon as I came up to him. "Where are you headed now, by the way?"

"The parking lot behind the stadium."

"Yeah, me too." We both started across the back quad, the empty space between Morrison, Angelo, the library, and the football stadium, which was dark in the half-lighting provided by the old-fashioned street lamps that, despite what parents were promised when they asked about on-campus safety, only worked on one side of the space. "Are you okay, Rowena? What did he want to talk to you about?"

"Um, about Madison," I said.

"His daughter? The one who's your student?"

"Uh-huh."

He relaxed a little. "Thank God. For a moment I thought he was going to proposition you or something."

"Well..."

"Shit! He didn't!"

"No," I said quickly. "Nothing like that. Actually, he was perfectly nice to me, much nicer than he was, you know, back in the meeting."

"Well, that wouldn't be hard," said Alex.

"I know. But, I mean, he was perfectly nice to me, nothing, you know, improper, but..."

"But what?"

"But he wants to meet with me next week. Me and Madison. To talk about her...options. Which is a little weird. I mean, I feel weird about meeting with a parent and discussing the student with them."

"Yeah. For sure. But she's going to be there, right? Like, of her own free will?"

"More or less. I mean, yes, she's supposed to be there, and supposedly it will be of her own free will."

"Okay. So if I understand FERPA, and I think I do, since I've done the fucking training, like, about six million times, it's okay to discuss stuff with a third party, including a parent, if she's given her consent. It's why we can send transcripts and write letters of recommendation and stuff."

"I know. And it's not really that. I mean, it's a little weird but maybe it'll help her. But, like...he also kind of, um, offered me a job."

"What?" Alex stopped. "You're fucking kidding me! The tenure-track position? He can't just do that! I mean, not that you don't deserve it, but you don't just hand those motherfuckers out. You have to torture people for months first until there's only one victor, standing on a bloody pile of dismembered bodies and sobbing brokenly with survivor's guilt. It's the law."

"I know. And not the tenure-track position, no. It really doesn't exist yet, at least I don't think so."

"Then...not Tom's job?! Or...have they created a second lectureship? That would be great!"

"No," I said. "Not that kind of job. More like, um, a babysitting job. Like, you know, watching over Madison."

Alex burst out laughing. "Oh Jesus," he said. "Seriously? You're not joking?"

"I'm not joking about the offer. I don't know how serious he was about it, although he seemed pretty serious."

"So, what, he was all like, 'Gosh, my daughter's so fucked up she can't even stay in this shitty college I got her into with my influence, so maybe I'll hire a goddamn PhD in Russian to be her personal babysitter and tutor?"

"Um...something like that, yeah."

"So would you live with them? What exactly do the duties of this job entail? Are you supposed to be filling in for Madison's absent mother in other ways as well?"

"I didn't ask."

"Yeah, and he's too smooth an operator to come out and say something like that straight out, at least not yet. But I saw how he looked at you, Rowena. I wouldn't put it past him to extend the invitation sooner or later."

"Um...yeah. I kind of got the same feeling."

"So? Are you thinking of accepting?"

"Um...I don't know! I mean, not that aspect of the offer, *if* it exists, obviously. But there's the fact that I really don't have anything else right now. I mean, despite just getting paid I currently have $300 to my name, counting what's left on my credit card limit, a car that can't shift into second gear half the time, a crabby cat with questionable bladder continence, and a very expensive diploma that won't get me a job at McDonald's. My other option is going and living in my brother's apartment in Jacksonville."

"Hmmm, yeah, I can see the dilemma. You could live in a shithole in the middle of nowhere and fuck a bunch of asshole Marines—and can I just say once again I think you should at least hold out for sailors, but I understand beggars can't be choosers—just to pass the time and make up for all that enforced celibacy of grad school and maybe put a few dollars in your pocket, because, unless the Marines pay a *lot* better than the Navy did, your brother isn't

going to be able to support you for long even if he'd be willing to.
Or you could live in Princeton, because that's where our fine Provost
lives, of course—no New Brunswick for him!—and fuck one asshole
academic with pretensions of grandeur and maybe sleep your way up
the ladder into the ivory tower, or at least get your MRS degree and
be nicely provided for."

"That's not what I'm going to do!"

"No, but those are your options," said Alex.

"Not my only options!"

"No? What's behind Door number 3, then?"

"Um...I don't know! Go teach English as a second language in
Russia?"

"Not a bad option," agreed Alex, nodding. "You'd be finished as
a serious academic, of course, or at least that's what I've always been
told whenever I've threatened to run off and do it in Marrakesh, but
it might be better than nothing."

"Is that what you'd do?"

"Me?" He flashed me a grin, his teeth white against the darkness
into which his stubbly face was disappearing. "I'd probably take the
Provost's offer, and I'm betting you will, too. And you want to know
why?"

"Why?"

"Because Madison needs you to, doesn't she? Right now I bet
you're thinking, 'But if I walk away from her, who will help Madison?
What will happen to her if I walk away from her?' Admit it. That's
what you're thinking, isn't it?"

"Maybe," I said.

"More than maybe. And you know what? You're probably right.
Somebody should take care of that girl, and it damn sure isn't going
to be her parents. Her dad's too busy bucking for university president
and that two million dollar salary, and her mom's too busy fucking

the ski instructor or whoever it was she ran off with. And like I said before, money don't buy you love, which is what that girl needs."

"So you think I should do it?"

"I think you should think about it," he said soberly. "I think you should think about it, and then you should demand a job title that will look good on your CV, and a contract that specifies time for research, and you should only sleep with him if you really want to."

"Um," I said. "Thanks for your advice."

"Anytime," he said. "So, you want me to be around when you meet with him next week?"

"Around?"

"You know, as a kind of invisible wingman? Just in case you need, like, someone to step in if things start getting weird."

"I doubt things would get weird with Madison there," I said.

"Tell you what: when's this meeting?"

"6:00pm, next Friday."

"Great. I'll be grading, or packing up my stuff, or whatever, then anyway, just as a way to avoid going home. So I'll walk you over to the meeting, and meet you afterwards, and walk you back to your car unless you tell me otherwise, okay?"

"Um...if it's no trouble?"

"Might as well put that Safe Walk training I did as a cadet to work," he said. "You know, escorting students around campus at night in matched male-female pairs of cadets? It seemed like complete shit to me at the time, but now I think it might have been the most useful thing I did, my entire time in the Navy. And it'll take me back to my idealistic youth to recreate that experience."

"Okay. If you don't mind."

"I more than don't mind. I insist."

"Okay. Thanks, Alex. I really appreciate it. I wish I could do the same for you when you go to Beirut."

"Oh Jesus." He groaned. "Don't remind me! But I'm afraid even a badass wingwoman like you can't protect me from what awaits me there. The humiliation will be mine alone to bear. Is this your car? You okay to get home from here?"

"Yeah, no problem. Where are you?"

"That piece of shit three cars down. You have an exam on Monday, right?"

"Right," I said. "8:00am Monday, Russian 101."

"Yeah, of course. See you Monday, then." He made an indecisive motion, like he was about to kiss my cheek, and then turned it into a squeeze of my arm before turning and going to his car. I waited until he had opened the door, swearing and kicking it to make it pop open, and gotten in, and then we drove out together in convoy, as if that would keep us safe from the intangible dangers that threatened us.

40

Nothing miraculous happened over the weekend to save me from whatever was awaiting me the following week. I spent some of my time working on another round of edits for the already-accepted article, which was slated to come out next summer *if* I could get the edits done in time. I wondered what Tsvetaeva would say to all of this. Probably insist proudly that she, as a true poet, was above all such nonsense, and hang herself rather than submit to the humiliation of living under a repressive regime. That option was looking more and more correct.

I also discovered by reading The Wiki that two more jobs and a postdoc I'd very laboriously applied for had all sent out their invitations to interview, and I hadn't gotten one. The Wiki entry for the postdoc was now a multi-page collection of wailing and lamentation, with applicants discussing everything from mailing the committee boxes of worn-out dirty socks (it would be cheaper, more satisfying, and remove old socks from the apartment, claimed the poster) to dropping out of academia and spending the rest of their lives gathering coconuts on a deserted island.

More realistically, many people were planning to go see if their local supermarket was looking for part-time baggers, and if they could move into their parents' basements, since whatever job they got, all their earnings were going to go to paying off their student loans. Probably to those on the outside it seemed somewhere between funny and pathetic. To those of us on the inside, it was very much a banality-of-evil experience.

To take my mind off my troubles I ran down to True Grit on Sunday morning and spent two dollars I shouldn't have spent on some coffee and conversation with Mike and Jimmy, where I couldn't help but feel them out about how they'd gotten their jobs collecting garbage. I'd never wanted to be a garbage collector before, but right now it didn't sound so bad. There was always a demand, and I could ride around holding onto the outside of one of those trucks, which might be fun, and end the day with the satisfaction of a job well done. And a long hot shower, providing I could afford to keep my water and electricity on, but at least it would be physical dirt, not an indelible moral stain. Easy to think when it's not your hands getting dirty. I wondered if white women with PhDs who looked vaguely like Elizabeth Taylor but with a yoga body could get jobs as sanitation workers. Almost certainly not, no matter how desperate we were. Back to high-class hustling and hooking, then, as my back-up plan.

No one in my 101 class was happy about the 8:00am final on Monday, and there was a lot of whining from some, a certain amount of falling asleep from others, and Vitya and Danila showed up half an hour late, smelling of cigarette smoke.

"For Christ's sake, you could have taken the test first and gone on your smoke break afterwards," I told them. "It won't take you more than half an hour anyway." Vitya and Danila were far from the best students in the class, at least when it came to the written work, but they never wasted much time agonizing over whether their answers were correct or not, which was normally the right choice on language tests. Vitya and Danila dashed off their test answers at stream-of-consciousness speed, and achieved results comparable to Ira, who carefully worked through every question—and then ended up writing something laughably illiterate anyway. Much to the heritage speakers' chagrin, learning to write in Russian involved learning all the spelling rules and endings, when it all sounded like a sort of "ee" sound to them. Instead of breezing through the course, they were having to work twice as hard as the non-heritage speakers in order to overcome their instincts, and were consequently doing poorly.

"Sorry, Prof," said Danila, not sounding very sorry. His steady string of B-minuses and Cs, not to mention my frequent expressions of displeasure at his behavior, rolled right off his back without effect, while Ira was in a state of angry despair over her B average, and jumped to find insult in my every word of praise.

"Yeah, sorry, Prof," echoed Vitya. "Can we have the listening comp questions?"

For a second I considered becoming one of those professors I despised and lecturing them on the sovereign importance of showing up to exams on time, and how they'd forfeited the chance to hear the listening comprehension questions by arriving at their final half an hour late, especially since they'd obviously been using the time to smoke, how my patience had limits, they had to learn to be more responsible, actions had consequences, blah blah blah.

"Sure, no problem," I said, swallowing down my worst impulses. Being a jerk to Danila and Vitya would only piss them off, hamper whatever acquisition of Russian they might have made otherwise, and generally turn me into a bully and a petty tyrant. "Why don't you go sit in the back corner, so it doesn't bother the others."

"Thanks, Prof; you're the best." Both boys gave me grateful smiles.

"No, I just enjoy drawing out your torment," I told them, which made them laugh.

Monday was the 15th, the last day of my contract. I had assumed that I would remain in the system long enough to enter my final grades, but when I went to enter them for 101 into The Den on

Wednesday morning, I was locked out and had to make a trip to
The Bear Cave to beg for help, which at first they wouldn't give me
because I was technically no longer an employee at TLASC. The fact
that for once the TLASC administration was working efficiently,
just when they needed it to work inefficiently in order to wring the
last drops of work out of me, was one of those funny little ironies in
life.

The 201 final was at 2:00pm on Friday, in the very last slot of
exam week. Lucky me to get the first and last exam times. After the
grading fiasco of Wednesday, I was afraid that I would be locked out
of the classroom, but TLASC's old-fashioned lock-and-key system
instead of card readers meant that I was able to let us all into our tiny
little room.

If anything, the students were even more surly than they had
been in 101. It was a cold miserable day, with a kind of a slushy
wet snow/sleet coming down, which had revealed all the leaks in my
boots and rendered ballet flats entirely out of the question, forcing
me to wear my sneakers. If anyone thought anything of the fact
that I was wearing electric blue running shoes to a final, they kept
it to themselves. Probably they were too busy thinking about how
they wanted to get this over with and go home. I had offered those
who lived far away the opportunity to take the exam during the 101
exam time so that they could go home early, but strangely enough,
no one had taken me up on that offer. Now, on this cold, dark
Friday afternoon one week before Christmas, they were regretting
that choice.

Afterwards Riva came up to me to give me a fistful of chocolate
Hanukkah gelt and tell me how sad it was that I was leaving and
would I be anywhere nearby next semester and what should she do if
she needed a letter of recommendation? I gave her my non-TLASC
email address—my TLASC email address was still working, but I
was already getting threatening messages about how it would expire

in 30 days—and told her I'd be happy to provide her with a recommendation whenever she needed it.

"Don't worry," I heard Adam tell her as they exited together. "Professor Cahill's really cool too." Which was nice but also sad.

Madison was the last to finish, and came dancing up to me with her completed exam, high, as far as I could tell, on natural exuberance rather than cocaine, although with her the two tended to run together.

"We'll be seeing each other again in just a little bit, won't we, Professor!" she said, shoving the completed exam into my hands.

"In just"—I checked my phone—"about two hours."

"Oh. Yeah. So, what are you going to do between now and then?"

"Probably get some grading done," I said, trying to sound more enthusiastic about it than I was.

"Oh, yeah, I guess so. Can I come with you?"

"To do what?"

She shrugged. "I don't know. I don't have anywhere else to go. I mean, other than my dad's office, but I can't go *there*. It, like, sucks."

"My office is a lot less nice," I told her.

"Yeah, but it's gotta be better than *there*!"

"Can't you, I don't know, go to the library or something?"

She looked so disappointed at my words that I backtracked and said, "It's just that there isn't a lot of space in the office. But you're welcome to come and hang out if you want to and you can avoid bothering anyone who's grading."

"Thanks, Professor H!"

But when I had walked and she had skipped along behind me across the leaking skywalk to the adjunct office, we found Alex, Emma, and Kate all there and all bent over piles of exams, looking harried. Madison took them in at a glance and said, without prompting, "Maybe I should go hang out with my dad, Professor."

"Probably a good idea," I agreed. "And I'll see you at six, okay?"

"Sure thing, Professor! See you then!" She skipped off like it was a beautiful morning in May, not a sleety December evening.

41

"**W**as that a student?" asked Emma, looking up from her frightening pile of exams covered in what appeared to be beginner attempts at Chinese characters. I wondered what would be worse: deciphering first-year Cyrillic or first-year Chinese. I looked over at Alex's pile of papers. Maybe Arabic beat us both out. "Why was she so cheerful?"

"She's just a cheerful girl," I said.

"Was that Madison?" asked Alex.

"Uh-huh."

"And you're still going to meet with her at 6:00?"

"Uh-huh."

"You're meeting with a student at 6:00pm on the last day of finals?" asked Emma. "What for?"

"She asked me to," I said.

Emma made a face. Alex refrained from saying anything about how it was really her father, the Provost, who had asked, but I could see him thinking it. Instead he stood up and offered me his seat.

"No, that's fine. I can"—I cast around for a place to work—"sit on the floor. You were here first."

"Nah, I need a break. I've been here for two hours and I can't handle another minute of it. And I have also agreed to meet with a student on the Friday afternoon of exam week. Justin," he added, looking at me significantly. "We're going to meet in the library in a

few minutes. So I'll just go on over right now, but I'll be back in a
bit."

"That's nice of you," said Kate, while Emma pursed her lips at
both of us as if our zeal personally offended her. Which it probably
did.

"Yeah," said Alex. "Okay, I'm off. Don't do anything I wouldn't
do. Text me if something changes, Rowena." He slung a bag over each
shoulder and left.

As soon as he was gone, Kate and Emma both turned to me. "Is
there something going on between you two?" Kate asked, looking
hopeful. An office romance would certainly brighten up everyone's
shitty semester.

"Not like what you're thinking," I said. "He's going to walk me
back to my car after my meeting. You know, like a campus Safe Walk
thing."

"That's so gallant," said Kate, a misty look in her eye. "I know
we're supposed to be feminists and everything, but I wish a man
would offer to walk me to my car sometimes when it's dark out."

"Using the buddy system to walk around dangerous places in the
dark isn't anti-feminist, it's smart," I said.

"Yeah...it's different if it's a *man,* though," said Kate, still with a
misty look in her eyes. "Not that I would know. I've been walked
home maybe once in my life, I think."

"Yeah," said Emma sullenly.

They both turned to me expectantly.

"It's a common thing in Russia," I said.

"Really?" said Kate. "You don't think of Russian men as being,
well, gallant."

"Either they're super-gallant, or they're predators," I said.
"Sometimes both. Either way they're probably going to insist on
walking you home. And rightly so, although most of the streets of
Moscow are probably safer than the streets of New Brunswick."

"Oh." Kate looked taken aback. "Well. That sounds...I don't know..."

"It makes you tough," I said. "Do you have a lot of grading left?"

We segued into complaints about grading, which ended with both Emma and Kate calling it a day, but with Kate making me promise to meet up with her for coffee at some as-yet-undefined time over the weekend, and Emma giving me a half-hearted "Keep in touch" as she went out the door.

At 5:30, when I had graded enough exams that I was starting to think about giving up and moseying very slowly over to Angelo as a way to kill the time, I heard people coming down the hall, talking.

I poked my head out the door, expecting to see Alex and Justin. Instead I saw Alex and John Greene.

"I really don't think it's appropriate..." John Greene was saying. I pulled my head back into the office, hoping they hadn't noticed me eavesdropping, but I could still hear them. Both men were speaking loudly, almost shouting, obviously well into what was turning into an argument.

"I have to be able to meet with my students somewhere," Alex said. "I don't have a private office. And you could say that the coffee shop is more appropriate than the office anyway. It's public. It's impossible for anything inappropriate to happen there by definition."

"But it looks like...socializing! It looks like it could be a, a...a date!"

"I hope I can tell the difference between a date and a meeting with a student. For starters, because in my case the first would take place with someone within ten years of my own age and of the opposite sex, whom I found attractive. None of the three applied in this case."

"Yes, but, you have to admit, it looks...it could be construed..."

"What could be construed? What are we going to do? Do we
need to perform thorough examinations of our students' sexual
preferences, as well as our own, before admitting them into our
classes, to make sure that our male instructors never have contact
with any gay men? Or with, because this is a much more serious
issue, female students of any sort? That doesn't strike you as a little
intrusive? For crying out loud, John, I was in the Navy! I know
all about these kinds of baseless rumors! And about the real abuses
that go on behind them! But what are you going to do? If you're
so worried about the possibility of a hint of impropriety from an
instructor meeting with a student in Starbucks, and you for some
reason think that private offices would be better—*which they won't*,
because they're private—then you damn well need to start providing
your faculty with private offices! Otherwise we're just going to have
to keep meeting with our students in coffee shops, if not our cars!"

"In your cars!"

"Haven't you heard? It's the new meeting place of choice for
today's adjunct instructor."

"Well...surely those rumors are greatly exaggerated..."

"Probably less greatly exaggerated than any rumors you've heard
about me! What rumors *have* you heard, anyway? Have there been
any complaints? And if so, why haven't *I* heard about it?"

"Well...no complaints...no complaints at all...but we all have to
be careful, Alex; you know that. We're like the Emperor's wife, above
even the whisper of suspicion. You don't want to find out how much
trouble even a baseless rumor can cause you!"

"I'm sure," said Alex more calmly. "I'm not denying that it could
be a problem. But seriously, John: where else am I going to meet with
my students? We have more instructors than chairs in the office now.
So what should I do? Set up trysts in the basement?"

"Don't call them trysts! Of course I realize you're in a difficult
position, and I wish there were something the department could do

to improve that...maybe when this new funding reaches us...but in the meantime...you just looked so *cozy* with him. You looked"—John Greene's voice took on a spiteful, envious tinge—"like you were friends."

"And we are. Of a very particular, Platonic sort. Look, John: I'm sorry if it seems...I don't know, if it bothered you. But there really is nothing inappropriate going on, and frankly *I* think it's inappropriate to assume that there would be. Especially since we can't go outing students without their permission!"

"You're right." John Greene was now speaking in a more conciliatory tone. "You're right. I'm sorry. I just...you know how much I care about the department. I don't want anything to jeopardize this funding that could come in. You must know, Alex, that if we don't get this money, we will be in serious trouble, and frankly, Arabic will be one of the first things to be cut. While if we *do* get the money..."

"I understand," said Alex dryly. "Believe me, I really do. And I'm not going to do anything to endanger the money, I swear on a stack of Bibles. Which is why I was meeting with this student on the Friday evening after finals."

"Really?" asked John Greene, sounding hopeful, like this would make him understand Alex better.

"No," said Alex. "I was meeting with him because he needed me to. But it did not fail to occur to me that it could also be beneficial to me and to the department to do so."

"Oh. Oh. Well, very good. I'm, um, sorry I snapped at you. It's just...it's been a very difficult semester, on so many levels. And I, uh, just had your best interests at heart."

"I'm sure you did," said Alex. I hoped the disbelief in his voice was less clear to John Greene than it was to me. "The department is lucky to have someone like you looking out for it."

"Oh! Oh, well, that's very kind of you, Alex. It's nice to feel appreciated for all the extra work you put in, as I'm sure you know all too well, working these extra hours as you do. Speaking of which: why don't you go home now?"

"In a bit," said Alex. "But maybe *you* should go home and get some rest. Like you said, it's been a heck of a semester."

"Oh! That's very kind of you. And I think I will, just as soon as I answer a few more emails. Goodness, is it almost quarter to six? My wife will be wondering where I am. She always likes to keep track of my movements, you know." John Greene emitted one of his high-pitched little laughs. "A sign of devotion, you know. We've been *very* happily married for, oh, almost thirty years now."

"You're a lucky man," said Alex. "Enjoy your break."

"Thank you, and, ah, you too, Alex." There was the sound of a heavy, ungainly man walking down the hall, and then going through the door into his office.

Alex came into the adjunct warehouse and threw his bags down on the floor. "Jesus fucking Christ, did you hear that?" he demanded. "John Greene damn near accused me of improprieties with a student! He came bustling up to me and Justin while we were sitting in Starbucks, said he *had* to talk to me right away and sent Justin away without so much as a fucking by-your-leave, and marched me back here, filling my ear with dire threats all the way! I cannot fucking *believe* that motherfucker!"

"Ah, well," I said. "I'm sure that was very unpleasant. But, um, John Greene"—I lowered my voice to a whisper even though I was sure he couldn't hear us—"may know what he was talking about."

"Really? Do tell." Alex sat down at the table, his face avid.

"Um, well...I heard...third-hand...that there were some emails...nothing substantive, you know, just some emails that *were* maybe a little too friendly, between him and a male student."

Alex burst out laughing.

"Don't tell him! I shouldn't have told you! There was nothing to it!"

"Yeah, but...oh, I promise I won't breathe a word of it, but it's just too delicious! Did you hear him, all that 'My wife is waiting for me' and 'Happily married for almost thirty years'?" Alex started laughing again.

"Yeah, I know. I kind of feel sorry for him."

"Oh, whatever. Speaking of inappropriate behavior, it's high time to get you to your meeting with the Provost, don't you think?"

"Let's go," I said. "The sooner you go to jail, the sooner you get out."

"Nice," said Alex appreciatively. "I'll have to start saying that myself."

42

The earlier sleet and slush had turned to actual snow, which ghosted down in magical swirls in the light of the old-fashioned street lamps and the Christmas lights that had been put up all over campus. Although the security lights didn't work in the more remote areas of campus, like the walk to the faculty parking lot behind the football stadium, the Christmas decorations here on the front quad were impressively lavish, and the lynching trees by the entrance had been transformed into fairy wonderlands.

"Fuck, it's cold," said Alex, pulling his collar around his neck. "Oh, sh...I mean, I didn't see you there, Justin."

"Sorry, Professor Miller! I didn't mean to startle you. I just...I mean, I guess I wanted to wish you a Merry Christmas. And make sure you were okay."

"That *I* was okay?" repeated Alex.

"Yeah. I mean"—Justin shifted uneasily from foot to foot, shivering in the snowy wind—"that guy, he, like, I don't know, he just seemed...really upset about something. I wanted to make sure you hadn't, like, gotten into trouble. Because of me."

"No," said Alex. "Everything's fine. But that was really nice of you, Justin."

"Yeah. And, um...I guess you're busy?"

"A bit."

"It's okay," I said quickly. "If Justin wants to talk to you, you should talk to him. I'll go myself."

Alex opened his mouth to object. "I'm just going to Angelo Hall," I said. "It will be well-lit the whole way. You can pick me up afterwards, and we can walk to the parking lot together."

Alex stood there in indecision for a moment, before nodding his head and saying, "Right. Text me if you need anything, okay?"

"Of course," I said. "Nice to see you, Justin."

"Yeah, you too, Professor Halley. And I hope you have a Merry Christmas!"

"Thanks," I said, and set off, head down, into the wind.

I crisscrossed the front quad, staying between the chains. I was cutting around Morrison Hall, preparing to cross the back quad to Angelo and checking my phone to see if I was already late, when a dark figure stepped out in front of me, startling me.

"Oh jeez!" I cried. "Oh, hey! Mackenzie! What are you doing out this late?"

"Oh, hi, Professor Halley! What are *you* doing out this late?"

"I have a meeting with Madison."

"Oh." Mackenzie made a little face, as she often did when Madison's name came up. "Well...that's very nice of you. Hey, have you seen Justin?"

"Justin?" I repeated. "Like, the Justin who studies Arabic? Tennis-player Justin?"

"Yeah, that's the one. I'm supposed to pick him up and drive him home."

"That's nice. I guess you're all still friends after everything that happened?"

"Yeah. I mean, yes, we're still friends, but we don't have a choice about it. Justin and I are first cousins."

"You are?"

"Yeah. You didn't know? Our grandfather is Vinnie Angelo. You know, who used to be mayor?"

"Oh," I said. Suddenly Justin's fear of his father seemed a lot more justified. I didn't know much about Vinnie Angelo, but I had to guess that, for all that he might crave WASP-y upper-class intellectual respectability, having a biracial, tennis-playing, gay grandson might be going a little too far down that road for him, and probably for his son as well.

"Funny that you're having a meeting, Professor," continued Mackenzie blithely. "My dad's *also* having a meeting right now! That's why I'm here. I'm supposed to pick up Justin and give him a ride home while his dad and my dad are at this meeting."

"Oh," I said. "Well, last I saw Justin, he was on the front quad, by Dreme, but he was talking to Professor Miller."

"Oh, well, maybe I should give them a few minutes, what do you think? I know he was supposed to meet with Professor Miller earlier, but it sounds like they're not done yet. I'll just"—she shivered—"I don't know. It's awfully cold." She looked over her shoulder, to where Angelo Hall loomed in the darkness behind us. "Maybe I'll go and sit in the lobby there and text Justin to come meet me when he's ready."

"Good idea," I said. I started walking briskly towards the front door of Angelo, acutely aware that I was now late for my meeting with Madison and her father. Not that being five minutes late should matter, especially since I was doing them a favor, but I was used to parceling out my day in tiny increments, and being even a minute late to a meeting with a student had been drilled into me as being one of the greatest of crimes.

But once I'd dropped Mackenzie off in the half-lit lobby of Angelo and hurried down into the half-lit basement, I found, not Provost Johnson waiting impatiently as I'd expected, but Madison pacing fretfully by herself outside the locked classroom.

"Hi, Madison," I said. "Where's your dad?"

"I think I did a bad thing, Professor H."

I walked over closer to her. A trickle of blood was coming out of one nostril, and her pupils were so dilated I couldn't make out the iris.

Don't scream at her! I told myself.

"How much coke did you just take, Madison?" I asked, trying to keep my voice level and non-judgmental.

She shrugged, which turned into a whole-body twitch. She was fidgeting from foot to foot, almost skipping in place, her hands roaming restlessly over her thighs like no part of her could bear to remain still even for a second.

"I dunno. A line. Maybe two. It doesn't matter." A tear started down from her right eye and trickled into the smear of blood around her right nostril.

"Yes it does. Here." I made to hand her a tissue from the packet in my purse. "Jesus Christ, Maddie, you're burning up!"

"I know." She crossed her arms over her chest and started jumping up and down.

"Seriously, Maddie, what's your heart rate? You look like you're ODing."

"I dunno. High."

"Can I check?"

Another tear trickled down from her right eye. "You shouldn't be so nice to me, Professor H." She uncrossed her arms and started pulling convulsively at her collar, trying to open it and get some air but too panicked and too high to make her hands work properly.

"Here, let me." I unzipped her jacket collar and the hoodie she was wearing underneath. When she didn't resist, I put my hand against her neck.

"Christ, Maddie, your pulse is really high. Where's your dad? I really think you should go to urgent care right now."

"Outside. I don't know. I don't care. I did a really bad thing,
Professor H."

"It's okay."

"It's not!"

"Let's not worry about it right now, Maddie," I said, making my
voice low and calm and my body unthreatening, as if I were talking
to a frightened animal. "We can fix it later, okay? Right now let's go
outside."

"Why?"

"To cool you down. You're overheating. You'll feel better once
we're outside. And can you call your dad?"

She shook her head violently. "No. Not him. Not him! And my
phone's dead, anyway. But don't call him!"

"Okay. Don't worry about it. Let's just go out, you and me, okay?
We won't bring your dad into it until you're ready. Can you walk?"

"I can walk just fine!"

"Great. Let's just walk, nice and easy, out the front door."

"Not the front door! *They're* out there! I saw them go by earlier."

"Okay," I said. "How shall we get out, then?"

"The back door."

She started jogging erratically down the hall. I jogged after her.
We went past empty classrooms and around a sharp corner into a
dark corridor with FIRE glowing redly above a door I could barely
make out in the gloom.

"No, wait, Maddie, that's a fire do..."

She burst through the door, and I sprinted forward and burst
through after her. Alarms exploded behind us, but we were already
out into the snowy emptiness behind Angelo Hall.

"What the fuck!" exclaimed a man.

There were half-a-dozen men gathered around in a semi-circle,
standing in the darkness where the security lights didn't penetrate in

the back of Angelo Hall. Where the dead janitor had been found, and where there were no security cameras.

"It's her! Grab her!" shouted one of the men.

My "danger" senses, honed through years of living in a bad place talking to bad people, went off louder than the alarms behind us. Thrusting my purse into the rapidly-closing door to stop it from slamming shut on us and locking us outside, I grabbed Madison's arm and, not waiting for the men to identify themselves or for Madison to give her permission, dragged her, our feet sliding in the slushy snow, back into the building, heaving open the door and heaving her through it with strength I didn't know I possessed, and pulled it closed as hard as I could.

"That was Mackenzie's dad," Madison said. Or I thought she said. Her voice was breaking up, like a tape being played at too high a speed.

"Come on," I said. Heavy fists were hammering and tugging at the door. "Come on, Maddie! Run, Maddie, run!"

We ran down the dark corridor, Madison's cocaine-enhanced muscles allowing her to keep pace with mine, honed by years of practice and training. I hoped her heart didn't give out before I could get her to a hospital.

We sprinted up the stairs and across the half-lit lobby. Snow swirled against the big glass windows in front. No dark figures were looming menacingly into view. Yet. They would have to go all the way around the building, sliding through the slippery snow on top of mud, and jumping over the black chains that kept miscreants from cutting across the landscaping.

"What..." Mackenzie was sitting in the lobby where I had left her.

"Get out of here, Mackenzie!" I shouted as I raced past her, Madison at my heels.

"What...Oh, there's my dad."

I slammed through the front door so hard I expected it to shatter, but it only flew open and bounced harmlessly against the edge of the frame. Hands materialized out of the dark, grabbing at me, grabbing at Madison, but we slithered out of them and then they pulled back, stopped by Mackenzie's voice demanding to know what was going on, what was her father doing, and should she call 911.

We sprinted across the back quad, Madison laughing hysterically as she ran behind me. The most direct way to where I wanted to go was straight across the quad, to the library. The library would have lights, emergency call boxes, maybe even helpful friendly people. The goddamn black chains were in the way. I hurdled over the first one without breaking stride. Madison, to my surprise, did so a step behind me. We ran straight across the quad, hurdling the second black chain and ending up back on the walkway. There was a beautiful blue emergency call box on a pole, there by the front door to the library.

As I got closer I could see that the library had already shut. I slammed my palm against the button on the call box.

"Hello!" I shouted into it. "Can you hear me? Hello! Hello!"

There was no answer and no dial tone. The box was dead.

43

"They're coming," Madison said behind me. "They're coming!" She tugged at my sleeve anxiously, but hysterical laughter still bubbled out from her lips, which shone darkly in the orange semi-light of the streetlights from the blood that was now running freely from her nose.

I looked back. The men were coming down the path after us, jogging almost casually, not bothering to jump the chains and cut across the quad as we had. Probably they thought they had us cornered.

"Come on," I said, and pushed Madison into the darkness.

There was a garden of boxwood shrubs in front of the library. The grounds crew had never gotten around to chaining it off, or maybe they had taken pity on people who needed to take the shortest way from the back quad to the football stadium. We ducked into the boxwoods, which were tall enough to shelter us, and wove our way back and forth through the slush between them, following the narrow footpath that had been worn down by generations of lazy students and faculty who couldn't be bothered with taking the real path.

We wound through the boxwoods around the side of the library, till the path dumped us out onto the main sidewalk. I risked slowing down long enough to take a quick look in either direction. No one. Maybe I was crazy and no one was chasing us. Maybe they weren't

chasing us very hard because they knew we had no way out of here
that didn't involve getting past them.

We ran at full tilt around the football stadium. Its wall seemed to
go on and on and on, a never-ending nightmare that would forever
keep us from safety, while revealing us to our pursuers as we ran
in our dark clothes against its high white concrete walls. Madison's
hysterical laughter morphed into hysterical crying.

"I can't run anymore," she said, grabbing my arm and trying to
slow me down.

"Just a little farther," I promised her. "Just there!"

I put on a last turn of speed, and she, inspired by me or maybe
by cocaine, leapt forward too. We dashed across the terrifyingly open
and empty doublewide sidewalk, and then we were in the safety and
concealing darkness of the faculty parking garage.

I had parked in the far corner of the ground level. I could even
make out my car through the twilight. I reached into my purse,
which I had somehow held onto all this while, and pulled out my
keys. Now we just had to make our way across the garage into my car
without getting caught, and escape. I was uncomfortably aware that
being in a car would limit our maneuverability. But it would provide
some protection, and once I got it out of the garage, we could speed
away to the nearest place where there were people, maybe friendly
helpful police officers...

"I don't feel good," Madison murmured.

"I'm not surprised. Come on. Let's go get in my car. Then I'll
drive you to the ER."

She groaned. I opened my mouth to tell her not to whine about
the ER and to get her ass moving towards my car. Before I could
say those words, she clutched at her chest and groaned again, even
louder.

"I don't feel so good," she said again.

"Okay. Can you make it to my car?"

She shook her head and, still clutching her chest, slithered down the wall she had been leaning against to end up sitting on the cold concrete.

"Can't walk," she said. "Chest hurts. Can't breathe."

"Okay. You wait here. I'm going to go get my car and come pick you up."

"Where the fuck are they?" said a man's voice.

"They gotta be in the garage."

"Go check around the other side of the stadium, make sure they haven't gotten out already and are heading into the woods. Then we'll set up a cordon, call for reinforcements, start searching for them. We can't let the girl get away; she knows too much. They both know too much, now."

Madison and I stared at each other in horror. I grabbed her arm, and without saying a word, dragged her into the only shelter I could think of, the stairwell to the upper levels of the garage.

"They're going to find us," Madison whispered.

"I know." My move had been the instinctive going to ground of the hunted animal, but now we were trapped in the stairwell, with no way to lock the door and nowhere to go but up onto the roof. I sat us down on the floor against the door. The window in the door was small and high up; maybe by crouching right underneath it we could stay hidden.

"I think they had guns," Madison whispered. She was shaking all over and still clutching at her chest, her breath coming in jerky, uneven gasps.

"Me too."

"Do you have a gun?"

"No. And the only gun I know how to shoot anyway is a Makarov."

"What's a Makarov?"

Why were we having this absurd whispered conversation when people could be about to shoot us with something just as deadly as a Makarov? But we were. "It's a kind of Russian pistol."

"Oh." Madison seemed to be calming down now that we were sitting down and talking. So I needed to keep doing it. No point in getting away from the bad guys only to have her drop dead from a heart attack. "How'd you learn to shoot one?" she whispered.

"My boyfriend taught me."

"Oh. I wish he was here."

"Yeah, me too. A semi-psychotic ex-OMON officer with a death wish would come in real handy right about now. But he's not here. It's just us, Madison. It's up to us to get ourselves out of this."

She hugged her knees up against her chest. "I don't think I can."

"You can."

She shook her head. "I don't think I should. I did a bad thing, Professor H."

"It's doesn't matter."

"It does."

"We'll worry about it later."

She shook her head again. "Maybe there won't be a later, Professor H. Maybe there shouldn't be. Not for me." Tears, blood, snot, and melting snow were all running freely down her face. She scrubbed at them, but only spread them around more.

"Fuck it," I said. "I'm sure as hell getting both of us the fuck out of here, no matter what *you're* planning."

She almost smiled. "How're you gonna do that, Professor H?"

"Shh. I'm going to see if they're coming for us." I slowly, so slowly it was like I was hardly moving at all, slid up the door until I could peer out the little mesh-filled window. Nothing. They must be circling the stadium and surrounding the garage before they started a methodical search. Or maybe they were bumbling around incompetently. But it would be safer to assume they were encircling the building before starting a methodical search.

"Okay," I said, sliding back down. "I think we're safe for the moment. How do you feel?"

"A little better."

"Good. Just keep taking deep, slow breaths, okay?"

"Okay."

I reached into my purse and pulled out my phone. Which was cracked almost in half. It must have caught the full brunt of the door, back when I had used my purse as a doorstop. I pushed hopefully on the home button anyway. Nothing.

"My phone's dead too," Madison whispered. "I forgot to charge it this afternoon. I was so excited about meeting you and talking about programs that would help me get my life in order." More tears ran down her face.

"Okay. It's okay. The police probably wouldn't get here in time anyway. We need to get to my car. Do you think you can walk?"

"Maybe."

"Good." I slowly slid back up the door and peeked out the window again. Still nothing. "Okay," I said. "This is what we're going to do. I'm going to run and get my car...no, we should go together. Once they hear a car start, they'll be right on top of us. We're going to run together to my car, get in it as fast as possible, you're going to crouch down on the floor, and I'm going to drive like a bat out of hell until we're out of here. Okay?"

"What about the gate?" she asked. "We'll have to stop for the gate."

"Not if we blow right through it."

She gave the ghost of a grin. "I wish I felt better," she said. "I wish people weren't trying to catch us. 'Cause then this would be fun."

"Yeah," I said. "That's the problem with stuff like this. Okay, you ready?"

She nodded. I put my arm around her and helped her get to her feet.

"Okay," I said in her ear. "I'm going to push open the door, and then we're going to run as quickly and quietly as we can possibly run, over to the far corner where my car is."

There was a soft noise, like someone opening a heavy door very gently. We stared in horror at our door. It remained shut. Then we both looked up. Barely audible footsteps were coming down the stairs. Someone had found us.

44

My legs were already flexing to push Madison through the door, when a voice called out softly, "Rowena? Are you down there?"

"Oh my God." My knees actually sagged with relief, and I staggered against the door, almost pushing it open anyway. "Stay here," I whispered to Madison, and started up the stairs.

Alex was sidling stealthily but quickly against the wall. When he saw me, he ran the rest of the way down and met me on the landing. "Oh my God," he said. "I thought..."

"How'd you get up here?" I asked.

"I saw you running from them and I figured you'd take cover here, so I crawled through the bushes around to the back of the garage, and then climbed up onto the top floor and started working my way down. Good thing I like rock climbing, huh?"

"Yeah," I said. "Do you know where they are?"

"Most of them are on the road outside the garage, hoping you'll come out and stumble into their trap. At least one is doing a sweep around the garage. So we need to move fast."

"Okay. Is your car here?"

"Yeah, on the first level, in the same bay as yours."

"Okay. We have to get out of here before reinforcements arrive."

"I couldn't agree more. You get Madison into your car and you both follow me out and then you drive like motherfuckers for the campus exit. Don't stop no matter what."

"What about you?"

"You need someone to create a diversion, draw their fire, act as bait, stuff like that. So that'll be me."

"Um...okay."

"I mean, that's what I was trained to do, right? Well not really, but sort of. I might as well put it to use. Time for me to release my inner Maverick, no matter how much he's been in hiding my whole life. I mean, I spent my entire deployment in an actual war zone sitting in a glorified filing closet writing reports and making PowerPoints. Now's the moment for Uncle Sam's training dollars to earn their keep."

"Um...I guess."

"Come on. Let's go get Madison."

We went down the stairs back to where Madison was waiting for us by the door. She was curled up in a ball on the floor.

"Madison!" I hissed. I ran over and shook her. She moaned.

"Come on, Madison, sit up, you have to sit up!" I pulled her upright and leaned her against the wall. "You might be, um, having a cardiac event. You need to remain upright."

"My chest hurts so bad," she gasped.

"Yeah. Alex! Alex. Go get your car. Go get your car right now!"

I thought Alex was going to argue, but after a second he nodded curtly, looked out through the window, and then slid through the door and set off, bent double and sprinting from car to car.

I knelt down by Madison. "Alex is going to get his car and bring it over here, and then we're going to load you into it and take you to the ER," I told her.

"Won't they hear us and come get us?"

"Alex is going to drive real fast."

"Okay. Real fast. They're bad people."

"I know."

She shook her head. "No. You don't. See, I did a bad thing, I told you. I didn't stop with the blackmail like I promised I would. I mean, I stopped with Justin, but then I found other stuff, other stuff from Justin's emails. I figured out who Justin's dad was. He's mafia. I mean, everyone's kind of mafia here, but he's really mafia, with casinos and drugs and all that stuff. And I followed the trail, got into his emails as well. And I found out"—her breath was coming in such short gasps I could barely make her words out—"I found out what they're doing. With Angelo Hall. They're taking money, Superstorm Sandy money they shouldn't be taking but also money, from, like, drugs and stuff, and laundering it through the building. They had a whole deal with the university. Pay for the building, and then get offices and stuff out of it, plus some of their money back. And stuff like Justin and his brother and Mackenzie and her brother got full ride scholarships. Half a million dollars' worth of scholarships. Is it really that expensive to go here?"

"Yes," I said. "So did you approach Justin about this?"

She made a spasmodic movement that was probably supposed to indicate "no." "I went to Justin's brother. I met him once through Brandy. We had a party...But the emails said he was in on it. So I went to him, and I asked...I asked for cocaine."

"And he gave it to you."

"A little. But then, this afternoon, after I left you, Justin's brother found me on the quad and said if I didn't shut up and leave them alone, they would do to me what they did to Brandy."

"What did they do to Brandy?"

"Benzos," she whispered. "Brandy was addicted to benzos. He'd take coke sometimes, for fun, and he liked to drink, but he was seriously addicted to benzos. That's what killed him. Justin's brother was his supplier, once his shrink cut him off. Justin's brother found out that Brandy was being a shit to him, and started giving him more and more, for free, hoping he'd get out of their hair. Brandy probably didn't mean to kill himself. The note about that bitch in the Russian club was just because he was pissed off with me for what I'd done, blackmailing him and all. But he was trying to get back together with Justin, so I think"—she swallowed—"I think someone, probably Justin's brother, went over to him and got him drunk and got him to take a bunch of benzos. Or maybe just made him feel so bad he took them on his own. And you know what happens if you mix alcohol with benzos."

"Uh-huh," I said.

"And so I went to my dad and told him everything! After I left you and Justin's brother found me, I was...I was scared, and mad, and so I went to my dad, and he got really mad and said I shouldn't have said anything out loud, some things are best kept quiet, and he sent me away and told me to go stay with you, so I wouldn't get in any more trouble, and he started making phone calls, and I...I got scared, I thought I needed something, Justin's brother had given me some stuff, and I thought: might as well get some use out of it. I thought it was just a little, it would just give me a little energy. But it gave me a lot. I think it might be stronger than I'm used to. Maybe on purpose. And now I don't feel so good."

The sound of a car starting up was followed closely by shouts.

"Madison," I said. "You've been very brave. Can you get into the car by yourself?"

"I think so."

"Okay. Let's get you up." I put my arms around her and lifted her to her feet, and then helped her through the stairwell door. Alex was driving up to us, his passenger door already open. Men were running through the parking garage gate, shouting and waving guns.

"When I push you into the car, I want you to throw yourself on the floor and stay down there, okay?" I said.

She nodded.

"Okay. Here we go!" I took the two steps up to where Alex's car was slowing down, Madison under my arm, and shoved her into the passenger seat. "Drive fast!" I shouted to Alex. "Get Maddie to an ER!"

"Get in!"

"You need someone to create a diversion, draw their fire, act as bait. That'll be me."

"God *damn* it, Rowena!"

The men were already inside the parking garage. I slammed the door shut behind Madison, stood tall for a moment to make sure the men saw me, and took off in the opposite direction.

45

I shot through the ground-level pedestrian exit, ending up back on the doublewide sidewalk between the parking garage and the stadium. No one. Maybe my plan hadn't worked and they were all going after Alex and Madison, shooting them down even now...no shots.

I ran around the stadium, its high white walls once again seeming like something out of an endless nightmare. I could hear cursing behind me. I looked back. Two figures were shambling after me, trying to catch me but slipping in the wet snow, hampered by their heavy clothes and their guns and their general lack of fitness.

When I came out around the stadium and onto the main campus, two more figures were rounding the stadium from the other direction. A car that looked like Alex's was speeding down the road with two more figures chasing after it on foot. One stopped and fired after the car, but missed, and the other figure started berating the shooter, maybe for missing, maybe for shooting and drawing attention to what they were doing.

I ran past the bookstore, which was dark and shuttered, and onto the front quad. There was a safety call box in front of Dreme Hall. Maybe it would be working better than the one in front of the library. Maybe not. Maybe it would draw the attention of my pursuers long enough for Alex and Madison to get away. I sprinted across the quad, hurdling the chains, and skidded to a stop in front of the call box, which emitted a reassuring blue glow.

Just as I was raising my hand to hit the call button, the front door to Dreme Hall opened.

"Rowena? What are you doing here?"

It was John Greene. Standing behind him was the Provost.

"Quick!" I said. "Call 911!"

"What? Why? What's going on?"

I looked back. My pursuers had slowed to a walk, and were advancing uncertainly across the quad.

"They're chasing me." I looked at Provost Johnson. "It's Madison," I told him. "They want Madison. And she's sick. Alex is taking her to the ER."

He pulled out his cell phone but didn't dial. "Which ER?" he asked.

"I don't know!" I looked back over my shoulder. The four men chasing me had now joined up and were walking across the quad, taking their time.

I dithered. Run inside Dreme Hall and hope to find cover? Or stay out in the open and rely on my superior speed? "They're coming for me!" I repeated. "Call 911!"

"Why are they chasing you?" demanded John Greene. "Are they rapists?"

"Maybe," I said, in the hopes that that would spur him to action. "Can we lock the door? Let's get inside!"

"I suppose we could lock the door to my office," said John Greene slowly, as if this were a classroom problem and we had all the time in the world to solve it.

"Come..." Before I could finish what I wanted to say, or grab him and run into the building, there was a shout. The remaining two men had joined the four slowly advancing across the quad.

"Don't run," one of them called. "Run and we'll shoot."

"Shoot!" cried John Greene in horror.

"Hands up!" the speaker called. He raised his hand. A handgun glinted in the light from the old-fashioned streetlamps.

John Greene raised his hands. So did the Provost. After a moment, so did I. After all, I couldn't outrun a bullet, and the longer I held them, the more time Alex and Madison had to get away and get to the hospital.

All six men came over to us and surrounded us.

"Mack," said the Provost. "Vinnie Junior. Nice to see you."

"You told us you had everything under control!" said a big man, the one the Provost had called Mack. "You told us you had *them* under control!"

"And I do," said Provost Johnson. "They're right here."

"Not your daughter!"

"She's not going to say anything."

"I don't know. She seems pretty mouthy to me."

A muscle in Provost Johnson's jaw jumped, but he said, still speaking as smoothly and calmly as if we were at some kind of a donor meeting, which we were, "I assure you, she won't say anything."

"Yeah. We'll make sure of that. What about her?" Mack nodded at me.

"You won't say anything either, will you, Rowena?" the Provost said.

I shook my head emphatically. "Your secret is safe with me."

"You see?" said the Provost. "Rowena knows how to be reasonable. Why don't we all go inside and talk like civilized people? There's no need for guns, I assure you."

Mack thought for a moment. "Okay," he said. "You and I will go inside and talk. I'm not feeling too good about this deal anymore. I want to hear you promise you're going to uphold your end of the bargain again."

"Of course. I'd be happy to. But in the meantime, why don't you let Rowena go? You don't need her."

"I think we do. I think we need to keep her and explain to her just how important it is to keep her mouth shut."

"I think Rowena understands perfectly well, don't you?"

"I do," I said. "This isn't the first time I've kept my mouth shut, anyway."

"Yeah?" Mack shifted around to look at me. "You're the Russian professor, right?"

I nodded encouragingly.

"Yeah, that's right. Well, tell you what: why don't you and Vova here go off and he can explain to you in a language you'll understand what will happen to you if you don't keep your mouth shut, and Vinnie and I'll go talk with the Provost. You can go with her." He jerked his head at John Greene.

John made like he was going to argue, but then followed along meekly as three of the men shepherded us away from the door, while Mack and two others walked Provost Johnson into the building.

"What are you going to do to us?" demanded John Greene, as soon as Mack was inside. "You can't do this! This is a crime! You...you should let her go! Rowena...Rowena's never done anything! I can't let you treat my faculty like this!"

"We let her go," said the man next to me. "First she understands."

We stopped under a streetlamp in the edge of the quad, next to the main road that led out of campus. A car was driving slowly towards us.

"We go for ride," said the man next to me. "Then we talk."

"Maybe we don't need to go for a ride," said the man next to John Greene. "We can just take care of 'em here."

"They will find them," said the man next to me. I could see his face in the eerie light of the streetlamp. It looked familiar.

"Like they did that other guy, that janitor who got too nosy?" The other man grinned at me. "They found him, but they never found us, did they? Open your mouth, sweetheart, and you'll end up just like him. Or worse."

"No," said the man next to me. "She not like him. She nice. She help my son. He—bad boy, but she—good girl. Help him. Danya tell me."

"I'm not going to say anything, I swear," I said, and repeated it in Russian for Danila's father's benefit. "I lived in Russia," I continued, still speaking in Russian. "I know how these things work. I won't interfere, I promise."

"See?" said Danila's father, poking me in the side. "Good girl. Not dangerous. Yes?"

"Yes," I said.

"Good. You and me—we talk. You." He nodded towards the other man. "You speak English. You talk to him."

The other man grinned. "Not a problem. You got a car nearby?" he asked John Greene.

"Yes...in the senior administrative parking lot...chairs get special parking privileges...normally I can't get into it but today it was half-empty...right over there."

"Great," said the other man, and he gripped John by the arm and started marching him briskly in the direction of the senior administrative parking lot, right on the edge of the front quad, only a few yards away.

"Come," said Danila's father, and jerked his head towards the side of the road. He took my arm and started walking me in that direction, the other man following along behind us.

"You helped my son," Danila's father said meditatively in Russian as we walked along. "He told me what you did for him at the final. You could have failed him but you didn't. That was kind. And you helped him in other ways, all semester. He liked your class. He even wanted to keep studying Russian. He's a good boy," he added. "Smart. But he doesn't understand about hard work and acting right. He doesn't know who he is: Ukrainian like me, Russian like his mother, Jewish like his grandmother, or American like his passport. And he's ashamed of me and what I do, but he goes to your expensive college on my dollars anyway, and brags about his mafia connections." He sighed. "I don't know what to do with him. What do you recommend, Professor Roe-eena?"

"Well...do you really want my advice?"

Danila's father nodded.

"Maybe send him far away? So that he's not here, getting drawn into your...work."

"That is good advice," said Danila's father thoughtfully. "I don't want him to follow in my footsteps, to be honest. We came to America so that he wouldn't. His mother wants him to be a surgeon, and I want him to be a programmer. But a legal one, not a hacker. I don't like crime, you know. I wasn't always a gangster. I was in OMON. You know OMON?"

"Yes. My fiancé was an OMON officer, too, for a while."

That seemed to please Danila's father, as I'd hoped it might. "You see! You do understand! So you also understand that you can't support a family on an OMON officer's salary."

"Yes," I agreed.

"So, bribes...private security work on the weekends...and here I am. We wanted Danila to have a good life. It's okay that I'm a gangster if he has a good life, you understand? But it's hard to get into America, and even harder to make a living here. I used to be a policeman, I used to be a good citizen and believe in the friendship of nations and liberté, égalité, fraternité, but now I'm a gangster, because that makes more money. It's the American way."

"I understand," I said.

"I thought so," he said in satisfaction. "Here's the car! Get in, Professor Roe-eenna."

"Where are you taking...where are we going?"

"For a talk," he said. "And Mack will want to talk with you as well. We'll go to his house."

That didn't sound good at all. I had a certain amount of faith in my ability to talk my way out of trouble with Danila's father, but much less with Mackenzie's father. I had the feeling that helping out his daughter was going to weigh a lot less with him than helping out his son had with Danila's father.

"Come on," Danila's father chided me, pulling me over to where the car had stopped in front of us. "Get in, Professor Roe-eenna."

I looked around. Two men, both armed, and another in the car. My chances of making a break for it seemed slim. Maybe Mackenzie's father *would* be grateful. I let Danila's father push me into the front seat.

"Let's go," he said in Russian to the man behind the wheel. By his profile I guessed he might be Vitya's father.

The car pulled forward, driving cautiously in the slush. We drove slowly past the three-sided main quad, where the lights in Dreme Hall still blazed, and towards the campus entrance, where the lynching trees that had been transformed into fairy gardens twinkled magically in the still-falling snow.

"They're behind us," Danila's father said, looking back to where a car, presumably John Greene's, had pulled out of the little administrative parking lot and was rapidly catching up with us. "But they're going too fast in this snow...Americans don't know how to drive in snow...Shit!"

The car behind us accelerated rapidly, fishtailing in the slush but still shooting forward with a screech of rubber.

"Go!" screamed Danila's father.

There was a loud *bang*, and the sound of metal tearing into metal, and our car jumped forward and then came to a dead halt, locked in place by the other car, which had plowed straight into it.

46

The driver was still untangling himself from his airbag, and the men in the backseat were still untangling themselves from each other, when I slithered out of my seatbelt, out from behind the airbag, and out, out, out the passenger side door.

For an instant I froze in indecision. I was sure that was John Greene's car that had plowed into us. Stay and help him? But what would I do? Better to get help. Run back across campus and try to get to my car and escape in it, hoping and praying that it wouldn't stall out?

The bright lights on the trees flanking the campus entrance winked on and off invitingly. Danila's father had managed to extract himself from the jam in the back seat, swearing and huffing but looking like he meant to grab at me. I threw my purse at him, startling him, and took off towards the entrance and the open road.

At first my only plan was escape. But after I had shot through the entrance and found myself on the sidewalk, I had to decide where to go. To the left of campus was an upscale neighborhood with single-family houses set well back from the road. I could run from house to house begging for help, and maybe I would get it in time or maybe I wouldn't, and maybe I would get shot as an intruder. To the right of campus were student apartments, now mostly deserted with the start of winter break.

I glanced back. Everyone was clustered around the two cars, which looked firmly stuck together. One man looked up and made as if to set off after me. I bolted across the road and straight ahead, on my usual route home.

It had been an instinctive decision, to get as far away from my pursuers and to head towards home, but after two blocks I realized no one had caught up with me. Their car was totaled, and none of them had been able to keep pace with me on foot. They would have to get reorganized, get another car, send out a search party after me...that would take them several minutes at least, and maybe longer. I could stop and call for help. If I had my phone. But I'd abandoned my purse, and my phone had already been broken. The only thing I had was my keys, still clutched in my right hand from when I'd taken them out back in the garage.

I slowed to a jog and looked up and down the street. In the space of two blocks I had left the façade of safety provided by campus, and entered the neighborhood of vacant lots and sagging porches and men who sat on them all day instead of working. But right now no one was sitting on their porch. No one was out in the street doing normal things, but occasional shadowy figures were clustered in dark street corners, maybe gossiping about sports, maybe doing drug deals.

I started running again, keeping my eyes turned away from the shadowy figures in the hope that if I didn't look at them, they wouldn't look at me. I couldn't go back towards campus. But I knew the way home from here. And on the way home there was a police station, only two miles from here. Even in my winded state and wearing dress clothes—thank God I was in my running shoes—I could do two miles in fifteen minutes. My followers would be hard pressed to catch me in fifteen minutes.

Sinister heads turned and watched my progress as I flashed past, but decided it was too much bother to molest me or help me. The

important thing was to get into a rhythm. I was gasping in panic and
from the sprint I'd just run, and I'd run myself out in another couple
of blocks if I didn't get that under control.

I forced myself to breathe slowly and calmly and focus on my
footsteps in the snow. I knew how to run in snow. Last winter, the
last time I'd been in Russia, Dima had been even more obsessed than
usual about keeping me safe by keeping me strong and fit, and along
with self-defense training, had chivvied me up and down Gorky Park
in the snow, shouting the names of female Heroes of the Soviet
Union in my ear as encouragement, until he'd finally collapsed, bent
double, the cigarettes he'd started smoking again during his last bout
of jail time for attending unsanctioned meetings catching up with
him, and I'd kept running just to show him how I felt about that
kind of treatment. That had been annoying, but it had worked. Hard
to complain about a little running when you have the names of
teenagers who'd been tortured by Nazis and died heroically for their
motherland, whose statues you saw every day in Revolution Square
Station, running through your head.

Nadezhda Volkova, I chanted to myself silently, in time with my
footsteps slapping against the snow. *Nina Sosnina, Zina Portnova,
Zoya Kosmodemyanskaya. Nadya, Nina, Zina, Zoya. Nadya, Nina,
Zina, Zoya. Nadya, Nina, Zina, Zoya.* It was soothing. I could run
forever like this...I could hear a car coming down the street behind
me.

It's just someone driving home after work, I told myself. *Nadya,
Nina, Zina, Zoya, Nadya, Nina, Zina, Zoya...*

The car swerved in my direction. I burst forward. The car
fishtailed in the slush and pulled left to avoid hitting a streetlamp,
and then swerved hard right again, jumping up on the sidewalk but
having to pull left, back onto the street, to avoid a telephone pole.
It stopped for a moment and let two men out, and then started up
again, revving its engine and accelerating ahead of me, surely to cut

me off at the next intersection...the police station was only a few blocks away. If I could just get through the next intersection without getting caught, I would be safe. Surely they wouldn't follow me into a police station.

The car had pulled into the next intersection and turned and stopped so that it was blocking the sidewalk. The two men behind me weren't gaining on me, but I wasn't losing them, either. I could try cutting across to the other side of the street, but they would follow me, and if I left my familiar route, I would be lost in a very bad part of town. Could I run around the car, or jump onto the hood and run across? Not fast enough. One of the men was drawing his gun.

I cut left with a suddenness that startled the others, and dashed for the other side of the street. Where was everyone? Why was no one out on the street at 7:00pm on a Friday? Because this wasn't that kind of neighborhood. And if anyone saw me, they probably wouldn't help me. What was that rumbling? Like a dragon, coming in to land...a huge truck was coming up the street behind me.

It can run interference for me, I thought, and slowed for a second to let it catch up to me.

It swerved left, towards me.

"Grab hold, baby girl!" shouted the driver.

It was a garbage truck. I sprinted up and grabbed onto one of the handles on the back. It accelerated faster than a truck like that should be able to accelerate, sliding through the intersection with a roar and thundering down the street, with me swinging from the handle on the back and my pursuers watching me escape, mouths open.

47

The truck dropped me off at the police station and then roared away, the driver giving me a thumbs-up out the window but not stopping to chat with the police, not even with the police of his own precinct.

When I ran in, I was confronted by an alarmed desk clerk who initially thought I was trying to stage a raid. It took me several attempts, as I gasped for breath, to explain to her that people were chasing me, and that I had run all the way from campus.

By the time they had mustered up a couple of available patrol units to look for my pursuers, they were long gone. I tried to convince them to go to campus, but I was told that multiple units had already responded to multiple 911 calls, and I should give a statement.

Giving my statement took a while, even after I got my breath back. Not certain what would they would find on campus, I stuck more or less to the truth but glossed over Madison's drug use and—doubting that I was doing the right thing, but doubting even more that doing anything else would be any better—her father's apparent complicity in what was going on. Instead I emphasized the involvement of Mack D'Annunziato and Vinnie Angelo Junior, which made the officer taking my statement groan out loud.

"Sorry," she said, covering her mouth. "But surely you know who they are?"

"Oh, I know."

"Yeah, well...we'll look into it, but, I mean, look at this place..."

I looked around. The shabbiness would have done a local Russian precinct station proud.

"You didn't hear this from me," she said. "But I don't know there's much we can do against those guys. I'll file the report, but..."

"I get it," I said. "I just want to have it on file."

She nodded. "Yeah, me too. So let's get it down right, okay?"

After that was done there was some discussion of whether I should go home. I still, miraculously, had my keys, which had cut deep grooves in my palm when I had grabbed onto the handles of the garbage truck, but no purse and no phone. After some calling back and forth, the officer who had taken my statement offered to drive me back to campus so that I could pick up my car.

"That's very kind of you," I told her.

"That's why I got into this, you know what I mean?" she said. "To help people. Let's go."

On the drive over to campus she told me her name was Janice, she'd had a child born out of wedlock at eighteen, and she was trying to save up for her daughter to go to college.

"I'd drive her past here and tell her if she worked hard in school, she could get into a place like this," she said as we pulled into campus. "Now I'm not so sure."

"Universities are pretty much like everywhere else," I said. "You don't leave wherever you come from behind when the gates to the ivory tower slam shut."

"Yeah," she said. "Look, we really will look into what you told us, but..."

"I get it," I said. "I really do."

"And anyway, you didn't tell us the whole truth, now did you?"

"I told you all the really important stuff."

"I get it. I really do." She smiled. "Is that someone you know?"

She pointed to where a skinny figure was standing next to the two crumpled cars, talking animatedly into a cell phone.

"Yes!"

"You feel safe for me to leave you here?"

"Yes. If you don't mind."

"We'll be in touch. Stay safe, now." She stopped and let me out of the car, and waited as I ran up to Alex.

"You're okay! How's Madison?" I shouted.

"Gotta go," he said into his phone, and threw his arms around me.

"You're alive," he said into my ear. "When you ran off...And Madison went into cardiac arrest on the way to the hospital and I had to perform CPR by the side of Route 1 with tractor-trailers roaring by..."

"Is she okay?"

"She was alive when I left her at the ER. Her dad came and found her, so I came back here to look for you, but all I found was John Greene being carted away in an ambulance."

"Is he okay?"

"He broke his arm when he crashed his car into yours." Alex laughed into my ear. "His finest hour. We can never hate him again. He figured he was going to be tortured and shot and so were you, so he rammed your car with his. He told me he saw you get out and run away."

"Yeah," I told him. "I got out and ran halfway across town, till I found a police station."

"John said they sent people after you."

"They couldn't catch me."

"I'm glad." Alex tightened his arms around me, and then let go and stepped back. "Shit," he said, looking at his phone. "I never hung up. You still there, man? Yeah, yeah, everything's okay. I found her. Actually, she found me. She's okay. You're okay, right?"

"What's a little run in the snow? I'll be fine. But I lost my purse. Have you seen it anywhere?" I went off to search around for my purse, hearing Alex telling the person on the phone that I must be okay because I was looking for my purse, and no, I wasn't the kind of woman who would value a purse more than her own life, and he had to come help me search.

"A buddy of mine from the Navy became a state trooper after he got out," he explained, looking slightly sheepish. "I've been screaming in his ear for the past hour to come help find you."

"No need. I found myself. And my purse!" I picked it up where someone must have found it and leaned it against a streetlamp. Even brand-new at TJ Max it had not been very nice. Now it was considerably less nice.

"I can never take this to an interview again," I said in dismay.

"Whatever. Buy a new one."

I gave him a look.

"Okay. But still, whatever. It's good that you dropped it when you needed to in order to run away."

"It's better than that," I said. "I threw it at someone and stopped him from coming after me."

"Good purse," said Alex, reaching out and giving it a pat. "You should hang onto it, keep it in retirement and feed it only the best treats."

"That's what I'll do, then. My phone is probably unsalvageable, though." I fished it out of the purse and held it up. Alex winced.

"Does it work?"

"It didn't earlier."

"Shit! That's, like, a $500 phone!"

"I know."

Our gloom and doom was interrupted by the screech of the two cars being pulled apart.

"We don't even have to be here," said Alex, as we watched the cars being winched onto the tow trucks. "We should go home." He paused. "Let me spend the night with you. Not like that! I mean, you don't have a phone. You couldn't call for help if someone came after you. And frankly, I don't feel like driving home to my parents' place tonight, and I sure as hell ain't spending the night in the office."

"Um. Okay. You're right. It's a good idea. I'm just not very set up for guests."

"You got a floor?"

"Sort of."

"Good enough for me. Let's go."

We checked with the single remaining patrol officer that we were free to go, and then Alex drove me back to the parking garage, and hovered anxiously while I got into the car, and followed me closely all the way home, despite my warning that he shouldn't get too close in case of sudden stalls.

Fevronia came out to greet me when I stepped through the door, but took one look at Alex, hissed, and ran away.

"Jeez," said Alex. "Am I that much of a mess?"

"Yeah, but I'm worse."

He eyed me critically. "True. Into the shower with you, and I'll order pizza."

"Pizza's expensive!"

"I've got, like, $167 left on my credit card limit. I can afford it."

"I have pasta."

"Pre-cooked?"

"No."

"I don't feel like cooking even if I could cook, which I can't. So delivery pizza it is. Plain cheese, right?"

"Right," I said. "I'll, um, go take a shower then."

When I got out of the shower, wearing, after a certain amount of dithering over the message it sent, my pajamas, the pizza was waiting.

We devoured it with unseemly haste, remarking over and over again how unbelievably tasty delivery pizza was when you hadn't had it in months, and lamenting the lack of beer to go with it, but beer was for people with real paychecks.

When we were done Alex broke a silence that was growing uncomfortable to ask if he could use the shower. When he came out, looking cleaner but no less awkward, we tried to stretch my meager bedding into something that wouldn't be horribly uncomfortable for him, at which point I burst into tears over the general shittiness of my life and all the adrenaline rushing out of my system.

"Hey, it's okay," Alex said, putting his arms around me. "I'll just get my coat or something."

"No! You can sleep in the bed."

"Um," he said, sounding as uncertain as me. "Okay. I'll just..." He let go of me and sat down gingerly on the edge of the bed. "I'll just sort of be on top of the sheets, okay, over here in the corner."

"Don't be ridiculous," I told him, sliding under the covers on the other side of the bed and motioning for him to join me.

"Yeah. Right. I mean, I'm supposed to have that whole officer and a gentleman thing going, right? Only without the looking like Richard Gere thing. But that's okay. Right now it's okay. And frankly"—he slid over next to me and put his arms back around me—"I'm too wired—that sounds better than scared, right?—to fall asleep by myself right now."

"Yeah, me too," I said.

"Okay. So, we'll just, like, relax and go to sleep like this, right?"

"Right," I said. For a long time I could feel the low-level quivering I always sensed when he was nearby vibrating through me, but eventually that stilled and we both fell asleep.

48

The next morning Alex got up, and, looking awkward and embarrassed, although I wasn't sure whether that was from spending the night in my bed or from spending the night in my bed without anything remotely sexual happening, said he should go home and let his parents know he was okay, but that he'd be back tomorrow, and that he should have an old flip-phone around somewhere I could borrow if I needed to.

"That'd be...that'd be great, actually."

"Great. I'll see if I can dig it out, bring it by tomorrow. Well, uh, bye." He tousled my hair as if I were a dog, and left.

As soon as he was gone I gave into the temptation that had been tormenting me since last night, opened my computer, and entered an email address that had been burning a hole in my brain the past year.

From: Rowena Halley
To: Dmitry Kuznetsov
Subject: You saved my life

> *Do you remember when we went running in Gorky Park last winter? It annoyed me then* [I originally wrote "I was boiling with rage," and then erased it], *but last night it might have saved my life.*

I expected either nothing, or an explosion of...something, but in fact what I got was an almost immediate reply.

From: Dmitry Kuznetsov
To: Rowena Halley
Subject: I'm glad
I'm glad. Keep running.

I stared at the response for several minutes, willing it to reveal its secrets to me and tell me whether I should be beside myself with outrage, throw up my hands and walk away, or hit "Reply" and start a reconciliation. The Russian teacher in me automatically noted that the form of "run" Dima had used had been the multidirectional form used for recreational running, not the unidirectional form used to mean "run away." Or "run to me." So maybe he was telling me to keep exercising, not to run away? But he also wasn't inviting me to run straight to him. And he hadn't even asked what I meant or what had happened to me. Righteous indignation filled me. If he wanted a reconciliation, he could ask for one, or at least ask why running had saved my life. *I* didn't care; it was all on him. Yeah, absolutely.

Telling myself this, I shut my laptop and examined my footwear options. My running shoes were still soaking wet from last night's adventure, and battered beyond repair. My boots were no doubt just as leaky as they had been the day before. I looked out the window. A good two inches of slush. Ballet flats were out of the question. I pulled on my boots, and, trying not to wince at the soreness that was making itself felt throughout my whole body, made my way at a slow walk to True Grit.

Just as I hoped, I found Mike and Jimmy there, eating grits and eggs and drinking coffee. I went over and sat down at their table.

"Thanks," I said.

They shared a look. "It was nothin', baby girl," said Mike.

"Just don't get us mixed up in it," put in Jimmy.

"Your secret is safe with me," I promised.

"We was comin' back from our shift, runnin' a little late, and we seed you runnin' down the road. Well, your bright blue shoes. And we seed that car comin' after you, so..."

"Thanks," I said. "Really, I don't know how to thank you enough. I don't know what I can do for you, but if there *is* something, just tell me."

Mike and Jimmy shared another glance. "I reckon buyin' us breakfast would be enough," said Mike.

"Long as you let *us* buy you breakfast back, baby doll," said Jimmy kindly. "There ain't a lot o' meat on them bones."

"Fat don't fly," I told them. "How do you think I outran all those people?"

Grins split their faces. "You sure did, baby girl! You outran all those men, and a car too! And you jumped onto our truck like you'd been doin' it all your life. You'd never think those skinny little white arms and legs could do a thing like that."

I winked at them. "We all have our secrets," I said.

There was some laughing and thigh-slapping over that, and then I let Jimmy buy me a plate of grits while I paid their bill, and we all finished our breakfasts and I promised once again that I wouldn't involve them with anything to do with either the police or the Angelo/D'Annunziato families.

The grits and coffee gave me a temporary carb lift that was sure to result in a carb crash later, but I used it to go home and go through all my emails. Nothing there of interest, except...was that a UNC-Charlotte email? From the chair of the search committee?

I opened the email, expecting a form rejection letter. At least that would be more than I usually got.

Dear Dr. Halley, I read.

> *While the committee regrets very much to be unable to continue with you as a candidate for our tenure-track*

position, we do have a temporary position opening up for the spring semester at our new UNC-Matthews satellite campus. We realize this is very short notice, but we are inviting our most impressive first-round candidates to apply to the job first. The job description and the link to the application are below. Please don't hesitate to contact me with any questions.

Brent Whittaker

Associate Professor of French

Department of Modern Languages

UNC-Charlotte

P.S. We greatly enjoyed speaking with you in particular during the interview in San Antonio, and we understand that you will be free for the spring semester, so if that is still the case, we particularly urge you to apply. I will be happy to answer any questions you have about the program. My number is below.

I punched the air in triumph, and then felt like an idiot for rejoicing over what was so

clearly not only a consolation prize but a terrible, crappy, awful job. I clicked on the link. Yep. Three courses, although only three credit hours each, so I would be teaching the same load as at TLASC, temporary part-time employee status, no benefits. But I should apply anyway. Or was I better off falling back on John's charity and spending the spring in his maybe-empty, maybe-not apartment in Jacksonville? I thought about how academics reacted to people who were "wasting their time" by being unemployed and out of the loop for even a single semester. Taking this job meant I could send out my spring applications on UNC letterhead. Okay, UNC-Charlotte. Okay, UNC-Matthews, which was probably one step above a community college, if that. But I should take the job anyway. If I could afford to. I couldn't even afford to hire a moving pod, let alone put down first and last month's rent on a new apartment. Maybe John could loan me the money.

I was just opening up a new email to send him a begging letter outlining the situation and asking for his help, whatever help he cared to offer, when there was a knock at the door.

Thinking Alex must have come back, I ran over and checked the peephole, grinning to myself at the news I had and—I had to admit—the idea of seeing him again. Screw Dima! Alex was the one who had come through when it counted. Plus, he was entertaining.

It wasn't Alex at the door. It was Provost Johnson.

49

"I just came here to thank you, Rowena," he said into the door. He held up his hands. "I'm here alone. It's safe, I swear."

A childish urge to tell him to go to hell rose up in me, but I quelled it and opened the door.

"How's Madison?" I demanded.

"She's stable. She"—his face pinched, making him look for a moment like a terrified father who'd spent the night in the ER with his only daughter—"maybe you heard, she went into cardiac arrest on the way to the hospital, and again in the ER, but they say she's stable now. I was with her all night. They sent me home around five this morning. Madison's mother is supposed to be on her way to sit with her today. She might even be able to summon up a little maternal concern for once. Can I come in?"

"Um. Okay."

I stepped back and let him in, acutely aware of how shabby and cramped my apartment was, and also that the empty pizza box was still sitting on the table, and the door to the bedroom was open, revealing the unmade bed. Normally I was a neat freak. But today I'd had other things on my mind. I almost said the words out loud, and then bit down on them. I didn't need to be apologizing to Provost Johnson for how I kept my own home. And maybe he should see how his instructors lived.

He looked around. "Is Alex here?" he asked.

"What makes you think he might be?" My voice was more prickly than I would have liked. I owed him no defensiveness for anything that might or might not have happened between me and Alex.

"He didn't come home last night. His father was calling me and demanding to know where he was half the night. I told him he was probably with you. He was, wasn't he? You didn't eat all of that pizza yourself."

"It's none of your business."

"Well, do you know where is? Is he safe?"

"He went home this morning," I said. "My phone broke," I added, relenting slightly. "Last night, during...Alex didn't want me to be by myself with no phone. And he didn't want to drive home so late, after...everything, either. But he left first thing, so he should be home by now."

"Good. Although it means another trip for me." He made an indecisive motion with his body, and then said, "Look, Rowena. First of all, I wanted to say thank you. You saved Madison's life last night."

"Alex saved her life. He was the one who did CPR by the side of the road."

"Yeah, but you did too. You both did. And I heard about what you did. How you ran off to act as bait so they would go after you instead of her. I wish"—he swallowed—"I wish I could repay you for that, but I can't."

"I didn't do it for money. Or anything else."

"I know. But I *do* want to help you, Rowena, so let me start with this."

He held out something. I took it. It was a folded check for $5,000.

"You've got to fucking kidding me," I said, and tried to hand it back.

"No, keep it. Listen to me! Keep it. You've more than earned it. For starters, it should have been part of your salary. You think I don't know how pathetically we pay you? Who do you think signs off on it? So consider this...reparations, or something."

"What do you want?" I asked warily.

"I want you to take the check, Rowena, and then I want you to cash it. It's good. Or is it not enough?"

"I don't know," I said. "I mean, by my calculations, that's just a week's worth of suits for you."

He laughed in spite of himself.

"But I really didn't do it for the money. And $5,000 isn't nearly enough for your daughter's life. So I don't know how to respond to it, other than to say you need to be making the same offer to Alex too."

"Where do you think I'm going next?" He closed his hand around mine, closing up the check inside it. I jerked my hand back, out of his grasp.

"Yeah, I wouldn't trust me either," he said. "But seriously, Rowena, listen. I have no doubt you hate me. I hate me too right now. But my offer's still on the table. Do you need a place for next semester? Or have you gotten something lined up?"

"No," I said grudgingly. "I mean, I don't have anything lined up for certain. But I was just invited to apply for a position this spring. The search committee for a tenure-track position I interviewed for but didn't get invited me to apply for a temporary position for the spring."

"Really? Where?"

"UNC-Charlotte. Their satellite campus in Matthews."

"Who's the head of the search committee?"

"Um...Brent something?"

"Brent Whittaker? Teaches French?"

"I think so. Why? Do you know him?"

"We were good friends in grad school, and we still keep in touch. Let me give him a call. Do you have his number?"

I stared at him, too full of suspicion and a mulish desire to be contrary to respond.

"Just a minute." He got out his phone, scrolled through the contacts list, and said, "Here we go. Hope he's up already—he never was a morning person. Hello? Brent, is that you? It's Erik. Oh, I'm doing okay, how about you? How's life in the 704 treating you?" He laughed. "The Dirty Dirty South agrees with you, does it? Great. Listen, I have a question. Are you doing a search for a Russian instructor right now? For the spring? You are? Fabulous. Because I think one of my current instructors has applied for it, or is planning to. Yeah, unfortunately we could only bring her in on a one-semester appointment; you know how it is. I wish we could keep her, but...yeah, maybe we'll loan her out to you for a semester or two, then bring her back. Her name? Rowena Halley. Graduated last year from Indiana. Uh-huh. Absolutely. No, we're all very impressed with her work. All the students love her. Even Madison. Yeah, she even managed to get Madison a little bit under control. I know, right? Madison...she's doing okay. You know how it is. Recommendation? Be happy to. I'll get it to you this afternoon. Okay, thanks Brent. Take care, man."

He hung up and looked over at me. "Brent said he's looking forward to your application. I promised him a personal letter of recommendation from me. And I mean it. I'll send it to him this afternoon. And I'll give you a general one. Do you have an Interfolio account?"

"Um. Yes."

"Of course you do. Send me a request and I'll upload it right away."

"Um. I guess."

"Oh, come on Rowena. What do you really want? Spit it out!"

"I want to get a job on my own merits, not through *blat*. Dirty connections," I clarified.

He laughed, but without a lot of humor. "Don't you know? That's how everything is done. What did you call it? *Blat*? Leave it to the Russians to have a one-syllable word for the concept. But it holds just as true here in the land of the free and the home of the brave as it does over there. Well, maybe not just as true, but that's also the way things work here, when it comes right down to it."

"I know," I said.

"And you *will* be getting a job on your own merits. I'm not doing this because, I don't know, you're blackmailing me. I'm doing this because by all accounts you really are a good instructor and a promising researcher, and Christ you're brave. And you used that bravery to save my daughter's life, when you didn't have to. She's a good kid, you know—"

"She's not," I interrupted. "*I* was a good kid. Even my brother was a good kid, in his own supremely irritating and rebellious way. But Madison is a poor little drug-addicted rich girl who's been given everything she could get except the chance to be a good kid."

"Yeah," he said slowly. "You're probably right. Fuck. Where did we go so wrong? We really did want the best for her, you know."

"Yeah," I said. "But all kids, even almost-grownup kids, need large amounts of their parents' undivided attention, and smart kids who like adventure and excitement and travel to Russia and programing their own video games don't always do so well in safe, highly structured environments. The more you try to keep them out of trouble, the more they take drugs and hack into other people's emails and generally wreak havoc. They need a little chaos and danger, and if you take it all away from them, they'll create it themselves."

"Yeah," he said. "It's just...I'm not arguing with you, Rowena. You're absolutely right. But...you know how it is. I'm not saying things were quite so tough when I was dissertating and on the market, but things were pretty damn tough. They don't just hand out PhDs like candy, and jobs even less. So I was all caught up in that, and Brenda—Madison's mother—she was angry that I was working so much and earning so little, while she was stuck at home with a toddler she'd had mainly because I thought...well, I wanted her, I really did, but I also thought it would be good for my career. They prefer single, childless women and married men with children because we're the most desperate and the easiest to control, you know that."

"Yeah," I said. "I know that. Poor Madison."

"Yeah. Poor Madison. None of it was her fault. And then I defended and got a job, and I *still* didn't have enough money to support a family, and I realized administration was the way to go if that's what I needed, so that's the way I went. Only somehow I lost Brenda and Madison along the way."

"I'm really sorry," I said. "That must be tough."

He looked like he wanted to roll his eyes at me, but stopped himself. "You *are* good," he said. "The sympathy almost sounds real."

"It is real."

"You're even better than I thought, then. So here I am, Provost before I'm fifty. But Provost at a university that belongs to the mob, body and soul.

"That must be tough too."

He shrugged. "No one to blame but myself. And I don't know if it's any tougher than anywhere else. It's all a snake pit, Rowena. Only in this case, the snakes have real fangs. But I figure: hey, at least taxpayer money *is* ending up at the university eventually. I mean, the upstanding citizens of New Jersey who spend their hard-earned dollars at the casinos and brothels and crack houses we have in such abundance *are* getting some return on investment. They're paying for their kids to go to college, whether they know it or not." He gave me a sideways look. "You probably think that sounds like bullshit. You probably think that nothing good can come from dirty soil."

"No," I said. "Moscow State University was built by gulag labor. Slaves, and of a very grim sort. They say you can still find inscriptions they left on the walls of the main building. And now it's a beautiful campus and Russia has the highest per-capita rate of college graduates in the world and students come from all over the world to study there, including from African countries that the West has been exploiting and oppressing for centuries. Sometimes things work out in funny ways, and while I don't believe the ends justify the means, I've spent enough time in Russia to be okay with graft and corruption. That's the only way it functions: you know; if everyone suddenly became law-abiding the entire country would grind to a halt within days. And we're not that different, just like you said. Rules aren't always meant to be followed. Sometimes they're just there to show what fine fellows we are, while we slip cash back and forth under the table with our left hands to keep things from crashing down around us."

"Wow. I actually don't know what to say to that. I think you may be even more cynical than me, Rowena."

"Yeah, but I'm a wimp," I said. "I can never hold my nose long enough to actually make a living under those circumstances."

"You're not a wimp. And maybe you can find somewhere where the stink isn't so bad. You should, Rowena, you really should! You really could have a fine future ahead of you. Not only that, but we need you, Rowena. I mean, academia needs you. Not just because we're desperately searching for women to fill those corner-office positions, even as we drive them out with our ticking tenure clocks, to show that we practice what we preach, but because maybe you really could effect some kind of meaningful change."

"Is that what you're doing?" I asked.

He shrugged. "I'm not going to get rid of corruption in Jersey," he said. "But maybe a few of Jersey's youth will learn to love Goethe, Keats, and Pushkin, and become better people because of it. And all paid for with mob dollars."

"Yeah," I said. "I don't actually disagree."

"So you'll take the money then?"

"Is it mob money?"

"It's from my personal account. I don't take personal kickbacks. So it's as clean as your paycheck."

"That clean, huh?"

"Yeah, that clean. Please take it, Rowena. Otherwise I'll feel terrible."

"Okay," I said.

"Good. I mean, thanks, Rowena. I really mean that. Let me know if you need anything. I really mean that too."

"Okay," I said. "Let me know how Madison does, okay? Here." I wrote my personal email on the back of an old envelope. "My email. My permanent email, I mean. Tell her to write to me if she wants to."

"She will. I'm sure of it. Well." He took a deep breath and straightened his shoulders. "That didn't go so bad, did it? Now to face Alex."

"I'm sure he'll be very polite to you."

"I'm sure. That's not the same thing as being pleasant, though. Good luck, Rowena. I hope to hear from you again soon."

"Sure," I said, and showed him the door.

50

Alex showed up the next morning, as I was trying, with an extreme lack of enthusiasm, to do some packing.

"Packing already?" he asked as soon as he stepped in. "Can't wait to get rid of us?"

"It's not that," I said. "It's that I might have a job. For the spring. I have an interview tomorrow. And in any case my lease runs out at the end of the month."

"An interview! That's great. So do I, actually. Also tomorrow. For a job I'm pretty much guaranteed to get."

"What! That's fantastic."

He made a face. "I guess. It's at Temple. Where my dad used to work. And it's because our favorite Provost made a few calls."

"Yeah, mine too, kind of."

"Well. If you can't beat 'em, join 'em, right?"

"I guess," I said. "Do you want to help me pack?"

"I *love* packing!"

"It's a good thing you're a professor of a critical need language," I said. "Because you'll never make a living on the stage with acting like that."

"Okay, I hate packing, but I'll help anyway. It will be good training for when I move to Philly."

"So you're not planning to live with your parents next semester?"

"Fuck no! I mean, I could. They're closer to Philly than they are to New Brunswick. But this is a lectureship with a massive, incredible, $42,000 a year salary, which after I make my monthly loan payments will just about rent me a couch in some skanky apartment near the university, so that's what I'm doing. But I will have to pack up and move at least some of my stuff down there." He surveyed my apartment. "Not as much as you, because my parents have perfectly good rooms for storing junk in, so they might as well get some use, but enough to be a headache."

"I know. Oh my God! I have the interview tomorrow, and if I *do* get the job, I'll have to find an apartment down in Charlotte, pack up everything here, have it shipped down there, unpack it—and like as not I'll have to do it all again next semester." I banged my head against the kitchen cabinet a couple of times.

"Hey. Hey, don't be like that." Alex put his hand against the side of my head, so that if I tried to bang it against the cabinet again, his hand would take the blow.

"I know. Don't give in to despair, yada yada yada, ladidadida. I just hate moving, you know what I mean?"

"I know what you mean." He stepped closer and put his arms around me. He was quivering with that pent-up energy he always had, at least when he was standing next to me. "I'm really tempted to ask you to fuck me right now," he said into my ear. "But I'm not going to, because I'm afraid you might say yes, and then we'd have sex on this nasty counter, and it would be lousy because we'd both be thinking about our interviews tomorrow and maybe other lovers past, and it would ruin what could be a beautiful friendship."

"I think you're right," I said.

"So." He released me and stepped back. "Rain check, maybe? Even though I don't look like Richard Gere?"

"Richard Gere is overrated," I said. "Real heroes help with packing."

"We do, don't we?" he said with a grin.

We pulled out the boxes I had broken down and stored away at the beginning of the semester, and taped them back into box shape—I was well trained in having a good supply of packing tape with me at all times. Then we started wrapping up dishes in dish towels and napkins and putting them in the boxes. It all went well until we ran out of packing material and energy, and there was still half the dishes left to go.

"How do I have so much stuff?" I demanded.

"I don't know. How *do* you have so many dishes? I have precisely one bowl, one fork, and one spoon."

"Yeah, but you don't cook."

"True."

"And people keep giving me stuff because I'm a girl and I like to cook and everyone knows that and tries to be kind and helpful by giving me presents of cast-off cookware. Which is nice, until I have to pack it up and haul it around the country with me."

"Yeah," Alex said. "I know this sucks. But it will get better."

"Really?"

"No. I'm just shitting with you. It's probably going to keep sucking for a long time, maybe forever. But it's what we do."

"*Why?*" I demanded plaintively. "Why are we doing this?"

"You know why, Rowena," he said with a smile. "Because we're saving the world. Two campuses at a time."

THE END

DEAR READER! THANK you very much for reading **Campus Confidential**. *Want to find out what happens next? Book 2 in the series,* **Permanent Position**, *is out now.*

And if you'd like to keep in touch, get regular updates and offers, AND get a free book, scan the QR code below to get your copy of the *prequel novella **Foreign Exchange** and sign up for my newsletter (but only if you want to!).*

About the Author

S id Stark lives a life very similar to her characters', only with more grading and fewer exciting chase scenes. She did once get held up in Heathrow on suspicion of being a Russian criminal traveling on an American passport, though, which was fun. She loves to hear from her readers, and can be reached by email at sidstark@sidstarkauthor.com, at her website at https://sidstarkauthor.com/, on Facebook at https://www.facebook.com/SidStarkAuthor/, and Twitter at @SidStarkAuthor.

Don't miss out!

Visit the website below and you can sign up to receive emails whenever Sid Stark publishes a new book. There's no charge and no obligation.

https://books2read.com/r/B-A-NVEK-HGLFB

BOOKS 2 READ

Connecting independent readers to independent writers.

Also by Sid Stark

Doctor Rowena Halley
Campus Confidential: An Academic Thriller
Permanent Position: An Academic Thriller
Summer Session: An Academic Thriller
Trigger Warning: An Academic Thriller
Honor Court: An Academic Thriller
Total Immersion: An Academic Thriller
Under Review: An Academic Thriller

Doctor Rowena Halley Boxed Sets
The Doctor Rowena Halley Series Books 1-4: Four Dark Comedy
Mysteries